# She'd rather have his scorn than pity!

Mary didn't want Ninian picking up any more pieces. She wanted no second bests. Ninian would never fall in love with her because he thought, as far as marriage was concerned, that she was cold and calculating.

And if she told him why, he would be stirred with compassion, which would compel him to offer compensation... pity, not love. Mary heaved a sigh.

"What's that huge sigh for?" Ninian asked. "You are the strangest mixture, Mary Rose. I don't understand you."

"You don't have to. I'm here for a purpose and when it's accomplished I'll be gone and this will be no more than a rather madcap incident in my life."

She turned quickly away from him. She must regain control of her emotions. She must not cry....

# South to Forget

by

## ESSIE SUMMERS

# Harlequin Books

TORONTO • LONDON • LOS ANGELES • AMSTERDAM
SYDNEY • HAMBURG • PARIS • STOCKHOLM • ATHENS • TOKYO

Original hardcover edition published in 1963
by Mills & Boon Limited

ISBN 0-373-00802-3

Harlequin edition published March 1964
under the title *Nurse Mary's Engagement*.
Second printing March 1964
Third printing April 1964
Fourth printing April 1976
Fifth printing July 1976
Sixth printing April 1977
Seventh printing January 1980
Eighth printing May 1981

Printed in Canada

# CHAPTER 1

THE patient's voice had a hint of amusement in it, and a challenge.

"Tell me, Sister Rose," he drawled, "are you really as cool as you look?"

She purposely misunderstood him, answered lightly, "As a matter of fact, Lieutenant, there's a trickle of perspiration running down my shoulder-blades this very moment. As a Canadian I find this Malayan heat every bit as trying as you New Zealand soldiers!"

He chuckled. "A clever answer, Sister. You're very practised at evading personal questions, aren't you?"

Her smile did not quite reach her eyes. "It's very necessary when one is nursing a lot of cheeky Kiwi soldiers!"

"Why? What's wrong with a spot of healthy curiosity about one's nurses?"

"Everything," said Sister Mary Rose crisply. "It's one of the first things you learn as a raw pro. *Not* to become involved with patients."

He grinned, doing up his pyjama jacket. "Yet it *does* happen."

"Not in my case, Lieutenant. I've steered clear of relationships with cases not only here but home in Canada too, even in my more susceptible days." She laughed. "We know so well that here in the wards a patient's world is narrowed to four walls, a patch of sky in a window, and half a dozen nurses. As soon as patients are home they forget us. And we forget them. Some patients, like yourself, have fiancées at home. We're just ships that pass in the night."

"Not necessarily. They tell me you're off for New Zealand soon. Enzed's a small country. You're bound to visit Mount Cook – all tourists do – and you'll pass our door. My people would love to see you, to thank you."

"There's nothing to thank me for, Lieutenant. It was all in the course of duty."

"Was it, Sister? Was it unadulterated duty that kept you at my bedside on off-duty hours? Hours when you ought to have been asleep?"

"Lieutenant, I think you're a little pill-happy. Antibiotics have a strange effect on some people. Or else you're excited that this last test has given you the all-clear. Other people besides myself fought for your life, you know. Doctor Mainwaring, for instance. He didn't get his full ration of sleep either. You were a world figure, a hero. You had survived incredible hardships. You made the headlines ... remember ? Missing for a year after the crash, in densest jungle. Then suddenly brought to that outpost by those natives ... injured still and in a high fever contracted on your gruelling trek. You were skin and bone. It was the biggest challenge of the nursing year to get you on your feet again."

He pulled a face, his brown eyes audacious. "And that was all," he mourned. "Enough to give a chap an inferiority complex for the rest of his life. Snatched back from the jaws of death merely to become an interesting entry in a case-book. To think that when I came back to awareness I regarded you as an angel of light ! Someone even told me that I'd not have survived but for you."

Mary removed the last of her instruments on to the trolley.

"Anyone else would have given you the same attention, Lieutenant. I wouldn't have been so constantly with you if it hadn't been for that bee you had in your bonnet that no one else was to nurse you. High delirium can do strange things to a man. You had mixed me up with your sister. And now, Lieutenant –"

He broke in. "Why don't you make it Ninian ?"

She sighed. "I don't believe in Christian names in the ward, Lieutenant."

"Then why do you call old Bill Bill ?"

She smiled suddenly. "I don't know. Bill is Bill. He couldn't be anything else but Bill. Ninian is a saint's name, and you're anything but a saint ! Convalescence is a difficult period, trying to the nursing staff too. You're not delirious now. You don't need humouring any more ... and in any case I doubt if you would have been humoured at all if you hadn't been a hero."

He scowled horribly. "If you mention that word hero again I'll throw my chart at you !"

Sister Rose picked it up, tucked it under her arm, disappeared.

Back in her office she went across to the window, stared out unseeingly.

Beneath Ninian Macandrew's banter there was genuine gratitude and real warmth, she knew. Yet had he but known it she had more cause to be grateful to him.

It had taken her mind off her recent heartbreak, filled in hours when she could not have slept, had given her a purpose in life, fighting death . . . and winning. It had been touch and go.

She had known it for just some queer kink in the nature of the Lieutenant's illness that had made him so set on having her near, but at the time it had meant more than he would ever know, that urgent-seeming, desperate, unreasoning need of her.

She remembered that first odd moment sandwiched in between two bouts of delirium when he had suddenly focused his eyes on her and said gladly, joyously, as one recognising someone loved and long parted from, "Oh, hullo. You're here . . . that's good."

It had stirred something in Mary's heart she had thought never to feel again.

*

If only life were all patients . . . and no fellow nurses. Life in the wards was quite different from life in the common-rooms, the dining-room of a large hospital. In the wards there was the lighthearted banter, the humour that cloaked the pain and bodily weakness, the gallantry and courage.

It was the off-duty hours Mary could not stand much longer. People – well-meaningly – tried to make you forget, took you to places to keep your mind occupied, made a fetish of seeing you were never alone, didn't have time to brood.

This tempering of the wind to the shorn lamb was no good. The lamb had to get used to the cold gales of circumstance.

Pity was demoralising, humiliating. Sister Mary Rose had reached the stage where she knew she could bear it no longer. She felt she went through life in this Singapore Hospital branded as the girl who had come out from Canada to be married, only to find her fiancé in the throes of a hectic love-affair with someone else.

It didn't help to realise it might never have happened had she come a year earlier. But she had been so desperately needed at home when her grandmother was in her last and prolonged illness. It hadn't occurred to her to doubt Francis's constancy. He had been so understanding always that it hadn't even seemed a problem.

Mary closed her eyes against the still sharp poignancy, the incredible disillusionment of walking into his flat, starry-eyed, prepared for his glad surprise when he saw her three days early. She had taken that cancelled flight so confidently, anticipating the joy in his voice when he would say, "Mary ... Mary, at last you're here!"

It hadn't worked that way. She had pushed the door open quietly, her heart thumping, her breath coming quickly. The silence of the flat probably meant that Francis was reading.

Francis had been there all right ... standing in the centre of the room, his arms crushing a tall slim girl with spun-gold hair, and there had been pain in his voice as he said, "Something's got to be done, Thea. I can't, I just can't let you go."

Her own reaction, in spite of her incredulity, the almost physical pain of it, had been instant.

"Then we'd better decide just what, hadn't we, Francis?"

Ten minutes later she had been outside in the street, despite all their protests, minus her ring, minus her future, minus any feeling at all.

Perhaps it would have been better to have gone home, but at the time she had felt she could not bear the sympathy of her family, her friends. To be pointed out to others as the girl who should have been married now, in Malaya, but had been double-crossed, had seemed unbearable.

Yes, at first it had been easier to pick up the threads of her life among strangers, in the busy, thought-banishing work of a big military hospital. There had been no one to whisper, to watch for signs of heartbreak, nerve-strain, no one to make quite useless attempts to bridge the gulf, to fill up the emptiness.

But after two weeks here she had found Anne in the hospital, just returned from leave up-country. Anne Redwood who had nursed with her in Toronto. And Anne, torn with compassion, had rallied her fellow nurses to "take Mary's mind off things".

By now she couldn't even sigh with weariness after a big day in her ward without someone cooking up an exciting outing or planning a party.

Mary had had three months of it. More than enough. Pity had no tonic, bracing effect. It was undermining, weakening, did nothing towards helping you to forget, to start a new life, to be philosophical. She wanted something more astringent, more challenging. Yet she still couldn't face going home. She wanted to go away as far as possible, see new places, meet new people, people who knew nothing about her.

Only the patients had really helped her, particularly these bright-faced, cheerfully impudent New Zealand soldiers and airmen. They had no idea she was other than heart-whole; they laughed, teased, plagued the life out of her.

It was natural then that in her plans for flight into forget-fulness her thoughts had fastened on New Zealand. That was about as far as you could go, they said; next stop was the South Pole.

Lieutenant Macandrew had said, joining in the conversa-tion, "Nurses seem to get around the world these days. Ours back home all seem to travel after they've done their train-ing. Go to the Old Country. Why not pay a visit to New Zealand some time, Sister?"

She had laughed, "I might, at that. I've always had a yen to go to the uttermost ends of the earth."

"Well, if you want to go beyond Maoriland, there are plenty of men who spend a whole winter isolated at the South Pole these days. Come to think of it, it might suit you. You're about as unyielding as an iceberg, anyway."

She had laughed with them. "I have to preserve a certain amount of starch! You Kiwi soldiers have undermined my discipline as it is, and this is the noisiest, merriest ward of the lot. One of us must keep you in your place!"

"Meaning that off duty you aren't so starchy?"

She had tried to look severe and failed.

New Zealand had sounded a little like home. Oh, not the North Island, with its hot springs and thrusting geysers, its sometimes active volcanoes; but the South Island. In fact, where Lieutenant Macandrew lived. Right in the middle of the Island, he had said, bang up against their highest mountain, in a huge mountain range. He had spoken of winter sports, sheep buried in snow, of fertile valleys, plantations of larch and fir. . . .

Not this pulsing, hot, lush country, teeming with the indescribable magic of the East, something that stirred your blood and set up longings best forgotten, that made solitude seem unnatural, even undesirable. She wanted to be somewhere at the other side of the world, somewhere where she wouldn't fear to meet Francis every time she entered a café, a theatre, a shop.

She felt better now her passage was booked. The sea journey might help. Oh, not romantic interludes on the boat deck in the moonlight, but meeting new people, seeing every day a new horizon, blotting out with distance all the memories that might disturb and unsettle her.

She had told Matron last night, and Matron, who also had had pity in her eyes, had agreed to let her go then, though she would have liked to have retained her services longer.

She had spoken so beautifully, expressing a belief in the healing power of time, the sound common sense of carving out a new life for oneself, of casting out bitterness.

It had been more than Mary could bear, even if she knew that in the same circumstances she would have spoken exactly like that to a member of her staff.

That sort of thing was going to be repeated over and over in this hospital for the next few days as the news flew round the grapevine of the Nurses' Home.

It was time she grew a tougher skin over that wound, met the veiled sympathy and understanding with a little hint of cynicism, something that would suggest she was looking forward to new adventures rather than trying desperately to forget.

She told Anne as they approached the deserted ward kitchen together. Anne stopped dead in the corridor.

"Oh, Mary, you'll be all alone. You'll know no one."

"That's exactly what I want. I can't make a fresh start here, Anne, with everyone knowing. That's why I'm not going home. I want to go as far away as possible . . . and that means south. And furthest south is New Zealand."

Anne caught her hand. "Mary, this means I'll have to tell

you. You mustn't go ... quite yet. There's – there's a chance that – that –" She flushed vividly red.

Mary smiled drily. "There's a chance that Francis's affair with Thea Secumbe is petering out, you mean?"

Anne swallowed. "Yes. How – I – I thought it was too early yet to tell you, but if you stayed on, you never know, it – how did you know, Mary?"

"He told me. A week ago."

"He told you! You mean – ?"

"Yes. Just that. He asked me if we couldn't make a go of it after all. Just imagine!"

Anne caught her hand. "But, Mary, these things do happen. You weren't here ... he was lonely, this is a different sort of life from home ... a glittering, social life, one you need partners for. It must have been infatuation, and it's over."

"It's over all right. With *me*. I have no feeling left for him. He isn't my idea of a life partner."

They both glanced behind them. One of the walking wounded was coming towards them. They moved into the kitchen, shut the door, stood looking at each other.

Mary said crispily, ironically, "You needn't worry about me, Anne. I can look after myself. I know exactly what I want this time and where I want to go."

Anne stared at her. Mary's voice sounded so hard.

She said, "You want to go to New Zealand, Mary. But I doubt if you know what you want."

Mary's voice was devoid of feeling, cold, calculating. "I do, you know. I want all that life can give me ... adventure, new faces, new scenes, high wages. I believe they're high there. I want amusement, a good time, the bright lights."

Anne was staring still. "Mary, don't you want the things most women want? The basic things? Doesn't marriage come into this? I mean in the years to come."

Mary allowed herself to be amused. "Oh, I didn't mean there weren't going to be any men in my life. I didn't mean I didn't want marriage, but none of this wide-eyed betrothal business, thanks, white veils and true lovers' knots and orange blossom and vowing deathless love. I don't believe in love. But it isn't to say I won't get married."

This was quite good. She was amazed at herself, at the

13

firmness of her voice, the cynical amusement in it.

"Mary!" Anne's voice was almost despairing. "But what is there in marriage if it doesn't mean just that? I can't believe —"

"There are other things, Anne. I'm not a romantic like you. Things that matter more ... comfort, security, kindred interests, a luxurious home ... oh, a host of things, much more lasting than this drink to me only with thine eyes business, fluttering pulses and a fastly-beating heart and pretending to friends and relations that you've met the love of your life, when it's nothing but a biological urge!"

What Anne would have said to that she never knew, for at that moment a buzzer sounded, sounded as if the patient was keeping his finger on it. Anne muttered something, vanished.

Mary put her hands to her forehead, pressed her cold fingers against her burning temples ... why on earth should her hands be cold in temperatures like these? ... shook her head slightly as if to free herself from her thoughts, moved to the table. She stood there, leaning her hands on it, gazing unseeingly at the wall opposite.

A wall with a door in it, a door that swung open slowly to present to her dismayed view the dressing-gowned figure of the famous patient, Ninian Macandrew. He had a glass of water in his hand. He stood and looked at her, his expression contemptuous.

"Well," he drawled, "eavesdroppers are supposed to hear no good of themselves. Sometimes, it appears, they hear no good of the speakers. That crack on my head must have addled my powers of discrimination. Or else you show one face to the patients ... to men ... and another to your fellow nurses. I'd taken you for a charming, devoted nurse. I thought you had high ideals, even thought you away ahead of all the others. And it was all a sham.

"I don't think we want you in New Zealand, Sister Rose. We built New Zealand on pioneers who were warm-hearted, God-fearing folk who put more into life than they got out of it, who planted trees they never saw grow to maturity, trees that would provide shelter and fuel for generations unborn, who married for love, who built families and tradition on that only possible foundation ... women who faced the rigours of backblock life because they *loved* their men, not because they had bank balances! They built their first homes out of the very sod ... there wasn't anything else to build them with. New Zealand life *is* good, how good I've realized only since I came here and saw how the underprivileged peoples live ... but New Zealand doesn't want women like you, believe me!"

His voice was like the flick of a whip. "Why, the women in that primitive village were worth half a dozen of you. They rescued me, tended me ... and even one more mouth to feed was a problem. What in the world is wrong with our standards of living?"

Mary held herself taut, braced. What could she say? Anne might have understood, she knew what lay behind this, but it wasn't the sort of thing you could explain to a stranger, to a patient you had nursed. Not even to Lieutenant Macandrew who had relied on you so completely, so insistently, when his life hung by a thread. She had found it so endearing. It had given her purpose in life again – but now he looked at you with contemptuous eyes.

You couldn't say: "Oh, I didn't mean it. It's just that I'm so hurt, that my world has fallen to pieces, that I want to pick up the bits myself, that I'm like a child whistling in the dark, pretending I don't care ... just that I don't want people prying, probing, pitying ..."

You couldn't say these things, even to this man who had been pulled back from the brink of death, who had suffered in service for the Commonwealth, whose family, far away, had mourned him as dead, fate unknown. Whose hand she had held in delirium, in unconsciousness, whose life she had battled for in company with other nurses, doctors.

So she said coldly, "If you'd not been out of bed when you shouldn't have been, you'd not have had the chance of eavesdropping. Maybe we've allowed you Kiwis just a little too much latitude. And I would remind you that my affairs are my own. What can my opinions possibly matter to you?"

He began to speak, checked himself, came forward and passed her without a word. He went into the passage, shut the door quietly behind him.

Mary swung round, stared at the door, mastered the ridiculous impulse to run after him, to say, "Mr. Macandrew, what were you going to say?" As if it mattered!

But in the next few days she had need of all her training and discipline to keep her mind on the ward duties and responsibilities, to make decisions, answer the men's quipping, appear outwardly undisturbed any time it was necessary to go near Lieutenant Ninian Macandrew. Thank goodness he was out in the ward now. If he had been in a private room he might have opened the conversation again. As it was he remained politely aloof, wrote letters, waited on the men who were still confined to bed, laughed and joked with the other nurses.

What did it matter? she asked herself desperately, scoldingly, as her mind returned to it when she was off duty. Soon she would be leaving all this. The men did get fond of their nurses, but it didn't last usually, and in this case the Lieutenant had been no more than friendly. He was an engaged man. The newspaper reports of his rescue had said that, so it did not matter if one soldier out of all these despised her. He would be flown home when his time came, as they all were, and she herself would have the healing tranquillity of long days at sea, the distraction of meeting new people, and then the adventure of new life in a new land.

It was the next day that the letter came for her. It had a New Zealand stamp and was post marked Lake Pukaki. Where was that? And who did she know? Could it be from one of the men she had nursed in her first days here? But she was sure none of them would write her. She stopped conjecturing, slit it open, drew out the letter, and turned to the back page for the signature since the printed "Mount Hebron Station, South Canterbury," meant nothing to her. Another envelope and the letter was enclosed. It was signed "Elspeth Macandrew." There was a line between Mary's brows now. It wasn't unknown for nurses to have notes of thanks from relatives, but they were mostly brief. This wasn't.

"Dear Sister Rose,

I must write to someone on the nursing staff about this matter, and I picked on you, not only because you are in charge of his ward, but because my son has written so much home about you. The enclosed letter is for him, and since the news isn't the kind one likes to send anyone, much less someone who has been so ill, I want to ask you to keep an eye on him for reaction after this.

"I am finding this most difficult to write. I would have come to tell him in person, even had my flight arranged, but I broke my arm and couldn't travel. I would like to tell you about it so you will know what to expect, and I have the feeling you will be the kind of person to understand, and who will stand by my boy in the next week or two till he is well enough to travel home. I would have preferred to tell him at home, but New Zealand is a small country and I dare not risk his being told this on the way home.

"I have a family very much spaced out and my son Ninian is much younger than his brother Roland. Despite that they have been good pals, always, though Roland has been married for years and lost his wife not long after Ninian first went out to Malaya. Ninian doesn't know that yet, we had reasons for not telling him.

"You know, of course, that he was lost all that time in the jungle, that at first his head injuries caused temporary loss of memory, that he was nursed back to health by those village folk we are so grateful to, and then, suffering many things in his struggle back through the jungle to civilisation, became very ill. We mourned him as dead; though, as all mothers do, I still carried round with me a faint hope that a miracle might have occurred and he be still alive.

"My son was engaged to someone he had known all his life, Nanette Williams. Exactly one day before we got the wonderful news that Ninian had survived, she became engaged to Roland. It was announced in the papers, so there has been no question of hushing it up. Someone would tell Ninian.

"You can imagine what anguish of spirit we have all suffered. My husband is many years my senior, and I would not allow him to travel on a mission as heartbreaking as this. Roland offered to come, but I was afraid of that. Afraid of a situation developing between the brothers.

"Roland has not had a very happy life, and apart from all that, Nanette loves Roland more than I ever feel she loved Ninian. I could be wrong, of course.

"Ninian has to be told. I've explained it as best I can in the enclosed letter. I am afraid to send it, yet I must. And I must rely on you to watch my boy, to help him. He may be deeply depressed. I am deadly afraid. The Ninian who left New Zealand could have taken this on the chin, I believe, but at this distance I am unable to gauge how his experiences in the jungle, and his subsequent illnesses, have affected him.

"He will not reproach Nanette or Roland, I know. He has an infinite capacity for sympathy and understanding, but I am afraid for himself. I do not know how deep it will go. I do not know if he will want to come home again. I have a feeling that in fairness to them he may stay away and never come home again. That, when fit, he may volunteer for dangerous duty, become reckless, uncaring, even bitter.

"When his last letter said he might be discharged very soon I knew I dared delay no longer. I have all a mother's fears. I don't really think he would do anything desperate, but – well, at times like this, one wonders if one really knows one's family at all. The only thing I can do is to put my trust in you. If you can in any way lighten the next few days for him I would be so grateful. I have found, all through life, that if one can only endure the first few days after a crisis, one finds strength for the rest. Once he comes home, if he does, I hope to find what he needs to help him most. Though I admit I cannot see my way clear to any solution at the moment.

"I shall be looking for a letter from you to let me know how he has taken this. I am sorry to put on to you the strain of such a distasteful task. The letter explains it all, but he will need someone to stand by after he reads it.

"With many thanks for what I am sure you will do on my behalf,

                    "Elspeth Macandrew."

Mary dropped the letter on to the table; her very fingers felt weak. She gazed unseeingly out of the window, closed her eyes against the brightness, trying to shut in her mind so that she might see with the eyes of the spirit how this Kiwi soldier would react. An instant and wild regret washed over her that so recently she and Lieutenant Macandrew had had a quarrel. Before that their relationship had been so pleasant, so normal, the teasing, amicable one of soldier and nurse.

It would have been so much easier had he respected her as

he had done earlier. It meant that any comforting words she might utter would be largely discounted by him because he didn't care for her attitude to life.

It showed that bitterness didn't pay. It not only harmed yourself but others too. In this case that entirely false attitude meant that she could not help this wounded and now-to-be-disillusioned soldier as she would like to have been able.

Nevertheless, action had to be taken. And soon. She would have to pick her time to give him the letter. It must not be done in the wards. She would consult with his doctor if she could get hold of him before his rounds. Ninian Macandrew could be moved into one of the private rooms. Later, not too much later, he must be moved back so that he couldn't brood too long. But he must be given time to get hold of himself.

Mary pulled herself together. She must not show too much pity. She herself knew how that could hurt.

*

Even so, she hadn't realised how hard it was going to be till she found herself in that private room and knew the giving could be no longer postponed. She was remembering that she had posted, only a few days before, a letter to this man's fiancée. A fat, bulging-at-the-seams letter. A love-letter. He would have been anticipating his return, their reunion, perhaps even planning their wedding. Mary steadied her lips, squared her starched shoulders.

Lieutenant Macandrew was sitting up against his pillows facing the door, and looked impatient, even a little apprehensive. He frowned when he saw it was Mary, said, "I say, Sister, nothing's gone wrong, has it? I asked the nurse why I was moved back in here, but either she didn't know or she was cagey about it. Why? Has something gone wrong? That last X-ray? I don't want anything to delay me now. The Colonel said he was arranging a flight as soon as the doctors give me the all-clear."

Mary swallowed. "Oh, it's nothing medical, Lieutenant. It's just this."

*Just this.* How idiotic could one get?

She moved to the bed, one hand in her deep pocket.

"Lieutenant, it isn't easy for me to do this, but it must be

19

done. I have a letter here from your mother, enclosed in one to me. She –"

His hand shot out, grasped her wrist. "Mother! Writing to *you*! Good lord, I know she's im –"

Mary shook her head at him with a gesture of authority that he obeyed out of sheer habit. "Please let me get this out, Lieutenant. There was something your mother felt you must know now that you're convalescent. But she thought it better to include it in a letter to the Sister-in-charge. No one is ill, or anything like that, but – well, here's the letter. I won't be far away. I know what's in it. If you want me, please ring. And if there's anything we can do for you, we'll do it."

She walked out of the room, her step as decisive and crisp as ever, but her knees like jelly, her vision blurred.

She had been through this herself.

Fifteen minutes later no bell had rung. Sister Rose knew she must go in to him. She didn't want anyone else to go.

The interval of waiting had done nothing for her knees.

*

The Lieutenant was turned away from the door, his face to the wall. He was quite motionless, too motionless. Something that spoke of rigid control.

For a horrible moment Sister Mary Rose felt she was going to be unable to find words. Her mouth was dry, her tongue felt too large. Pity appeared to be going to overwhelm her. Although she knew so well how pity stung, now she could understand all those bumbling, hurting, well-meant gestures that had come her way when she herself had known dis-illusionment, though at least she had had the inestimable blessing of being able to lick her wounds in privacy those first few days.

The Lieutenant turned. His eyes were quite steady, his voice controlled. It must be costing him quite an effort. But Mary's experienced eye took in his pallor, gauged the shock.

"A mess, isn't it?" he commented. Before she could speak he added, "Poor Mother, what a letter to have to write!"

That got Mary by the throat; she sought for words.

Before she could get them out he said, "In fact, poor every-one. What a homecoming this is going to be. Agony in A major for everybody."

20

Mary said crisply, her fingers on his pulse, "I'm going to get you some coffee. Naturally this has been a shock. There are all sorts of things I should say, but most of them would be platitudes, I'm afraid. Things like saying this won't always be as poignant, that time makes a difference, and that sort of thing, but you won't be able to believe that yet, though I know it's true. Doctor Steedman will come in to see you presently. If there is anything he or I can do, please ask us."

He ignored the last part of her words, gave a short sardonic laugh. "So you know it's true, you said? What can you possibly know about this sort of thing? You've got no more decent feeling in you than a potato. It's a hell of a situation. I'm fond of my brother. I'm —" he broke off. She supposed he could not yet mention Nanette's name. He continued, "And nobody like you, so cold, so calculating, so devoid of warm human emotions, could possibly understand. You don't believe in love, remember? Only in comfort, security, suitability, bank balances!"

Oddly enough it didn't particularly hurt Mary. This would get it out of his system, lessen the shock. This railing against her was really railing against Nanette, against the fate that had brought him back to his world at the very time his fiancée had found comfort with his brother.

They decided they would not move the Lieutenant back into the ward till after evening visiting hours. Mary should have been off duty, but stayed on. She wouldn't feel satisfied till she saw the Lieutenant asleep for the night; he was to be given a shot in the arm. And she was going to be particularly careful to make sure he had no access to any drugs. Certainly they were always careful, but it wouldn't hurt to double-check. Lieutenant Macandrew had had the run of the ward the last week or two, and shock could have a depressant effect.

Mary was glad she had not gone off duty when she saw Ninian's Colonel enter the ward passage. His Colonel, who was Colonel Secumbe, Althea Secumbe's father. If this man had not brought out his daughter to taste the gaiety of Malayan life, Francis and she might have been married now.

She went swiftly towards him. "Oh, Colonel, might I have a word with you before you see the Lieutenant?"

She opened a door.

The Colonel said, "Nothing wrong with him, is there? I've come to tell him I have his flight arranged. The doctor —"

She interrupted him without apology. "That was what I was afraid of, Colonel. He — he's just had bad news from home. Not bereavement, but — you see, they thought he was dead. And his fiancée had meanwhile become engaged to his brother. It was announced in the papers the day before they got word he was alive. But they could do nothing while he was so ill."

"Good God!" said the Colonel. "What a ruddy mess!"

"I had a letter from his mother, enclosing the one for him. He had it this morning, and has taken it reasonably well. We put him in a side room, but will put him back in the ward after you've seen him. We'll make sure he sleeps."

The Colonel nodded. He cleared his throat, looked at her, said unexpectedly, "Well, Sister, he couldn't have anyone finer than you to help him over this bad patch ... since you've been through the mill yourself."

Once again Mary was bereft of words. She didn't know the Colonel had known about his daughter, Francis, herself.

He added, "I've always wanted to say something, but I thought I'd better not. I could have spanked Thea. I didn't know it was going on. I'd told her not to flirt with the men in the regiment, so she looked outside for entertainment. Maybe it's better not to meddle, but feel I must say this. At first Thea took it all very lightly, but suddenly she's developed a conscience. She isn't seeing Francis any more. These things do happen, you know. Sudden infatuations and the tropics — and loneliness — are the very devil, you know. So there's a chance things could go right for you yet."

It all seemed incredible to Mary. As if it wasn't happening to her, as if it were happening on a screen.

The Colonel was tall, broad, a magnificent specimen of a man. She looked up at him, said gently, "Thank you, but ... it's all over between us," and to her horror, her eyes filled with tears.

She put up an impatient hand to brush them away, the Colonel took a step nearer her, took her chin in his hand, said, "Oh, my dear," then spun round as a voice, cold, controlled, said, "Were you looking for me, sir?"

They had started so noticeably it looked like guilt, though it was only embarrassment at being caught out in so emotional a situation, highlighted by the fact they were both in uniform. Yet neither of them realised how it looked to the man outside, how that last sentence of Mary's had sounded. Some of their awkwardness sprang from the fact that they shared with the Lieutenant his painful knowledge of a most poignant situation back in his homeland.

The Lieutenant looked directly at Mary. "I had thought you might be explaining things on my behalf and finding it far from easy, so I thought I would spare you that. However –".

His tone indicated his contempt. Mary felt alarm. This man was the Lieutenant's superior officer. This wasn't done, to use a tone like that, even if she had heard that New Zealand and Australian soldiers were the most casual in the world. And it could be that the Lieutenant was in the mood to be reckless.

She said quickly, "That's exactly what we were doing, Lieutenant, and I'm afraid I was being a little upset about it."

The Colonel, quite unaware of what his subordinate had read into the scene, said, looking his Lieutenant in the eye, "It's very natural she should be upset. Any right-thinking woman would be. Now let's go into one of the side rooms and discuss your return home. This may have altered things."

Half an hour later Mary went into the room. The Lieutenant was sitting on the edge of a vacant bed, smoking. He looked up, sounded irritated. "Now for heaven's sake treat me ordinarily. I've had a knock. So what? I can take it! There's only one thing that worries me – my return home. How will it affect the family? How will people treat me? I can imagine it all. We're a closely-knit commnity, even if the sheep-stations are far apart. That's the way of it in the country.

"I can just imagine how people will watch us ... Roland, Nanette, myself. I would write and tell Roland for goodness' sake get married and get it over, but knowing my brother – he has all the patience in the world – he'll probably want to put it to the test, have me home and make Nanette choose. It will be ghastly. She will want to choose him but will never be able to convince him, and Rol hasn't had the easiest life as it is. Mother and Dad will be torn between the two of us. No parent should be. It will be hell. But there *is* a solution, and you could help."

Mary was so surprised she sat down sideways on a hard chair, rested her hands on the back and her chin on her hands and regarded him dazedly.

Then her surprise lessened. "Oh, do you mean I could write to your mother – tell her you've taken it philosophically?"

He shook his head. "No. You intend going to New Zealand, don't you? I want you to come with me, pretend we've fallen in love. I'll make it worth your while."

On the heels of Mary's utter and bewildered surprise came the thought that she seemed to have spent the last two days seeking words and not finding them.

Finally she said, "I'm afraid I don't understand. What else would that mean to your family than that the hurt had gone so deep they would think you'd done it in chagrin? It wouldn't deceive them a moment."

"If it was done like that, yes, Sister. But if I wrote my mother a letter – in fact two letters, one to Nanette, dating them by yesterday's date, telling them I'd met someone I'd fallen in love with, quite madly, and breaking off my engagement ... with suitable regrets of course, even if it bore today's postmark they would think it was posted before I'd got the other. The times would be near enough."

This time Mary's silence was a considering one. This plan had something of genius in it. There were snags, of course. The fact that she was even considering it came as a surprise to her.

Her hair lay in wet strands on her forehead beneath her veil in this humid heat that was almost unbearable tonight. She pushed it up, let it fall back.

"It would solve the immediate embarrassment, soldier, but cause complications later."

"Such as?" His eyes were very bright, too bright for a recently very ill man, but it might be only because he was realising she wasn't turning him down flat. He had to talk it out, she knew.

"Such as?" he repeated.

"Well, engagements usually imply something. A contract

24

to marry in the future. Something would have to be done about that."

His lip curled. "You aren't prepared to go as far as that, I take it?"

Her blue eyes flashed. "Hardly. How perfectly ridiculous. Imagine you even thinking such a thing!"

"It's your own fault. Is there anything wrong with my thinking that a woman who said she wasn't looking for love in marriage wouldn't flinch from one that would provide her with the things she deems of greater importance ... comfort, security, etcetera. Marriage with me would provide all that. My people have a very large sheep-run. What more could you want?"

It took all her time not to flinch perceptibly. She swallowed and said steadily, "I could possibly want a husband who didn't despise me as you do."

"I see. I know too much about you. You mean you'd deceive some poor bloke into thinking you did love him?"

Mary made a gesture of distaste, impatience. "Lieutenant, this is getting us nowhere. We aren't discussing marriage – or my character. We're discussing a most absurd proposition you've just put to me. I was just academically interested in how you proposed to manage the situation later. Meaning that if you turn up with a fiancée the family will expect wedding bells sooner or later. How would you deal with that?"

"It wouldn't be difficult. I could want to settle down quietly after arduous adventures. You could say you wanted to find out if you liked the New Zealand way of life. Then later we could quarrel, or if that seems – at the time – unnecessarily dramatic, we could just announce that we had discovered we were not really suited. People would merely say these sudden attractions don't stand the test of time, that patients often fall for nurses, but it doesn't last. Or you could say you were homesick for Canada, drift back home, then write breaking it off.

"And if you're wondering about finance, I have shares in the estate, I would pay you a wage equivalent to – even in excess of a nursing salary."

Sister Rose gazed into space, considering it. He took her lack of response for distaste for the whole thing, reluctance to be involved, and he turned away, his voice rough.

"All right, Sister, forget it. I might have known you wouldn't. After all, it's not your concern, is it? Doesn't matter to you if the whole family is going to suffer great anguish of mind, if all our lives get snarled up. You don't have good warm blood in your veins. You do everything on a coldly calculated basis. Let it go."

She stepped after him, caught him by the elbow. He swung round, his brown eyes wary. "Now, don't trot out something about it being time I got off to bed. Bed can be torture if you can't sleep. And I don't want to be doped, either."

Mary found herself smiling, almost the first time she had smiled this horrible day. "Maybe it's my duty to see you do go to sleep with an easier mind, just the same, soldier. All right, I'll do what you want me to do. Since you have all the methods of terminating our business arrangement worked out, I'll consent." Her eyes met his coolly. She didn't know what prompted her to add mockingly, "You could hardly expect me to turn anything so advantageous down, could you? The chance of seeing a new country, of earning my living in the easiest way possible ... it's going to be money for jam."

He began to say something, no doubt in the way of some scathing retort, but must have realised it would not pay to offend her and checked the words.

"Okay then. I'll get cracking on that letter if you leave me here till it's done."

"You can stay here for the night. It will disturb the ward if you're moved back in too late. I imagine those two letters will take some writing. And I'll slip out and post them for you. I'll tell Staff Nurse you're not to be disturbed. I'll think up something to account for it, and I'll come back in an hour and a half. Not longer, mind, or I'll be in trouble myself."

Mary went out of the room. She was glad when the time was up. She felt so unsettled she would find it hard to sleep tonight.

She found he had only one letter ready, a fat one, addressed and sealed.

"To your mother? Where's the one to Nanette?"

"Inside that, of course."

Her surprise was far from mild. "Good heavens, you don't know much about women, do you? Even if she seems to prefer your brother, and this may be a way out of an impossible situation, I don't think women like letters as important as this handed on by the man's mother."

He semed at a loss for a moment, then he said, "That way it doesn't need a postmark. Mother won't be quite so astute – she'll never pick it."

Mary considered it. "Yes, that could be better."

"And they will both be greatly relieved when the letters arrive."

Mary thought his mother would be relieved. A terrible thing for a mother to feel torn between two sons, knowing one was bound to lose the woman he loved. Yes, it was a wonderful solution in that respect, but ... how was Nanette going to react?

Ninian Macandrew was quite sure she loved Roland the more, but did she? Might it not have been consolatory? He would be sorrowing for the loss of a wife, she a betrothed. They might have found comfort in each other, even in shared memories, but now – Ninian had returned from the ranks of the missing. His whole story was a romance and it had been blazoned all over the world. The girl might be chagrined, hurt in her pride, if not in her heart, to have the engagement terminated because he had fallen for someone else. Men didn't have these nuances of feelings. But it didn't matter now. It was her duty to see he had a good night's sleep.

She picked up a syringe from a kidney bowl she had brought in with her.

His dismay was comical. "Sister, that's quite unnecessary. I'll sleep now I have the problem resolved."

"I'm taking no chances on that," she said firmly, "and I might point out to you, Lieutenant, that you're in no position to argue with me."

She was swabbing his upper arm as she spoke. In went the needle.

He said reproachfully, with a return of the old manner before their personal problems had obtruded into an easy relationship, "And you'd better stop calling me Lieutenant, if we're going to get engaged."

She withdrew the needle, swabbed the prick, said coolly,

27

"We won't be engaged till we're on the way. I want no one here to know anything about it."

His eyes narrowed. "I get it. You don't want the Colonel to know."

"Well, the Colonel and others."

"You know, I think you mean the Colonel most of all."

Mary realised what he meant. The Colonel could suspect that it had been cooked up to save face on Ninian's return. It was best kept a secret between the two of them.

"Yes . . . particularly the Colonel."

"You don't mean to tell him at all ?"

"Of course not. No need to tell him, is there ?"

"No. After all, at the earliest, I should think he'd not be back in New Zealand till the end of the year."

Mary frowned. He was making quite a thing about this, wasn't he? A bit puzzling. But what matter? This man needed sleep now. Perhaps his thinking was already muddled. His lids drooped.

"Goodnight, Lieutenant," she said.

The lids lifted, mischief lit the brown eyes. "You ought to get a bit of practice in, Sister. Kiss me goodnight."

Her Ward Sister voice returned. "That isn't in the contract. We can appear affectionate in front of your people convincingly when we arrive. That's all."

But as she went out she thought : "Well, at least he has retained his sense of humour. He'll see it through." She looked back as she reached the door. He was already asleep. But even as she posted his letter Mary knew she herself had little chance of sleep that night.

As she tossed and turned she asked herself what she had committed herself to. Close involvement in what could be a very sticky situation ? It was fraught with all sorts of complications. A thought obtruded itself, an unwelcome thought . . . the knowledge that, although she had tried to tell herself she would have done this for any man in like situation, that was not exactly true. Wasn't it the truth that against her will, despire the hard words he had flung at her, despite the fact that this man's heart was given to another, she *wanted* to go with him ? She knew a strange reluctance to let him go out of her life. She wanted to be the one to play the part of his bogus fiancée !

28

# CHAPTER 2

THEY decided to go back by ship. If they both left by air it would cause comment, since it was known Mary's passage was booked, and also it would give the family time to adjust themselves to the idea, though the Lieutenant's mother's letter had been full of joy at the way things had turned out.

There had been a letter from Nanette too, an extremely prompt one, Mary had thought, but naturally Ninian Macandrew had not shown that one to Sister Rose. He had been quiet after reading it. Sympathy on her part would have been out of place, and in any case, as she told him, she wanted no gossip, so was spending no more time with him than formerly.

He was completely convalescent now, allowed many privileges, and had been out several times. No one appeared to connect the sailing date with any purpose. The Colonel had been told he was going by ship to let his family get used to the idea of his return home. He thought it a good idea, so did Doctor Steedman, who was the only other one who knew Nanette was now engaged to the Lieutenant's brother.

The doctor said to her one morning, "I'm so glad you'll be with Macandrew on that trip over. Could you do a bit of unobtrusive watching? That infection he had was an obscure one, as you know, and the sort of thing to flare up again, if he should get depressed and run down. He took that fancy to you – thought you were his sister and so on – and he won't know anyone else aboard, I suppose, so naturally you'll gravitate together.

"See he enters into the social life on board, doesn't brood. And you could acquaint the ship's doctor more intimately with his injuries – full case-history, in fact. I think he's pretty fit, and he's rallied from this shock better than I'd expected, but there could be a delayed reaction, so watch for it."

Anne said one day, "I'd have thought the Lieutenant would have wanted to get home as soon as possible."

Mary said lamely, "Well, he's taking a car home on that ship. I believe they aren't allowing too many new cars into

New Zealand just now. Most of the soldiers take one from here."

Anne looked at her. "Aren't you quaint, honey! He doesn't have to conduct it personally."

Mary laughed. "No, silly thing to say. I daresay he thinks the sea voyage will set him up, complete his convalescence. In fact, the doctor suggested it. He's been through something, you know, even if he does look fit now. And he can see a bit more of the world."

"Don't fall for him on the way, Mary. You know what moonlight on boat-decks does. He's got a fiancée waiting for him back home."

"I know. Besides which, he's not exactly my cup of tea."

Anne whistled. "I'd have thought he'd have been anybody's dream – tall, broad, loose-limbed, rugged and brown."

Mary laughed, went away. She paused by the Lieutenant's chair on the balcony.

He said in a low voice, "Pick up that letter on the locker, would you, Sister? From Mother. She thinks you may feel diffident about coming home with me, so that's to welcome you." He grinned. "She thinks you may feel awkward, since we're supposed to have fallen in love while I was still engaged!"

She slipped it into her pocket. "How very nice of her. Thank you."

The Lieutenant glanced round. The other men were all busy.

"Since I'm allowed out and about now, how about meeting me tonight and having dinner together?"

"No, it wouldn't do. We'd be bound to run into someone from here. We shall see more than enough of each other when we get to New Zealand. Besides –"

"Besides what? It won't –"

"I have a dinner engagement, Lieutenant."

His eyes narrowed. "With whom?"

"Does it matter?"

"Yes. Singapore isn't exactly some little backwoods Canadian village, you know."

Her lips twitched. "I may have been brought up in the backwoods, Lieutenant, but I nursed in Toronto. I imagine it's much larger than any of your New Zealand cities."

He ignored that. "But there are some very iffy types about, and you have such peculiar ideas, you –"

Mary's eyes had lit with pure mischief. "Your Colonel would love to hear himself described as an 'iffy type', I'm sure!"

"The Colonel! You're having dinner with the Old Man? Well, I'll be –"

"He's not particularly old, you know. In his prime, in fact."

"Prime! He's got a daughter as old as you!"

Mary closed her eyes against the stab of that. The Colonel's daughter. His lovely daughter. Althea, whom Francis loved.

She rallied. "Then the Colonel must have married very young. I find him charming. Besides, I much prefer older men. They're not so rash, so hasty. And as escorts I find them quite delightful."

The Lieutenant made an impatient gesture, sweeping her comments aside. "Anyway, I didn't mean to enter into a discourse on his age. All Colonels get called The Old Man. I mean I don't think –"

"What *do* you mean? I find this conversation pointless. What has it got to do with you whom I go out with? Just because we're entering in upon a bogus engagement it doesn't mean you can pick my . . . friends."

"I want to make this engagement look convincing, so you'll jolly well –"

"I find you absurd. That doesn't enter into it, because the engagement doesn't begin till we reach New Zealand."

He said violently, "Are you having dinner at his flat?"

"Hardly." Mary's thoughts were wryly humorous. That would never have done. That could involve having dinner with Althea too. She thought this gesture of the Colonel's very kind. He was endearingly perturbed about the situation, yet the poor pet had about as much idea of handling it as a pig trying to pick up a cup and saucer.

She said lightly, "We're going to some quite fabulous place. I'm looking forward to it."

The Lieutenant snorted. "All you girls think about . . . glamour and excitement!"

Mary said mildly, looking up, "Oh, there's Nurse Macmaster. I want to see her," and she whisked away with the starched finality peculiar to nurses.

She supposed the Lieutenant was afraid lest, to the Colonel, she drop any hint of their plans. That must be it.

\*

She quite enjoyed the sea trip. There were few passengers, most of them elderly, so little formal social life, and other servicemen invalided home had been flown, so there was no one to remark on their association and it seemed natural for an ex-patient and a nurse to gravitate together. It was gloriously hot without being oppressively so, and even Mary's pink-and-white skin, that contrasted so with her shining cap of black hair, browned a little.

The Lieutenant was naturally brown, with tawny-fair hair, and after weeks in hospital, he turned quite bronze. More than one of the middle-aged couples watched them indulgently.

This was a good sightseeing trip; it took in four Australian ports, Fremantle, Adelaide, Melbourne, Sydney, and the ship spent several days at each.

"We shop for a ring in Sydney," said Ninian Macandrew, the night before they berthed there.

Mary looked startled.

He sounded annoyed. "Didn't think I could take you home without one, did you?"

"No-o. I hadn't thought much about that part. But there's no need to buy one. I have a diamond dress ring, a cluster. I could wear that."

He said slowly, "I don't particularly care for diamonds. I like colour. The family know that. They would think it odd."

"They could always be told I preferred diamonds."

"Don't argue so much." He sounded really angry.

She gave in. "Oh, well. Since in any case it will be returned to you."

He did not answer, and she wished she hadn't said it. Perhaps he was thinking of another ring that would be returned to him.

Sydney excited Mary, it was so different, so cosmopolitan, glittering and grimy, unbelievably beautiful and ugly all mixed up together, with the clear hot light of Australia washing the whole scene.

The Lieutenant spent far more on the ring than she wanted him to. When the salesman moved away she said so. He said impatiently, "Oh, don't be so stupid. It has to be better than the one I bought Nanette. Besides, it's out of character for you to protest about the price."

Mary remembered with surprise that she was supposed to be an opportunist. She said coldly, "But it won't be mine . . . eventually, so it is a wicked waste." She subsided because the salesman had returned.

Evidently from now on the acting was to start, for Ninian Macandrew smiled suddenly and said, "Exactly the colour of your eyes, Mary. That's why I wanted a sapphire."

The jeweller beamed on them and presented them with a case of teaspoons, which made the Lieutenant laugh when they regained the sunlit street.

"A memento for you, Sister, of a mad episode in your youth. No doubt if your grandchildren ever ask you where you got them from you'll not tell them!"

As they walked away, the new ring felt heavier than ever Francis's ring had felt. Then Ninian said suddenly, "That ship's going to be here three whole days yet. Let's see if we can fly across, Sister. I've a sudden yen to get home."

Mary panicked. Till now meeting Ninian's family had seemed so far off, unreal. But now she would be pitchforked into this man's family, and despite the welcoming letters they had received at every port, it might not be all plain sailing. There would, naturally, be tensions and undercurrents. With the ship lying here three days, and the prospect of the four-day crossing of the Tasman Sea, it had been a whole week away.

She swallowed, clutched his arm. "I don't know. How long would it take us to fly?"

"Four hours Sydney to Christchurch. Although, as we're two hours ahead of Australia, by the clocks we arrive six hours after, you gain two on the way."

She said slowly, "We may not be able to get a flight. And besides, Ninian, is it really wise?"

He looked puzzled. "What do you mean?"

"You – you always take the risk of catching folk at an inconvenient time when you take them by surprise. They may prefer to know when you're coming, to arrange a welcome home."

Remembering her own frantically tragic moment of surprise, her eyes were almost black.

"Good heavens, girl, I'm not dropping in unexpectedly upon acquaintances ... I'm going *home*. Apart from everything else, it could be, with the situation as it is, they get het up about my actual arrival, act unnaturally and so on, so I just want to breeze in with you and all their apprehensions will scatter. I think it will dispel the last shadow for them."

Mary was still uncertain. The last shadow for them, yes, but what of the man himself? How was he going to feel when he met Nanette again? Would he be able, even for the sake of his brother, to conceal any hint of bitterness? Might not his love for her swamp his mood of self-sacrifice? If she wasn't perfectly happy he would worry about her. If she was blatantly so, he would resent it.

His eyes were on her, puzzling at her worried frown. "It will be all right. Your being with me will ensure that. Things are nicely tidied up. Your co-operation has made this possible. Let's go and see if Qantas can book us in."

*

Now that dream of a harbour with its shining span of bridge had been left behind and they were flying across the Tasman. Mary shivered suddenly. He looked at her curiously.

"What was that for?" he asked.

She said slowly, "New Zealand looks so far on the map, so small, the last outpost of civilisation and only the South Pole beyond that. I've flown a lot, but all the other flights have had vast land masses as their destination. This is the first time I've ever felt nervous."

The Lieutenant smiled, rather nicely. "Oh, there's quite a tidy bit of New Zealand really. She's about the size of United Kingdom. And she makes up in height for what she lacks in area, so she stands up a bit above her long white cloud."

"Long white cloud?"

"The translation of the Maori name for New Zealand. Aotearoa. You accent every vowel equally, you notice. Makes a musical language. Means the land of the long white cloud – not that you notice that so much coming in by air as by sea. We could get a glimpse of our highest mountain, the mountain that dominates my home. Aorangi. It's over twelve thousand feet high. Means the Cloud-Piercer or Sky-Piercer."

"I thought Mount Cook was your highest mountain."

"Aorangi is Mount Cook. What a blessing you're used to snow and snow sports. You'll be in your element at our place, and coming right into autumn, it will be the best time."

"Yes, it will help pass away the next few weeks."

He turned sharply in his seat, his eyes raking her. "Sister, it may mean more than that. We can't break this up too soon. It would look suspicious. I want Nanette and Roland safely married. They've waited long enough."

"Long enough? What do you mean? Why, it's no time since your brother's first wife died, is it ?"

His brown eyes met hers squarely. "My brother loved Nanette when she was a pixie of a child at twelve. He was thirty-two. When she was seventeen he wanted to be engaged to her, he was prepared to wait for marriage, but her parents wouldn't hear of it. Not only that, but they persuaded Rol that it wasn't fair to Nanette. She'd never had a chance to meet many young men of her own age – he had always been around. That there were too many years between them. That if he really loved her he would go away and let her meet someone her own age. And because he adored her and thought it really would be for her own good, he did just that. He went up to the North Island with a stock and station agency firm, and left her to eat her heart out for him. And out of nothing but pity he married someone who was being slowly crippled with some obscure disease. Actually they were happy enough together, if not exactly as Nanette and Roland would have been. I've always had an idea that Nanette got engaged to me mainly because I reminded her of Roland. So you see . . ."

She saw. Perhaps more than he wanted her to. But there was one question she could not ask. She could not say, "And how much does it mean to you ?" And yet quite suddenly and inexplicably she very much wanted to know.

"So you see, Sister, how important it is that we play our parts. Not only that, but play them well."

Her lips twitched. "Then in that case, may I remind you,

*Lieutenant*, that you've called me Sister twice in the last five minutes. The name is Mary!"

Laughter united them briefly.

He said, "To play the part really well it will have to be 'darling' quite often, and 'my love.' I trust you won't find that too distasteful?"

"Oh, no, I'll remember you'll have your tongue in your cheek. I'll remember the epithets you'll mentally be framing will be 'gold-digger' and 'go-getter'."

"You certainly have a shrewish tongue, Sister darling. I find it in me to pity those poor devils of nurses under your care."

"It could be I'm shrewish only to you."

"Well, if that's your true nature perhaps it's a relief to you not to have to try to appear the sweet, rather unselfish girl I first took you for, even if at times you were a trifle distant."

Their eyes met. Mary's gave nothing away. "You ought to be glad I'm not," she pointed out.

He sighed. "Another cryptic speech!"

"I mean that had I been the type you first took me for, you probably wouldn't have had the nerve to propose this deception. But as you decided ... by what you overheard ... that I was self-seeking, mercenary, hard, I was ideal material for what you wanted."

"That's true." The drawling amusement of his voice maddened Mary, but she would not betray it. "After all, it would be a bit risky to attempt something like this with an ordinary decent girl. One might fall in love with her, or she with me."

"I shouldn't think it very likely, Lieutenant. Not the latter, anyway. To put it crudely, you aren't everybody's cup of tea – censorious, with old-fashioned ideas about women."

"You mean because I still expect women to marry for love?"

"Yes, I've not much time for love. It snarls the lines, destroys one's judgment, blinds us to more lasting things."

Mary was conscious of inner astonishment at herself, even as she uttered the words. They were so opposed to all she had always believed in. What was there about this man that so roused her? Why did she find it so necessary to impress upon him that she was not attracted? Simply because he had overheard her being silly? One moment she was wretchedly sorry for him, the next she was being cruelly cynical.

"You mean more lasting *material* things, don't you?" he persisted. "The outward signs of comfort and security. The things that mean a man has arrived, isn't still making his way. The reason why you prefer older men. When's the Colonel coming back to New Zealand? I heard just before we left Malaya that it might be earlier."

Mary blinked at this sudden change of subject. That would mean he wanted to get away from the too personal.

She said hesitantly, "Well, to me he only said he thought early next year. Why?"

He ignored that. His mouth twisted. "Oh, well, that will give you time to be free of me. We'll have our little fiasco all washed up."

She turned a puzzled face to him. "If you're trying to find out if I told him what we planned to do, the answer is no. It was completely your business."

"Why did he ask you out to dinner?"

She couldn't help it, she snorted with laughter. "Do you realise how derogatory that sounds? As if I wasn't the sort men ask out. I expect the Colonel was a bit lonely. He's not the type to be keen on the sort of feminine company so eagerly offered in the East, and as he's a widower he hasn't the comradeship some of the men have who have their wives stationed there with them. His daughter is a gay little piece, and besides, I really think the Colonel quite likes me. We found a lot in common."

"Oh, *like*! That's about the strongest word in your vocabulary, isn't it? A milk-and-water word."

She said helplessly, "Well, you don't want me to say I cherish a strong passion for him, do you?"

But he didn't laugh, he said, "No, even you aren't a big enough hypocrite for that."

Mary suddenly knew she was losing her temper, and you couldn't in an aeroplane thousands of feet above the earth, close to other people.

She said, in a controlled voice, "I'll just watch the scenery for a bit . . . or the lack of it. I much prefer it to these sarcastic exchanges."

She turned to the window to look down on the grey, foam-flecked lonely sea that seemed to be crawling below them.

\*

Christchurch was bathed in autumn sunshine as they circled round and came in. They were soon through the customs and taken into the air-centre on the airport bus. It was late afternoon, and the time of year had turned the willows and poplars to torches of flame beside the stream of the gentle Avon that wandered through the flat city.

By common consent they were now playing the part of any engaged couple, well aware that soon they would be playing it all day. Ninian said of the willows, "Actually they're all descended from willow shoots brought here from Napoleon's grave at St. Helena."

"Oh, I love to hear things like that. You feel as if you reach out and touch a page of living history. Living things, not dry chronicles."

He regarded her assessingly. "Mother is going to be enchanted with you. She's that way, too. How strange life is! If I'd been in love with you I'd have been quaking in my shoes wondering how the family would like you, and ten to one they would have found something to disapprove, to dislike. As it is, I could bet my last button you're a howling success."

"And only you will know that under the veneer I shall cultivate to convince them that our engagement is a bed of roses. I'm really a most obnoxious type of female."

He ignored that. "You even have the right name to endear yourself to the family. I ought to have told you. They might think it odd I haven't mentioned it to you. We had a little sister called Rosemary. She died when I was twelve. The sweetest kid. Dad was never quite the same."

Mary swallowed. In his delirium he had taken her for his little sister. He must have heard her name. Mary Rose. Rosemary.

"Oh, won't it be a bit poignant for them?" she asked.

"I've an idea they'll be so grateful to you for this solution to the family mix-up, they'll love it. Now, when we get into the city we'll make arrangements to get a rental car to drive down in tomorrow and book in at a hotel for tonight.

38

Perhaps we could do a show."

"No, thank you. I feel we'll have more than enough of each other's company the next while, and I'm woefully tired. I'll buy a paperback and go to bed early to read."

If she expected him to be insulted she was disappointed. He laughed, said, "You give no quarter, do you? I find it refreshing."

All the way south next morning a sense of unreality persisted with Mary, as if she had been propelled into this situation without making any decision herself. What would happen when she met Ninian's people was most unpredictable. Mary felt suddenly as nervous about it as if she really did intend to marry into the family.

They were going across the Canterbury plains, crossing a river more than a mile wide, the Rakaia, when she suddenly thought of something.

"Ninian, will we be meeting Nanette and Roland right away?"

"Not unless by some ill chance they're at Mount Hebron today. Roland is a stock and station agent at Fairlie, and I believe Nanette is there just now, with an aunt. Her people are gone now – they had a place near us when we were all small – but she has numbers of relations in South Canterbury, and she's so perfect a housekeeper that she's always in demand. She has other relations near us, around the lake."

"And we don't go through Fairlie?"

"Yes, we do. We're going due south to Timaru, which is our nearest city ... not a large one, but a seaport ... then we strike west into the Mackenzie country. From Fairlie we start going through the mountain passes, interspersed with large river-flats. But I don't intend to stop at Fairlie."

Mary was silent. He couldn't bear to – yet, she supposed. She broke the silence by saying, "That has a familiar sound ... the Mackenzie country. Reminds me of our Mackenzie River. Was it named after some famous pioneer?"

Ninian laughed. "No, quite the opposite. After an infamous sheep rustler. But we're very fond and proud of Mackenzie just the same. Maybe time and distance has lent glamour – plus the fact that *our* sheep were never stolen."

"When will we get there?" Mary asked.

"Oh, late afternoon. It's about two hundred miles, and

39

some of it slow going. Rough shingle part of the way, and mountain passes."

There were a thousand questions she wanted to ask him but some she dare not. He must be raw still from finding out Nanette was going to marry Roland. He seemed sure she would still want to. But how much did any man know a woman's heart? Roland may always have loved Nanette, but. . . .

Mary kept the conversation to the scenery, which was easy to do in beauty like this. The great wheat fields of the plains reminded her of home, flat, rich golden, with great red headers lumbering through, and far across to the west an unbroken line of mountains upflung against a brilliant sky. Here on the plains were mostly English trees, and autumn was splashing the leaves with flame and gold and russet. Back in the hills, Ninian said, was dense native bush, evergreen, but the pioneers had found the plains bare except for tussock, with never a stream nor a tree to break the monotony, except against the mountains and right at the sea edge. Only the big sprawling rivers had intersected the featureless stretches, holding up the settlers for weeks at a time when in flood.

Mary asked, "Is there much land west, beyond the mountains?"

"No, much less than this side . . . just a narrow strip comprising the West Coast Province, with some of the most varied and spectacular scenery in the world."

"And where you live, can you cut over or through the mountains there, to the West Coast?"

"No, it's quite impassable there. There are very few roads. There is the Lewis Pass in North Canterbury, Arthur's Pass straight out from Christchurch, with the Otira Railway Tunnel in the same area, and below us, by Lake Wanaka and Lake Hawea, there is one only recently put through, the Haast Road, named after a famous explorer and naturalist, Julius von Haast. A magnificent undertaking, it will soon push its way up to South Westland townships, and it will mean a great tourist attraction, a circular route.

"Below that, coming up from Invercargill way, is one of the finest scenic roads in the world, cut through native bush and rain forests, completely unspoiled, the road to Milford

Sound – a fiord really – through the Homer Tunnel. Dad will want to take you there, it's his favourite holiday."

She said drily, "But you won't take holidays in winter, will you?"

"No. We stay round because of the snow sports at our back door. Besides, you can't go to Milford by road – only air – in winter. Avalanches thunder down on it."

"Then I won't be seeing Milford. I won't be here in your spring! When is your spring ... August?"

"Starts in September. But you *will* be here. I hope you realise that we've got to be convincing enough long enough to get Roland and Nanette married before we stage our parting?"

"Surely it shouldn't take as long as that?"

Ninian looked straight ahead, a furrow between his brows. "Roland is so patient, knows so well how to wait. He wouldn't take his happiness at the cost of mine. We'll have to be most loving, I'm afraid, or he'll see through it."

He turned his head, his eyes met hers, amusement flickering in his brown eyes. To her dismay Mary found herself blushing vividly.

"That's much better," said Ninian approvingly. "You look far more lovely like that ... all confused and pink. Much more like a prospective bride meeting her in-laws for the first time. Not icy disdain and keep-your-distance-soldier, all hospital starch and no quickened pulses!"

Mary felt a spurt of temper. "May I point out to you that I'm only playing a part? You aren't likely to quicken my pulses or put me in a flutter. This is all pretence. I'll do my very best to appear ... er ... fond of you, but you can't expect me to look all dewy-eyed and shaken every time you come into a room. What's the matter? What are you stopping for?"

"This," he said briefly, and moved nearer.

Alarmed, Mary looked up. Her uplifted face gave Ninian maximum opportunity. His arms imprisoned her. She tried to turn her head. His mouth came down on hers, hard.

The pressure was quite merciless, his fingers were like steel biting into her upper arms. She was quite powerless to move, and her captor took his time.

He lifted his mouth from hers, but still held her in that

41

strong grasp. A car went past, hooting derisively. He took no notice. His brows, brown with a tawny glint, were quizzical.

"Well?" he drawled. "So I can't put you in a flutter, eh? Can't quicken your pulse? Now I could bet your pulses are racing at the moment. In fact, you're absolutely breathless, and your colour is even higher than before."

Mary found her voice. "You can put it all down to temper, Lieutenant. I'm not being used to being kissed against my will. The fluttering, the pulses, the breathlessness, the colour ... they all add up to one thing: I'm in a flaming rage! Don't you ever dare do that again!"

His voice was rich with amusement. "Oh, come! You know perfectly well there will have to be a few tender scenes, or they'll see through our little stratagem."

"Don't be ridiculous. The odd caress, yes, the occasional endearment; but not a kiss like – that. They aren't usually given in public!"

It seemed impossible to abash him. "Yes ... it *was* quite a kiss, wasn't it?" He looked as he had done sometimes in hospital before the news about his brother and fiancée had come through – mischievous, daring.

Mary bit her lip. "A one-sided kiss," she said.

He was still too close to her for her colour to subside, her breath to return to normal. He laughed maddeningly.

"Was it really so one-sided, Mary?"

He felt her stiffen, laughed, and with one swift movement imprisoned her arms. "You'd like to smack my face, I know. But you won't. Instead you'll freeze again, treat me like an iceberg. Don't you wish you were in your starched uniform? Anyway, why should you be so furious? You were going to set out to look for a Kiwi husband with all the advantages. And you weren't going to admit to him that love wouldn't be entering into it, so you'd have to put up with kisses, love-making, wouldn't you?"

Mary couldn't remember ever in her life having felt such fury. With every taunting speech he made it more and more impossible to tell him she had only said those things out of bravado.

She steadied her voice, put contempt into it. "You forget one thing, Lieutenant. I may be looking for love, but I would hardly be likely to marry anyone I detest as much as I detest you. And *will* you drive on? That's the second car that has hooted."

"Yes, I'll drive on, Sister. I've had my fun."

They drove in silence till they reached Timaru, sweeping down to the still, perfectly-curved waters of Caroline Bay with its man-made harbour.

Ninian said, "It's rather too early for lunch, but I'd prefer to have it here if they can put something on for us. I'm too well known in the other places, west, and I want none of this 'see-the-conquering-hero-comes' stunt till after I've been home a few days. I suppose I'll have to put up with it then; that's the penalty of belonging to one of the pioneer families. Would you mind having a meal so early?"

"Am I in any position to mind anything?"

He stared at her from under his brows. "What an odd thing to say!"

"Is it? But I thought from your behaviour earlier that you always pleased yourself."

He whistled. "You really have got your dander up, haven't you, honey? Well, it's a nice change. I thought you were deuced attractive when I first came back to an awareness of the world about me in Singapore, but you were such an ice maiden. I longed to apply a bit of heat, to see if the ice was six foot thick."

"Well, you've certainly done that. Right now I'm at boiling point. Everything you say ties up with my analysis of men. You've only got to appear aloof to have them eager, but once they're sure of you –" She stopped. She'd reveal more than she meant to if she didn't make an effort to regain her temper.

His eyes were still exasperatingly audacious. "Then it *was* only skin-deep?"

She sighed. "What do you mean?"

"You said *appearing* aloof."

She looked up at him. "Lieutenant, as far as you're concerned, aloof *always*. I find this conversation ridiculous. I was generalising, not being personal. Let's eat. I'm hungry, I find."

"Fair enough, there's nothing quite like fighting to sharpen the appetite. Come on, sweetheart."

Her eyes sparked. "There's no one within hearing distance,

Lieutenant, so you can keep your tongue-in-the-cheek endearments till your people are present. I don't think I've ever met such — such impertinent, vain, hard-bitten soldiers as Kiwis in all my life!"

"Haven't you nursed any Australians?" he queried amiably, putting a hand under her elbow.

"Yes, I have, and I still think Kiwis can beat them hollow!"

They could have a grill, they were told, and a cold sweet.

"And the lady would like a very long, very cold drink," Ninian said sweetly.

"Any particular flavour?"

Before Mary could answer the quick-lunch attendant, Ninian replied for her, "Oh, she prefers something acid . . . lemon or lime, which shall it be, darling?"

Mary's eyes met his. She disengaged them, said to the girl, "I've changed my mind. I won't have a cool drink, I'll wait for the coffee."

"That," said Ninian, pulling out her chair, "is what is known as cutting off one's nose to spite one's face." He peeped under her hat-brim in mock contrition. He went across to the counter again. Mary kept her shoulder turned. She would *not* betray any interest in what he was doing now.

A glass appeared before her, tall, green, frosted. Ice tinkled musically against the rim, lemon floated on top and a sprig of mint. She looked up caught his rueful eye, and suddenly laughter had its way with her.

"Thank the lord," said Ninian with genuine feeling. "I thought I'd gone too far. A sense of humour is a good thing and all."

"Were you afraid I'd walk out on you and leave you in a sticky situation?"

"No, I wasn't. I think you may have a hard streak in you, but I don't think you'd do that. Not for my sake, but for my mother's. You liked her letter, didn't you, Mary?"

"I did. I can imagine how she must have felt when —"

"When I was returned from the dead and Nanette was engaged to my brother."

The full poignancy of the situation, its utter dreadfulness, swept suddenly on Mary. No one would ever know how much that mother had suffered. Perhaps Nanette had suff-

44

ered deeply too ... was still suffering. How odd that she could not – quite – feel any great sympathy for Nanette. She averted her face a little, studied the menu.

Ninian pulled a face. "Not very inspiring, is it? I'd rather have taken you to a hotel, but it's much too early. We don't have a reputation for very marvellous restaurants, though some of the wayside ones are improving greatly as we become more and more aware of our great tourist potential. But I'll give you a really fabulous meal at the Hermitage some time."

"Hermitage? It sounds monastic, not luxurious."

"It's the luxury hotel at the foot of Aorangi. Years ago, in the early days, it would be just a lodge in the wilderness."

Mary found she enjoyed the meal just the same. They headed back north a little, then west. The plains had given way to green rolling hills and wooded valleys, with a background of mountains. They crossed and recrossed snow-fed rivers tumbling over rocky beds or spreading out over great shingle surfaces in a myriad streams. Here and there were stooks of corn in contrast to other vast paddocks where bags of wheat from the headers were stacked.

"Nice to see a few paddocks still reaped. Dad always does a few too, simply for sentiment's sake. He uses great hay barns for the bales. But there is one spot near the Hebron stream where he always builds a haystack for the kids. Says every child should be able to remember the simple delight of lying in hay, after a bathe."

It sounded idyllic. For the first time Mary felt stirring within her, pleasurable anticipation. She said impulsively, "I'm going to like your people. I'd been dreading all this, but suddenly I feel it could be fun."

He smiled. "That's better, and it's the only way we'll act naturally."

Something struck Mary. "You said 'kids'. I thought that as your brother was so much older than you, you'd be the youngest."

"Oh, I am. At least Rosemary was younger, but I meant my sister's kids. They're always there. They have a farm near. Roland and Isabella were much older than Rosemary and myself, almost like two families. Isabella and Gil – my brother-in-law – are not home at present. Gil won the plough-

45

ing match and went to Europe to compete, so they're having an extended tour. They thought they might as well, since Gil's fare was paid. So Mother's got the family, two girls and a boy. Isabella didn't want to go, she's very chicken-hearted about being separated from the children, but Dad insisted. He reckoned it would take Mother's mind off the fact that I had appeared to have had it. I guess it would too, at that. Barbara's all right, but Josephine and Jonathan, the twins — oh lord, they're handfuls!"

Mary glanced at him sideways. "I could guarantee you're secretly proud of them, though."

He laughed, admitting it. "But you never know what they'll do next."

They were in rolling downland now, with here and there triangles of native bush tucked into the gullies of the foot-hills. Over the mountains the clouds had been swept up-wards by the hot nor'wester wind to a long roll of curtain, leaving the sky above the jagged peaks a clear golden-green.

Mary said, trying to get her bearings, "The sun will set over there? That is due west, isn't it?"

He nodded.

She said in a voice of wonder, "It looks as if you could actually stand on a high peak and see the sun rise over the Pacific in the east and watch it set over the Tasman in the west. What a narrow country. How different from Canada, where it takes days to cross from one ocean to the other."

"Yes, I believe nowhere in New Zealand is more than about seventy miles from the sea. You'll notice a difference."

"Yes, yet in small things it's so like. The serrated tops of those pines against the Alps, the larch woods we passed back there."

Warmth that was partly from the sun, partly from a new-found sense of contentment, stole through Mary. She closed her eyes against the brilliance of the light. She really didn't want to miss a bit of this fascinating new land, but she'd just close her eyes for a few moments.

She woke to find the foothills much nearer and her face against a rough tweed sports jacket. It was comfortingly masculine, smelling of tobacco and Harris tweed, and for a moment she didn't know where she was. She thought it must be a dream and she was back in the days when she had

46

snuggled her face against the tweed of Francis's jacket. She sat bolt upright immediately she realised it was Ninian's.

"Oh, I've missed so much scenery. I hope I wasn't a weight on your arm."

"Oh, no, it looked very much in the part we're playing, and in any case we'll be through here often. We come down to Timaru very frequently."

It gave Mary a queer sensation. It did look as if there were going to be months of this.

"We're coming into Fairlie now. Isn't it a lovely, sleepy little township? But lovelier still when it's under snow."

Fairlie. Where Roland lived and where Nanette was staying. Where they would live when – if – they married. Just one main street and crossroads straggling back into the hills and down to the Opihi River, buildings shabby and smart, old and new, hills circling it watchfully, an air of golden peace about it all.

## CHAPTER 3

THEY pulled up on a crossing. Half a dozen people were coming over it. Mary had turned to ask Ninian something and saw him stiffen, a stiffening that was forced, as if he braced himself. His forefinger lifted from the wheel, pointed to the two people last over the crossing.

"My brother – and Nanette!" he said in a low voice. "Oh, damn, they're going to see us."

As quick as thought, Ninian had pressed the horn in gay salute as if he had meant to do just that, grinned, gestured them over, crossed the crossing, drew into the kerb.

His fingers touched Mary's briefly. "Play it up like hell, won't you?" he asked.

Her eyes met his, reassured him.

They sprang out.

Mary was suddenly and quite illogically glad Roland wasn't like Ninian. He was black-haired, blue-eyed. There was no doubting the delight with which he greeted Ninian. His two hands gripped his brother by the upper arms, and he said, "Why, you old son-of-a-gun ... how'd you get here

47

so quickly? Thought it'd be another week."

Ninian grinned. "Well, we were so thoroughly enjoying the leisurely trip, bit of a change from flying, then all of a sudden I felt I must get home. Don't let the folk know, will you? I want to surprise them."

"Can't anyway, Nin. Storm back in the hills last night. Power lines down everywhere. I tried to get them this morning and couldn't. They hope to have communication restored by night-time."

Ninian's hand came to Mary's elbow, drawing her out of the car. He really did it very well. He even had a proud smile on his lips.

"This is Mary!" he announced.

Roland's delight was obviously sincere. He smiled, the tired patient lines on his face disappearing; he took her by the shoulders, bent, brushed his lips against her temple.

"Welcome to New Zealand, Mary. This is a great moment. It makes the Macandrew family complete." *Complete. Not divided against itself.*

"And this is Nanette." Ninian's voice gave nothing away.

Mary, acknowledging the introduction, took in the utter charm, the appealing, fragile charm, of Nanette. She would have a little-girl appeal when she was very old, she thought. Daintily built, she came only to Roland's shoulder, her face was heart-shaped, her hair a rich golden-brown that curled enchantingly about a wide, smooth forehead, golden-brown eyes the colour of sherry, lashes that curved upwards in thick points, curled naturally. A pale coral lipstick, and a creamy pallor that was quite fascinating. Not the sort to blush. An exquisite skin, matt-surfaced.

Suddenly the pallor was chalk-white. It was the only thing that betrayed her. She made the conventional greeting as if she had never been engaged to Ninian, asked how he was, said how thrilled the family would be that he was here sooner, began asking Mary what she thought of the scenery, how it compared with Canada.

Mary noticed Roland take a sideways look at her, stand a little closer, protectively. She was the sort men would want to protect. She, Mary, must remember that all this, Ninian's plan, was done to protect Nanette ... though why she found it necessary to prod her memory, she did not know. There were women like that, who instinctively demanded – and got – chivalry. Maybe they had something there, perhaps they brought out qualities in their men that other, self-reliant women didn't. It boosted a man's ego. Good heavens! What was she thinking on these lines for? She'd lose the thread of the conversation if she wasn't careful, and Ninian would be rightly annoyed. He was depending on her, that was the only reason she was here.

At that moment another car drew to a halt beside them. Someone leapt out, came across, face beaming, hand outstretched.

"Well, for goodness' sake, old-timer, I thought it was you! Ahead of the official welcome, aren't you? Good show. And my word, you look fit."

"Rob! Good to see you. You must come up as soon as possible. And this is Mary. Have you heard about Mary from the family?"

"I sure have. Mary ... an old friend's privilege." He bent and kissed her cheek. He said to Ninian, "You certainly are to be congratulated, old man." His eyes narrowed. "I say, I just realised something ... Did I or did I not pass you parked by the side of the road somewhere north of Timaru this morning?"

His dark eyes were alight with teasing laughter. "Aha, I need no answer! Mary is going pink! Not to matter, Mary, I adore girls who blush." Robert Fulton turned laughingly to Roland. "I saw this pair in a terrific clinch and hooted derisively as I passed. Gosh, Ninian, had I known it was you I'd have broken it up!"

Mary caught a glint of something that flashed for a moment in Nanette's eyes, something that disturbed and dismayed her. Perhaps Ninian Macandrew should not be too sure that Nanette would be relieved he had brought a sweetheart home!

Ninian took it all in good part, laughing most naturally, then he said, "No ... thanks all the same, we aren't going anywhere to celebrate, we only want to get home."

Robert said, "Are you very tired with all this travelling, Mary?"

She shook her head. "No, not now. I dozed off after –"

She had been going to say after Timaru, but Ninian broke

in, "She dozed off after our clinch. She's a great lass for cat-naps. Wakes like a giant refreshed after them. I never knew anyone with so much go. They were horribly short-staffed in the hospital, and she was always taking extra duty and coming up fresh as paint after four or five hours' sleep."

Robert looked knowing. "She may have had her reasons, of course. Might have wanted to spend more time with her favourite Kiwi. I gather that, all round, your hospital stay was far from all pain and discipline!"

They parted laughingly, turned left up into the hills, began to climb in real earnest and soon were into Burke's Pass with foothills and mountains all about them.

Mary forgot the antagonism she felt towards her companion, the complex nature of the pact she had entered into with him. It was similar enough to her homeland, with the great belts of pine showing raggedy tops against jagged mountains that gleamed whitely against the sun, yet with subtle differences that had all the charm of novelty.

"I'm glad you're so interested in it all, Sister Mary Rose. It will go down big with Dad, he'll be wanting to whisk you off all over Maoriland to show you things."

"Is he keen on travel? So many farmers feel they can't leave the place often."

"That's so, but not Dad. He's a good employer, works on a bonus system over and above wages, and builds good houses – not just cottages – for the workers and families. He and Mother are characters. They suddenly take it into their heads to go somewhere and off they go. I can just hear Dad trying to sell you New Zealand. He'll say, 'Aye, but you must see Fiordland, lassie, that's where the scenery is vertical . . . aye, positively vertical'. It is too. The mountains plunge right down to bottomless fiords."

They came to Tekapo, the lake stretching out from below the road, a turquoise blue sheet of water, to far, lovely mountains. There was the great power-station and a long low stone cottage with an unpronounceable Gaelic name on it. It fascinated Mary.

"Would you know what it means, Ninian?" she asked.

"Yes, my people saw to it that we all knew a bit of the old language. It was built for old T. D. Burnett of Mount Cook Station – a grand old man. I knew the stone-mason who built it. Great chap himself. He put up the name too, and said Mr. Burnett told him it meant a point of land overlooking water. The stone-mason added: 'There is only one language that could express so much in one word. Laconia is not the only place where they saved their breath.' You don't get many folk talking like that these days, do you, Mary? He said he hadn't much education, but like most Scotsmen was rocked in the cradle with the classics."

Mary was suddenly visited with the realisation that Ninian Macandrew was a kindred spirit. No wonder she had been drawn to him when he was a patient. What a pity that she had ever uttered those cynical observances. Though in any case there was still Nanette. . . .

His voice went on, holding real regret now. "Tekapo House is gone, submerged for ever under the waters of the lake. It had to be done. Unlimited electricity is such a boon to the families of the Mackenzie, but something was lost that can't ever be regained − a link with the past. We bought some of the furnishings for the homestead."

He waved towards the church. "But we have the kirk, the spirit of Tekapo itself. Care to see it?"

She was uncertain. "But you wanted to press on home."

"Not really. Didn't want to prolong that meeting in Fairlie. I expect you can understand that."

"Yes, I can, Ninian. You don't have to be savage about it. I do have *some* decent normal feelings."

He looked at her curiously. Had there been a break in her voice?

He grinned. "Anyway, since this is where our wedding will be supposed to take place, they'll wonder if I don't show it to you."

They got out of the car, gazed up at the rugged little on the bleak, rocky, tussock-tufted hillside. Gnarled spikes of matagouri struggled for existence on it, blown permanently in the direction away from the prevailing wind.

It was built of lake boulders, laboriously carried up from the shores. They were used in their natural state, unhewn, with lichens still clinging. The church seemed to fling a challenge to the elements, braving alike the swirling dust-storms of the nor'-westers of summer and the white blinding blizzards of winter.

"The Church of the Good Shepherd," said Ninian. "Very fitting in this wild sheep country."

He undid the back door, and they went in to see before them the same magnificent sweep of lake and mountain that they had seen outside, save that now it was framed by a plain glass window with an unornamented brass cross and candlesticks silhouetted against it. Mary felt immeasurably moved. It was so simple, so austere, the stone altar, the solid English oak beams and rafters. You could well imagine the summer hikers in short pausing here for worship, shepherds with their dogs tied up outside, mountaineers leaving packs and skis at the door, snow flaking off the treads of the boots to melt on the floor.

They hadn't much more than twenty miles to go through Simon's Pass before they came to Lake Pukaki.

There was great satisfaction in Ninian's voice. "It's how I wanted it. So often we bring visitors for the first time only to find Aorangi so living up to its name that it's lost in cloud. There she is, at the head of the lake. Isn't it the perfect setting for her? Last night's storm cleared it, I guess, and in any case it's probably whiter for the storm."

This lake was sapphire, girdled by tussock-gold foothills leading back to grape-blue heights above, and over them again, peak after peak of dazzling purity. Had Aorangi been alone, rising from a plain, its height would have been breathtaking. As it was it was just the biggest giant of them all.

"Our house is on the left side of the lake, well up from the road, but built so that you get a perfect view of the tentridge of the mountain," Ninian explained.

They skirted the tiny township, Mary noted the Post Office where Ninian's mother had posted her letter, then they were taking the lake road. The homesteads were few and far between and the properties reached right back into the mountains. The runs would have to be large here because in winter the carrying capacity would be smaller. Some of the homesteads could not be seen at all, they were tucked into the folds of the hills, hidden in great shelter belts of trees, but sheep-pens and woolsheds seemed to be nearer the road in many cases.

Ninian seemed more relaxed since the meeting at Fairle. A good thing it had happened, giving no one time to grow tense with anticipation, fear, dread.

Ninian turned the car in over some cattle-stops, and the track began to rise between larches that reminded Mary of home. "We'll not risk the second lot of cattle-stops, they rattle madly, as you notice, and I don't want them to get warning. I want to give them a complete surprise. I'll park the car under those blue gums."

"Won't the dogs give tongue?"

"They may, but we'll have to risk that. The older ones shouldn't. They should recognise my step."

They came together up the white dusty track. Mary felt apprehension feathering within her, and sternly squashed it. If this had been true instead of pretence she might have known more than a touch ... any girl meeting in-laws for the first time would have known a shaking within her, clammy hands, tenseness, the need for making a good impression.

To ease her feelings she grinned, "I have the maddest inclination to tip-toe."

He laughed with her, took her hand. At her faint suggestion of withdrawal he said, "The whistle's gone, Mary, the game is on. They may catch a glimpse of us through the trees. We must remember to play up not only when we're being watched but when we're not. It's got to come naturally to us."

Mary said hastily, "I think we could amend that. Playing it when not watched makes it a full-time affair. You'd better make it when we're being watched and when we think we might be."

The track wound round and upward, twice it crossed a creek by a couple of humpy-backed bridges made of local stone. The sun was slanting now, tall shadows lying across the bright green turf, sheep dotted every hillside, birds sang, but Mary could not identify them. She wasn't trying ; all her thoughts were on the coming meeting, her heart was thudding against her side. It was not going to be easy, trying to appear a loving couple in front of an intensely interested family.

The house appeared before them, white and black wooden with a grey slate roof, uncommon in this country of corrugated iron roofs. It was two-storeyed, with quaint dormer windows in a row on the top storey. The garden ran downhill, an extensive garden, bright with geraniums, late roses, stocks and carnations. They would get frosts early here, the chrysanthemums would be nipped almost as soon as they bloomed, and everywhere the Lombardy poplars were torches of living gold. In one corner an aspen poplar quivered with delicious laughter, a silver birch moved its branches in the gently stirring wind till its leaves looked like a shower of golden sovereigns. A magpie called chatteringly, a cascade of silver chimes sounded from the kowhai tree. "A bell-bird," said Ninian softly. "As soon as winter comes they come to Mother's bird-table for honey."

They opened the gate in the cyclone netting fence that kept the stock out, stole through, tip-toeing now in real earnest. A path marked out brokenly by rocks set into the lawn weaved across it and over a flowerbed to the side of the house that was beautifully sheltered from the south-west by a hill that rose up beside it. As they stepped on to the house path a strange noise came from the right of them and above.

A rushing, skidding noise, it was. Trees cloaked the tiny, smooth track that wound uphill, and they had both just begun to look up when there was a terrific warning shout from two pairs of lungs.

"Look out! Look out! LOOK OUT!" and the next minute something shot against the back of their legs, scooped their feet neatly from under them, shot their legs into the air, and they came down on their back in a medley of arms and legs, and other human beings.

Their own yells of alarm had been at the top of their lungs. The noise subsided, their breath returned, their wits with it. Mary rolled over, sat up, leaned over Ninian, who was lying sprawled on his back.

"Ninian, are you all right? Your back? Your shoulder? Your leg. Tell me, are they all right?"

Her face was white with concern. This could undo all the healing.

He managed a faint grin. "Yes. No bones broken, I know. Just . . . just winded. Your head, I think, got me in the midriff. But you – are you all right, Mary?"

His voice was drowned out by an agonised wail from a dusty towhead struggling up from the debris.

"Holy cats!" it said. "Jo, we've scuppered the hero!"

54

He dashed a forelock out of his eyes, essayed an apprehensive grin, gulped, said, "Oh, hullo, Uncle Ninian . . . er, welcome home. Sorry we bashed into you with our trolley."

His uncle thrust his head forward aggressively, grabbed a shoulder in a none too gentle grip, began to say something, but at that moment Mary went into peals of laughter.

"Welcome home," she gurgled. "*Welcome home!*"

Another towhead reared itself up anxiously beside the first "Hullo," it said uncertainly, then both children subsided into uncontrollable mirth, and after trying to maintain his angry glare Ninian caught Mary's eye and collapsed himself.

"Thank heaven," said Jonathan with feeling. "This one's got a sense of humour. Just imagine if it had been Nanette. *She'd* have shattered. Oh, positively *shattered!*" It was quite illogical for Mary to make up her mind that instant that she was going to like Jonathan.

His uncle leaned over and clipped him. "That'll be enough from you. And what the devil do you mean coming down that track on to the house-path in an infernal machine like that? You might have killed us. You might have broken our limbs. You might have taken every bit of skin off us."

"Hardly that, Nin. Bit difficult to do with your clothes on."

He drew back at the glint in his uncle's eye. Mary put a hand on Ninian's arm. "Oh, no, you don't, Ninian. It was a pure accident. Nobody's hurt, so why get in a flaming temper?"

She turned to the children. "Your uncle's not himself yet. He's been very ill. This has shaken him up, I expect."

Ninian's mouth had fallen open. "Well, I'm darned! Anybody'd be mad to have the feet taken from under him the minute he gets home. Anyway, Mary, it was you I was alarmed for. You came a frightful toss. Are you really unhurt, sweetheart?"

"Yes. No doubt a few bruises will result. But there's no need to fuss. It will spoil your homecoming. I'm all right bar a few ladders in my stockings. Are you two children hurt?"

"No. Just a bit chipped. We're used to chips. The main thing is the trolley's not harmed." Josephine drew back hastily from close proximity to her uncle.

But now Ninian was laughing. "Well, I did say I didn't want the pipe-band out, but there are limits! Mary darling, let me dust you down before you meet Mother." He hauled her to her feet.

"I rather think it's too late," she said.

Ninian swung round to see his mother and Barbara running across the lawn from the front door, giggling as they came, obviously trying to sober up but not managing it at all well.

"Look at them," he said in disgust. "Talk about a welcome! Mother is the most awful giggler you ever met."

But as Mrs. Macandrew reached them her face suddenly changed and crumpled. "Oh, son," she said. "Oh, Ringan, Ringan!"

*Ringan.* The old Gaelic name for Ninian.

Elspeth Macandrew clung to her son for a moment. He was patting her back, had his face pressed hard against hers. Then she disengaged herself.

"And this is Mary Rose," she said. She took the girl's face between her fingers, looked searchingly and deeply, then smiled.

"It is well, very well, I think. Thank you for bringing him safely and *happily* home, Mary." The brown eyes, so like her son's, were misty. Mary knew what she meant . . . for making it possible for Ninian to come home. Suddenly Mary was glad she had consented to this mad masquerade.

Barbara was ordering the twins to take their wretched trolley away from the house. "Next time you might not get off so easily. You two are a terrible responsibility. Gran and I don't know what you'll do next."

The twins shrugged, picked up their trolley, started for the hill again.

Ninian's incredulous voice halted them. "You don't imagine for one moment that you can do it all over again?"

"Why not? You know we're doing it now, so you would watch out . . . and Granddad never comes this way, or anyone else for that matter. What *were* you doing sneaking across the lawn like that?"

"Trying to give Mother a nice surprise!" Ninian's voice was rueful, it trembled and he started to laugh again. "All right," he relented. "I know it's a bully place for that – I used to do it myself – but tell you what. Off to the workshop and make yourself a notice: 'Danger – kids on trolleys,' and stick

56

it on a stake right here."

Elspeth Macandrew called after them anxiously, "And don't use any chisels. Your grandfather can't abide them being gapped. Come awa' in, Mary lass, the house is surely glad to welcome you the day."

"I'll bring our luggage up later, Mother. We got a rental car in Christchurch. It's under the gums. Of course a lot of our luggage is following by sea. By the way, we saw Roland in Fairlie. Nanette was with him. Rol's sending you up an outsize salmon. About nineteen pounds, I think he said. Had it given to him yesterday. It'll be on the mail bus tomorrow. He wanted me to go round to the house to get it, but I didn't want to stop, I was dying to get home."

Mary noticed Ninian's mother give a quick look at him. Then she said calmly, "Oh, well, that's one hurdle taken, best to get the meeting over and done with." She turned to Mary. "I was praying things might turn out like this. Right from the time when Ninian first began writing home about you after he was rescued I began to suspect he'd fallen for you. I was so afraid it was only wishful thinking on my part – I know full well patients often fall temporarily for their nurses – but when his letter came I was overjoyed. If only I'd been able to recall mine!"

Ninian smiled a very nice smile, tucked his mother's hand in his arm, said, "Oh, no need, Mother. It only made Mary surer of her welcome, coming so soon after I'd broken it off with Nanette. Otherwise she might have been very nervous wondering how you would receive her, being the cause of a broken engagement."

Mary blinked. Ninian was quick. That sounded most reasonable. It certainly seemed to convince his mother.

"I think Providence had a hand in this," said his mother quietly.

Looking up, Mary saw the corner of Ninian's mouth twitch, his eyes flicker appreciatively to hers. A gleam of amusement in hers responded to it. Good job he had a sense of humour, she had an idea this family was going to be most candid. Ninian would need all his humour to see him over the next few days. The hurt would be deep, but if sometimes he could smile over things, it would help.

"What a blessing I made cheese scones not half an hour

57

ago. Not to be compared with a fatted calf, son, but we'll soon fix that, too. Only it's not veal, but venison."

Mary's eyes sparkled. "Venison! I've not had it since I left home."

It was a lovely old homestead, warm and welcoming in the late afternoon sunshine striking through the windows. On the ground floor they had modernised it in the best possible way, letting in more light. A richly patterned Persian carpet covered the hall and spread out up the dark spindle-banistered stairway to the upper regions. One was conscious of the clean smell of beeswax, well-laundered chintzes, big deep chairs and couches with loosecovers, magazines flung down, knitting, overflowing bookshelves.

They went straight into an enormous kitchen; it ran the whole length of the house at the back and was, one knew, the heart of the home. It looked out on to a natural rock-garden at the back where the hillside sloped upwards. On a rocking-chair at the end where a fuel stove purred and glowed, two huge cats lay curled up together, one glossily black, one tiger-striped.

Barbara pulled the kettle on to the fire. "Gran darling, I'll make some tea, you talk to Nin and Mary. Then I'll dash up the hill for Granddad. He's working up there. I'll put the eats out first."

All the usual things were said, and a few Mary didn't expect. They weren't going to have any well-bred notions of ignoring the situation. They had got a great deal of satisfaction over the way things had turned out.

Elspeth clucked over Mary's nylons, bending down to inspect the damage.

"Truly it doesn't matter," Mary assured her. "These things happen in the best regulated families."

"And ours is far from that," chuckled Barbara.

Elspeth looked up into Mary's face. "Eh, lassie, but you *are* like our Rosemary."

Mary caught her breath. It might sadden Elspeth Macandrew to be reminded of a child loved and gone, but there was only delighted surprise in the lined face near hers.

"Did ye no' see it, lad?" she asked Ninian, lapsing in the excitement of the moment into the brogue she had mostly lost. "The same Highland colouring like your father's, the black hair, the blue eyes, the cheekbones high and well set, the wild-rose colouring. Why did ye no' tell me?"

"I did see it, Mother. But I wanted you to find it out for yourself. It's quite striking, isn't it? I think it was what first attracted me."

His eyes, twinkling, met Mary's. She was saved from a reply by a sudden entry into the kitchen. No doubt at all but that this was Ninian's father and he had been running some distance. A giant of a man. He must have seen his son from some vantage point.

But he had not.

He gasped out: "Betsy's bad. The foal's come ower early and it's the wrong way round. Babs, saddle up Witch and ride to Redgrave's. Go as hard as you can – get them to drive to Lake Pukaki and see if they're connected and can raise the vet. It's a bad thing the wires are down just when the men are away." He broke off, stared. "Why, Ninian lad, where did you come frae? Och, and this no welcome to you at all. It will hae to wait . . . but go for your life, Babs."

Ninian said, "I've a car at the gums, Dad. A rental car. I'll take that. I'll try to get the vet."

Ninian's father turned to go out. Mary stood up, reached his side. "I may be able to help, Mr. Macandrew. I've not only done maternity but many's the calf and foal I've helped into the world at our place in Canada. It's just possible I may be able to turn it."

He looked her up and down, seemed to find her acceptable – or maybe he was just desperate. Mary tugged off her hat, flung it on the table, said to him, "Come on!"

They wasted no words on the way up, needing their breath. But once in the stable Mary sized up the situation. The mare seemed exhausted. That would be because the foal wasn't coming easily and her pains were getting her nowhere. That foal might suffocate if they didn't get it turned quickly. Well, if the mare was exhausted at least it would mean she would not thrash round too much. Although animals were wonderful, they seemed to sense you were trying to help them, even if you did not share a common language.

She flung her jacket on a bale of straw, pushed up her blouse sleeves. She made an examination, came to a decision.

"Have you some disinfectant handy? A bucket? And some fairly clean rope, not too thin."

"You mean use a rope to turn it? I've never seen that done. You'll have to instruct me, lass. I've turned plenty of lambs, but never a foal."

"I'll turn it," said Mary. Ninian's father was busy, running water, putting in disinfectant, producing a rope for her scrutiny.

"Lassie, it's no sort o' job for a woman."

Mary smiled at him. "It is for a midwife. Nursing isn't all clean uniforms and starch and sterile conditions. And I've a very strong stomach."

"You're going to need it," said Joseph Macandrew.

Mary moved to Betsy's head, began fondling her muzzle, talking softly to her till Joseph had things ready. She scrubbed up thoroughly in the bucket, got more disinfectant, soaked the rope in it.

"I'd have said wait for the vet if the phone had been in order, Mr. Macandrew, but it could take hours for Ninian to locate him, I suppose?"

"Aye. He may not run him to earth at all."

It wasn't easy. It was tricky, painful for Betsy, difficult for the girl working with the aid of the man. It was some time before they got the foal turned finally. Their first attempts had resulted each time in the foal slipping back into the same position before the mare had a chance to expel it.

"Be ready to clear its nostrils as soon as it's born," said Mary to Joseph, breathing heavily as she endeavoured once more. "It may have got a lot of mucus in its nose. If need be we can give mouth-to-mouth resuscitation. Come on, Betsy lass, come on. That's fine ... a bit more, a bit more ... Aaahhh! Mr. Macandrew, give me that cotton waste."

Betsy, panting, gave a feeble whinny of joy, turned to try to lick her offspring. Barbara and Mrs. Macandrew had come up from time to time with more buckets of hot water, coming in quietly, leaving their offerings, going back for more, but Joseph and Mary were alone at that moment.

Joseph took a closer look. "A filly," he said with great satisfaction, "and as black as her mother. As black as your hair! We will be naming her Mhairi after you."

Mary lifted her face, glistening with sweat, toward him,

smiled. "I'll be honoured," she said. She caressed the little foal, which seemed none the worse for the difficult birth. "It's all right, Betsy – there, she's all yours now. She'll do." The mare began licking the gleaming satin coat.

Mary stood up, looked down on herself and laughed a laugh of real mirth. "Nice way to meet your son's fiancée," she said.

Ninian's father smiled. "Baptism by blood," he said aptly. "You're one of the family from now on, lassie. As if you were already my daughter-in-law."

Mary experienced a queer feeling. For the first time she realised that it wasn't just a matter of playing a part for the first few awkward weeks of Ninian's return ... it was getting involved with these people, people it was going to be easy to love.

She swallowed, knew a moment of really swamping apprehension about the immediate future, then thought: I must take things as they come; reached up to him, kissed him.

He smiled down at her with sheer affection. He looked flattered and twinkled.

"That makes me feel forty years younger. I can forget I'm eighty come Hogmanay."

Mary's surprise was unmistakably genuine. "Eighty! You couldn't be!"

Joseph looked delighted. "I don't feel it," he admitted, "but that might be because of being married to a woman so much younger than myself."

"I'd not realised there was such a difference ... I don't mean I think your wife looks old for her age, just that you look so young you must have closed the gap of years."

"Aye, Elspeth vowed it would be so. Said there was a fair chance of her catching up if we had a big enough family, that childbearing and managing a man would be sure to add years ... ah, but she was a saucy lass, and a bonnie one." He added with a swift change of subject, rather startling Mary, "You're the one for our Ninian, I can see."

Mary's one dimple flashed to team up with the twinkle in her eye.

"Because I can bring a foal into the world?"

He pinched her chin. "You're a saucy lass too, I see. Nay, it's not that. But you couldn't be a greater contrast to that other whey-faced wench!"

Mary caught her lip between her teeth. Whey-faced wench! Nanette. Lovely, lovely Nanette with her creamy pallor. She wanted to laugh madly. Nanette was something to rave about, yet old Joseph Macandrew disparagingly called her a whey-faced wench.

"She'd never have done for our Ninian. He wants a lass wi' spirit – like you. Wi' a bit o' Highland colour. Black hair, blue eyes, bright cheeks ... aye, and a quick temper too, I'll warrant."

Mary laughed. "You'd be right, Mr. Macandrew. It's up in a flash."

"And down in a flash too." It was a statement, not a question.

She nodded. Suddenly, the first time for months, she felt gloriously alive. Ever since she had seen the Colonel's daughter in Francis's arms she had felt frozen save for those few furious moments on the road to Timaru, and that had been so fleeting it hadn't counted, had been just a flare leaping up to die as quickly. But with this, now, all tenseness had gone. She realised how taut she had held herself mentally, what iron control she had exercised. She had an idea that with these people you could be yourself. Up one moment, down the next, what matter? They would still love you. Except, of course, with Ninian. No changes of mood there. It wouldn't be wise.

She said, without apology for curiosity, "But you don't mind Nanette marrying Roland?"

Joseph shook his great leonine head. "Nay. Our Roland needs someone to protect. A clinging vine. But Ninian wants a woman to fight with occasionally, like Elspeth. My certes, we've had our moments, glorious moments, lassie. Right royal rages and grand makings-up. And the children too learned to make up quickly. Not to sulk. But Nanette ... what a shilpit creature she is!" The shaggy eyebrows shot up. "D'ye ken what shilpit means?"

Mary nodded. "I do and all! My grandfather used it. A wishy-washy creature, always shilly-shallying."

Joseph looked immensely gratified. "There were times when I'd hae liked to put a bomb under her, messing about, making a shambles o' our Roland's life. Ought to have stood up to her parents, ought to have told them she'd wait till she came of age. But no guts. After all, that's what we did, Elspeth and me. Her folk were against it too. Same grounds – age. Don't really blame them for thinking a younger man'd be better, but we knew, Elspeth and me. It was for ever.

"And what did Elspeth do, you ask? She just said, 'I can understand you feeling that way. This attraction may wear off – I'm willing to put it to the test, say three years. I'll be twenty-two. If it's not worn off, I'll marry Joseph then.'

"Well, they accepted that, hoping. It didna wear off, they were still against it, brought along a chap nearer her age ... a namby-pamby sort of chap. Verra, verra ladylike! It was the last straw for Elspeth. She said to them, 'You'll drive me to elope with Joseph if you will not give me your blessing,' and she said to me, 'Let's cut and run. We'll go to Timaru, get married there, come back.' I said, 'Nay, lass, we'll be married in our ain kirk, and if your father and mother will not give you your wedding feast we'll put it on in our ain home.' So we told them we were getting married on a certain day. They accepted that, gave her a splendid sitdown, and made me maist welcome in the family frae that day on."

He chuckled. "Puir things, they had an awfu' setback a year later. The ladylike young man embezzled a lot of money and they felt their daughter had had a lucky escape."

"And you feel if Nanette and Roland had done just that, all would have been well."

"Yes. Families always come round. They have to accept these things. Instead of which Roland married someone who needed him, but it wasna the love of his life ... and in time our Ninian, the young fool, picked up the pieces and tried to put them together again."

Suddenly Mary knew there was something she *must* know. –"And if this had not happened, Mr. Macandrew, do you think it would have worked? That Ninian and Nanette would have been happy?"

She found she was holding her breath awaiting the answer.

It was prompt. He hadn't needed to work it out.

"Nay. Nanette would never have forgotten she had loved and lost. There are women like that, ye ken. She enjoys being martyred. Ah, pah! And my lad would never have kenned what it is to be loved properly. I'm no' the kind that thinks a good marriage can be based on friendship and respect. I'm red-blooded like Ninian. I think there's got to be friendship and respect, aye, a marriage falls to pieces without that. Aye, and kindred interests too and a bit of contrast to even things up. But there's more between a man and woman than that. A sort o' spark. And you're right for our Ninian."

Mary turned her head away sharply. Respect was the very thing Ninian did not have for her. *Nor had he anything else.*

The old man cocked his ear. "Here they come." He chuckled mischievously, "Some folks are guid at turning up when the stramashing is all over!"

He put an arm about Mary's shoulders, turned her to the door. The vet and Ninian arrived in the doorway, took one look at the smile on Joseph's face and Mary's and knew all was well. The vet went straight to the mare and foal, Ninian, playing his part, to Mary.

"You clever, clever girl! Darling, has it been too much for you?"

His father snorted. "Has it been too much for her? Losh, man, do ye no' realise what a winner ye' picked this time? I dinna ken how she did it, but do it she did. A filly, and named for her."

Ninian chuckled, "Oh, I can see she's going to get the whole family under her spell, the witch!" He picked up a lock of hair from Mary's forehead, tucked it neatly behind her ear. "My love, what a mess you're in. I'll have to buy you a new suit. Come on up to the house and get changed."

She shook her head. "Not yet, Ninian. I want to see what the vet has to say. I daresay he'll want to give the mare an injection to guard against infection. We had to work too quickly to be a hundred per cent hygienic."

They stayed about twenty minutes longer. The vet smiled. "I'll take you on as an assistant any time, Miss Rose."

"Oh, that you will not," said Joseph. "They'll be getting wed in two shakes of a lamb's tail. Have you thought where you'd like to build your house, Ninian? I'd thought about having the old orchard cleared. It's well sheltered from the sou'west and there's a grand view of the mountain."

Ninian burst out laughing. "Give us a bit of time to get our breath, Dad! We're not all whirlwinds like you. Some of us have to live at a pace to suit our age."

The old man looked at him. "If I had a betrothed as bonnie as your Mary I'd be wanting to make sure of her. Well, come on up to the house for a meal. But I'd get out plans as soon as I could were I you ... builders tak' a gey long time nowadays. Though you could always bide in the shearers' quarters till your home was ready. I ken the homestead's big enough for us all, but I dinna believe in young uns being in with the auld."

Ninian tucked a hand in Mary's arm. "See what a managing family you've got yourself, sweetheart? We'll be married before we know where we are. Come on, Jock, you've done nothing to deserve a meal, neither have I, but we'll cash in just the same."

Mary walked to the house, feeling more than slightly dazed. It had seemed fairly simple back in Malaya, in fact the only thing to do, but now she had a sense of having been lifted bodily by a tornado, whirled along. These people weren't thinking in terms of a long engagement, they were anxious to get Ninian married as soon as possible. Were they afraid of Nanette? Of her power over Ninian? Were they wondering if, now Ninian was returned, she might crash Roland's world in ruins again?

They found a tasty snack prepared in the kitchen.

"We'll have the venison tomorrow," said Elspeth sensibly. "I thought if anything happened to Betsy, no one would want to eat. But all is well."

"Aye. All is well, thanks to our Ros Mhairi," said old Joseph, reaching for a scone.

A silence fell. Ros Mhairi ... the Gaelic name for Rosemary. The name of the little loved daughter.

Then Elspeth said calmly, "So you have noticed it, Joseph, the resemblance?"

"Och aye. Who wouldna'? The Hieland colouring, blue eyes, black hair. Her ancestors would be Hieland folk, emigrated to Canada, as ours did to here. She even knows our queer old expressions."

"Such as?" inquired Ninian.

Mary held her breath. She didn't think Joseph would be given to mincing matters, he would call a spade a spade.

65

What if he repeated that Nanette was a shilpit creature? He would do it in all good faith, thinking Ninian no longer loved Nanette. He would not guess how he might wound his son.

But Joseph merely said, "She kens what I'm saying when I say 'thole' and 'thrawn'."

"How did you come to be using those words, Father?"

Joseph was a match for Ninian any day. "I said to her, 'You're a fine nurse and all, I can see that, but how you tholed Ninian as a patient is beyond my ken. He's a thrawn de'il even when he's well!'"

Ninian's laughter outdid the twins. "Oh, Dad, you get no better! It's good to be home."


CHAPTER 4

AFTER the meal Ninian said, "Now we'll take Mary's cases upstairs. The pink guest room, I suppose?"

"No, son. The long room with the two dormer windows. Rosemary's room. Mary isn't a guest, she's a member of the family."

Mary caught a look of incredulity on Ninian's face. It made her guess that that room had never been used since. It stabbed at Mary, this warmth of welcome, and she was nothing but a cheat . . . even with the highest of motives.

Elspeth was going on placidly, "Barbie and I did it out last week, fortunately. But as we didn't expect you so soon we've not got all the books and things moved out yet. We can do it tomorrow, and give you something more to adult taste. Come on, Mary, we'll take you up."

As soon as Mary entered she knew why Ninian had looked so incredulous. The room, though spick and span, looked as if it had been tenanted only yesterday. There were drawings pinned up on the walls, a pram with a sleeping doll in it, Beatrix Potter books, A. A. Milne, L. M. Montgomery, exercise books bulky with pressed ferns, leaves, flowers.

It was quite charming, had evidently once been two small rooms, but now it went right across that end of the house, from gable to gable.

"Rosemary wanted a room she could see sunset and sunrise from, so her father and Roland took out the walls and incorporated part of the passage too."

Mary said, a shake in her voice, "I've never seen anything more lovely. Those darling windows ... the rag mats ... I feel – so – so honoured. Are you sure you –"

Elspeth took Mary's hand, pressed it. "Very sure, my dear. Just accept it, won't you?" And Elspeth Macandrew walked swiftly out of the room.

Mary bit her trembling lip, walked to the west window that would frame the sunset behind Aorangi, gazed out through a blur of tears.

She felt an arm come round her shoulders, and grew rigid.

Ninian's voice said into the back of her hair, "Don't be so ashamed of those tears, Mary, you're doing very well. They like you."

She said in a stifled voice, "I feel such an impostor, such a hypocrite. They're so sweet. They're giving me their all. I – I –"

She choked, couldn't go on, put her head down on Ninian's shoulder.

She heard him laugh a little. "Even you can't stay hard-boiled in this atmosphere, can you? But cheer up, Mary, we aren't always as sentimental as this. And don't forget your imposture is making my homecoming possible for them. Possible and happy."

His hand came up to the back of her glossy black head, stroked it gently. "Aren't we doing well? Those imps of twins are up in the Lookout Tree and most frightfully interested. Let's give them something to really get a kick out of."

He tilted her chin, kissed her lips, and laughed as she sprang away from him, dabbing at her eyes. Then she laughed herself and came back to the window to see where the children were. It was an immense aspen poplar with broad spreading branches and had a rough platform with three sides and a roof built into the fork above the massive trunk.

"Rosemary and I made that," said Ninian, and there was no pain in his voice at all.

*

The rest of the evening went very pleasantly. Mary still had feelings of unreality occasionally and soon came to the conclusion that you could easily, in a situation like this, slip into accepting it all as true. It was odd, that, because she had thought she would feel strange, apprehensive, embarrassed. Perhaps it was because they were all so wholeheartedly delighted that she felt she must play the part with all that was in her.

But perhaps she felt at ease because Roland and Nanette were not there. They remained as a faint remembered cloud on the horizon. They were in communication by phone again. At seven-thirty Nanette had a call from Fairlie. His father had answered it, called out, "For you, Ninian, Roland on the line."

He was a long time, seemed quiet when he returned, dropping into his chair by Mary.

"What did Roland have to say, son?" asked his mother.

"It wasn't Rol. It was Nanette. He just got the number for her."

"Oh." Elspeth's voice was absolutely flat, disapproving.

The silence that ensued was awkward, heavy.

Ninian broke it. "She's coming out here to stay with her cousins next week."

"What for?" Elspeth's lips were tight.

"Oh, because Roland will be in the district on his rounds. He'll stay here, of course."

Another silence.

Barbara broke it. "Crumbs! Gran, we'd better get that dress of mine for the concert made before she gets here."

Ninian turned to stare at her. "No need for that, surely, Babs. You couldn't get a better dressmaker than Nanette. She'd help you."

Mary wondered if that was a note of pride in his voice. He knew they rather despised Nanette because she was ultrafeminine, liked to be waited on hand and foot. She didn't like farm work or gardening, she'd gathered that much.

Elspeth said ruefully, since Babs had decided not to answer, "That's just the trouble. She's so good she makes us feel ninnies. Barbie and I only dressmake when we can't get out of it. We muddle along and somehow it usually turns out right, but more by good luck than good management. The

68

lord only knows how much unpicking we've done. We certainly get there by means Nanette doesn't approve of."

Mary tried hard not to feel so pleased. It was silly. After all, this engagement was only a bogus one, a temporary one, so it couldn't matter to her. But it did make it easier that they liked her more than they liked Nanette. It must be a flaw in her own nature to feel like this. She'd never suspected herself of petty jealousy before.

She said hesitantly, "I'm not very good at dressmaking myself, but maybe I could help. I'm likely to get the left sleeve in the right armhole and all that sort of thing, but though I hate the putting together, I do love the finishing-off. Any good?"

"Good? It'll be a godsend. Barbie's supposed to be an animated lampshade in this concert. There are miles and miles of bobbly tassels to sew round the skirt. You mean you like hand-sewing?"

"Yes, like mending and darning and hemming. It's matching up bits and pieces that gets me rattled."

Barbie was impressed, "Gosh, Gran, she'll do us, won't she? Nin, you've picked the right sort this time for sure!"

Ninian reached out a long arm, brought his hand down in a resounding slap on Barbara's bare knee. "What a family! That's the lot of you now. You've got it off your chest. Stop comparing Mary with Nanette, it isn't fair. One after the other ... the twins first, Father, Mother, and now Barbara!"

Mary said, "Your father? But you weren't there, Ninian. Oh –!"

She clapped her hands over her mouth like a schoolgirl, crimsoned.

"Exactly," said Ninian grimly. "But I guessed he would. He wouldn't have been able to help himself. Mary coming along and delivering the foal. Him and his talk about Scots expressions ... there are quite a few I could imagine he would use about poor Nanette."

*Poor Nanette. The little helpless one. The clinging vine. The one who enjoyed being misunderstood, who enjoyed having loved and lost. Who couldn't make up her mind which brother she wanted. Nanette, who still held chief place in Ninian's life.*

Ninian turned swiftly, too swiftly, looked into Mary's face,

69

saw distress and embarrassment, was evidently afraid the
family would notice, and said laughingly, "It's all right, darling, I'm used to this indecently frank family; you aren't.
They've all got it off their chests by now and will probably
stop embarrassing you."

Elspeth said placidly, "Mary isn't embarrassed at all. She's
probably ever so glad we like her so much better than Nanette. Any lassie would be. She'll be living on the property,
Nanette won't, so it's a fine thing and all that it's worked out
that way. I can take Nannette in small doses. And your engagement to her was a lot of nonsense. I can't think how you
ever got round to it. It was nothing but pity. You and Roland
both let your compassion get away with you. But now we'll
stop talking about it – Mary Rose, I want to know about your
people. Are they both of Scots descent? The Roses, now let
me see, they'd come from round Inverness way. What's the
name of the Castle . . . Kilravock, was it?"

Mary looked delighted. "But how could you know? I mean
many folk don't even know their own clan connections,
much less anybody else's."

Elspeth said, "Oh, I was a MacGillivray from that way.
But three generations back. Yet I remember talk of the
Roses. Wasn't it said you could always trust a Rose? Some-
thing to do with their motto?"

"The motto is *Constant and true*," said Mary quietly.

Old Joseph looked over his spectacles. "Have that engraved
on the inside o'your wedding ring, lassie. A fine motto."

Mary swallowed. Constant and true, and she at this moment living a lie!

*

After that the evening proceeded on less touchy lines.
Mary felt surrounded by love and comfort. They had hot
savoury toast at ten, Barbara serving it. The twins were long
since in bed. Then Joseph and Elspeth rose. Joseph knocked
out his pipe, put it in the rack above the rough lake boulder
fireplace, stretched and yawned.

"Well, time we were off to bed. I expect you two want an
hour or so to yourselves. Haven't forgotten my own courting
days yet. Goodnight."

He stooped and kissed Mary's cheek. "Goodnight, Ros

Mhairi, and God bless."

Elspeth kissed Mary and her son, went with Joseph, smiling, tucking her hand in her husband's horny one as they reached the door.

Mary watched them, smiling. She turned back to find Ninian regarding her closely. "They are sweet, aren't they, Ninian?"

"Aye. Even if lamentably outspoken."

In a flash the thought of Nanette was back between them. Mary stirred uneasily. "I think I'll go up too, it's been a long and tiring day."

"Oh, no, you won't. They'd think it odd. They were giving us the opportunity for a little billing and cooing. Don't disillusion them, even if we only read."

Something in his eyes disconcerted her. It was challenging, derisive, and she didn't know why.

She stood up. "I'm sure they'd understand I was tired." She walked briskly to the door.

She had not thought Ninian could move so quickly. He was at the door before her, turned the key. "I said we'd stay, as they expect."

"You're just being tiresome," she told him in her best Sister manner. "I've never known anyone to want his own way so much. You are thrawn, just as your father said. I should think Nanette was well rid of you!"

The next moment she looked aghast. "There! I've done it too! It's catching, this bluntness. Ninian, I'm sorry. And I'm sorry for all the things they said too. They don't mean to hurt you. It's this ridiculous situation. They think you fell out of love with Nanette, and into love with me. It's a terror. And I don't see that we can do one thing about it!"

He had turned his head away, but just as quickly turned it back again. "It isn't particularly easy, Mary, but it was the only thing to do ... this pretence we planned ... wasn't it?"

She held his eyes sincerely. "Yes, I think it was the only thing to do. It would have been unthinkable to have come home otherwise – and if you'd stayed away your parents would have been very sore at heart."

"Then keep playing it up, girl. Come and sit down for a while. We can read."

"All right," she said, and found difficulty in keeping her

71

voice from shaking. Why? What did it matter to her? She must not identify herself more closely with this problem than she need.

She regained control, managed to say with a hint of amusement, "You'd better turn that key back. It would seem very odd if one of them came back for something forgotten."

His eyes met hers, also amused, but with an awareness in them that made her colour rise. "Yes, they could think all sorts of things."

He turned it back. Mary went to the rocking-chair. "I love these things, though I warn you I shall probably drop asleep."

"You aren't going to sit in it. As you remarked, they might come back, and they would find it decidedly odd to discover us with the hearth between us. Sit by me on the couch. I'll put another log on. There's an article in this digest that intrigues me. I'd like to read it to you, get your opinion. It's a medical one."

At eleven-thirty Mary said, "I'd like to have a look at the mare and foal before going to bed. I know you and your father went up at nine, but I'd feel easier if we did."

"All right. It may be a bit frosty out. It had the feel earlier. Slip on Mother's old Inverness cloak. It's on the back door."

It had a hood too. He wrapped it round her, buttoned it under her chin, lifted a fur-collared jacket of his father's down, put it on, put a hand under her elbow and they stepped out into the night.

The air met them, bracing and clear, a crescent moon hung above Mount Hebron, the starlight was silver-white, the Milky Way a blaze of light. Ninian pointed out the Southern Cross, other stars and constellations Mary did not know. Her uplifted face gleamed palely in the moonlight.

"I can now realise I'm Down Under, in the Southern Hemisphere, with strange stars above me."

They turned towards the stables, facing the great alps beyond, faintly luminous in their snows against the midnight blue sky. The stable was warm, steamy with breathing. The little foal was snuggled into the hay, its mother lifted a contented head, bent down, gave a lick or two at the ebony flanks, whinnied a welcome.

They came down the hill in silence, the magic of the night about them. On the verandah they paused. Ninian said, "Mind if I have a last cigarette?" They leaned on the rail together. His arm was warm against hers.

The scent of tobacco mellowed the air, comfortingly masculine, at least it was masculine if you did not smoke yourself; she felt at home, drowsily content.

Suddenly something in the fragrance of the tobacco woke a memory in Mary. Francis ... leaning with her on the verandah at home, kissing her with just that fragrance on his breath. She moved abruptly, the spell broken.

Unknowing, Ninian stubbed out the cigarette, tossed it in the air, where its dying glow described an illuminated arc like a miniature fireworks display, fell on the concrete. Nevertheless he trod it out.

"Come, we'll go in." He looked at her sideways. "It's just occurred to me you know most things about *me* ... I don't know a thing about *you*."

"You don't need to," answered Mary as he closed the back door. "Five or six months to get Roland and Nanette safely married at the very outside, then I'll be out of your life."

"For heaven's sake, don't even whisper such things. You can see how sharp the family are. You must play the game every hour of the day. But if ever you feel you have to talk frankly or bust, we'll saddle up and go over the hills and far away beyond eavesdroppers."

The upstairs landing was quite small. The doors were very close together.

"My room is right next to yours. That's the parents' room, that's Barbie's and Josephine's, that's Jonathan's." He bent down and whispered, "The girls' door is moving. I reckon they're behind it. Let's give them something to thrill the little brats."

He bent the rest of the way, gathered her into his embrace, kissed her soundly, then said quite distinctly, "Goodnight, Ros Mhairi, my darling."

Mary fled into her room, closed the door, stood against it for a moment, annoyed to feel her heart thudding so violently. How foolish! He had been a really tough Kiwi soldier patient, he was just a teasing son and uncle. It didn't mean a thing. She was quite mad to let it affect her so. The trouble was, she told herself, she ought to have gone out and about more, experienced more casual kisses. How absurd and stupid to be breathless and fluttery and . . . and to feel that kiss burning right through her. Maybe any man's kiss could thrill you. Till now she had thought only Francis's had had that, for her. And it would make this next little while difficult going. As she fell asleep Mary was conscious most of all, when she could banish the memory of that caressing "Ros Mhairi, my darling," that she was burning up with resentment . . . resentment that a kiss given so casually and teasingly by Ninian could have stirred her so.

*

The following days were not so bad. Ninian was out more with his father. He said laughingly, the first morning after breakfast, "Well, much as I hate to leave you, my love, I must. Work awaits. Anyway you'll get to know Mother more without me. But I'll take you riding this afternoon."

Mary said crisply to Elspeth, "Now, Mrs. Macandrew, I don't suppose you like people hanging over you in your kitchen any more than most women. Tell me what duties you'd like me to take over and I'll get cracking."

"Well, I like to cook my own dinner, but if you like to do Jonathan's room and Ninian's as well as your own, and the upstairs bathroom, I'd be immensely grateful. I daresay you'd like to poke round Ninian's room, anyway. Most women are curious about their husband's early life. It's rather endearing. All his school photos are up there, and all the evidence of his hobbies. Take all the time you like."

Mary did the other rooms first. Something in her flinched from going into Ninian's room. Finally she made herself. He had made his bed, that was all. His cases were lying strewn about, contents straggling over the edges. Mary stuffed them back, lifted them on to the bed. One wall was lined with books, many of them on mountaineering and on the flora and fauna of New Zealand. They tempted her to dip into them, but she worked steadily on.

There was a gun-cupboard, locked, with a notice on it, "Kids keep out." There was a toboggan standing on its end, snowshoes, skis, golf-clubs. The walls were covered with photos, black-and-white and coloured, almost all of alpine peaks. There were trophies for skiing and skating. The floor was of knotted pine, well polished, with old-fashioned rag mats on it, beautifully designed.

Elspeth Macandrew came upstairs, poked her head in "Mary, would you be kind enough to unpack for Ninian? He'll just never get round to it, or else he'll stuff everything in the wrong place. His shirts and things can go in the compactum, the big things in the wardrobe and the odds and ends in the tallboy. Thanks a lot."

Mary didn't like doing it. It would have been so different had she loved Ninian. Any woman took a pleasure in putting away her man's clothes, matching socks, shaking creases out of shirts, extracting cuff links and sitting them side by side, folding pyjamas. As it was, she felt a Pauline Pry.

She stacked everything into neat piles. She opened the top drawer, put in handkerchiefs, pulled open the second for the socks – oh yes, there were some socks here already. But on top of them, face down, was a photograph in a silver frame.

She lifted it, turned it up, and as she had suspected, Nanette's face stared up at her. Nanette and Ninian. Ninian had his arm about her shoulders, she was laughing up at him under a smother of apple-blossom in the old orchard.

She gazed at it, conscious of feelings she could not understand. A sound at the door made her look up. Look up and start guiltily. Ninian stood there.

She felt the tell-tale colour sweep up into her cheeks. "I – I – I – your mother asked me to put away your things, Ninian. I didn't want to, but she seemed to think I'd like to. I'm sorry. I didn't mean to pry."

He crossed to her, took the photograph from her, not gently. "I'll get rid of this promptly," he said savagely, and put his foot on it. He picked up some paper from the bed, put the fragments in it, wrapped it carefully and put it under his arm. "Destination rubbish-bin," he said, recovering. "Morning tea's ready, Mary. Mother sent me to get you. We always have a cuppa and fresh scones at ten." Mary suffered herself to be led down.

Elspeth was sitting behind the big teapot, musing, her chin in her hands. She looked up, announced happily, "I've been planning things, Ninian."

"Then heaven help us," said her son. "When Mother starts plotting the rest of us take cover!"

His mother looked at him severely. "I'm trying to be helpful, son."

He groaned. "I know. That's always the trouble." He turned to Mary. "There was a book of Anne Hepple's once – I wonder if you've read it – where the heroine was described as the sort that not only helped lame dogs over stiles but also induced perfectly contented, stay-at-home cows to jump over the moon! That's Mum in a nutshell, isn't it, Dad?"

"Aye. 'Deed it is. But somehow those cows always end up having the time of their lives, so just leave your mother alone, son."

"See!" Elspeth shot Ninian a triumphant glance, "and the Roses will just love this.'

"Roses! What do you mean? Can't be time for pruning them yet? No, we always do that in August. Is it manure?"

"Manure! Ninian Macandrew! What on earth are you talking about? *I'm* talking about your in-laws."

"My what?"

"Well, if you want to be a purist, your *future* in-laws. Mary's folk. They're farming too, so their quiet time would be winter, and as winter in Canada is summer here, it will be ideal. I thought if they arrived about November our lambing would be almost over, you could get married and have a honeymoon and be back before shearing starts. In fact before Christmas. Wouldn't the Roses love a hot Christmas! If only we lambed early like they do away from the mountains you could have been married in September, of course. But never mind. Mary, do you think your people would be able to stay four or five months? I'd like them to see the whole country properly."

Ninian started to laugh. "What did I tell you, my sweet? Now, go easy, Mother. Mary, don't let her stampede you into anything. We'll fix a day later. Hang it all, I've only just got home!"

"Stampede! Why, I'd have thought you'd have wanted it earlier, but I do realise it would be easier for Mr. and Mrs. Rose to get away after their harvest is in."

Mary looked bewildered, alarmed. Ninian came to her rescue.

"Look, Mother, Mary's father naturally wants his daughter

to be sure of things. After all, he probably doesn't know much about New Zealand. He'll want her to get used to the way of life here, so we'll not make any dates at all. Give Mary a chance to get settled, then if she suddenly decides she can't live without me a moment longer, we'll settle on a date. I know in the cities you have to book receptions months ahead, but I guess we'll just have the reception here, won't we?"

He sounded so convincing, for one mad moment Mary found herself beginning to wonder should she have lace or brocade, realised what she was doing and suddenly choked over her scone.

The twins, always approving anyone who took the giggles, joined in. Elspeth and Barbara followed suit.

"What are they laughing at?" Ninian asked his father helplessly.

"I dinna ken, but never fret about the women laughing, son, it's far better than crying." The subject got changed.

But not for long. Morning tea finished, old Joseph said, "Ros Mhairi, come on up to the old orchard. I want you to have a good look at the layout up there, see what you think about it for a site for the new house."

In a dream, Mary got up and followed him and Ninian. The twins brought up the rear.

Josephine said anxiously, "Mary, we've got a hideout in a tree there, you won't want that cut down, will you? And there's a row of old macrocarpas that ought to have been trimmed into a hedge years ago ... you won't want it cut down, will you? Because an owl lives there. It's a beaut owl. We did have hopes it might have been a laughing one, but it isn't, but we love it just the same. Laughing owls are practically extinct."

"If need be," promised Ninian solemnly, "we'll build the house round the owl, courtyard style." He winked at Mary, bearing up bravely and making an endeavour to look as a bride might, viewing the site of her future home.

Old Joseph was in his element. Ninian found himself being bulldozed into agreeing and disagreeing and in general behaving as any son might in similar circumstances. It was too much for Mary. She wandered off with the twins to see where the owl lived. She was up the tree with them when she spied another building, old and grey, through the branches.

"What's that, Jonathan?" she asked.

"Oh, the old homestead. The one our great-great-grandfather built when he first took up land here."

Josephine bobbed up beside him. "It's not! The sod cottage is."

Jonathan said, "Shut up. Mary was asking me. Not the first home but the first homestead. At first, because there wasn't any wood for building, he had to dig sods and build a cottage of that. Just a but and a ben, thatched with raupo reeds. It's at the back of that one. We use it for a playhouse. Then, as they could afford it, they built the first homestead. Ours is designed the same. By the time ours was built dormer windows were going out, Gran says, but Granddad's mother loved them and wanted the new house built like that. But this old house up here is very small."

"But it looks like stone. Is it?"

"Yes. He dug the stone out of the hillsides."

They went up to see it, through a hole in the hedge, and there was the old house before them, dreaming in the sunshine. The chimneys were half tumbled down, but the contours were good and the walls looked sturdy. It was rough, undressed stone, with deep window embrasures. Cottage roses clung to it here and there, still blooming. Hollyhocks, seeded from the first planted there, year after year, had tried for a hold on the walls, but the winds off the lake had broken them down and they bloomed brokenly among the long grass in crimson and rose splendour. Larkspur had seeded everywhere, making a sea of blue, asters starred the dry seed-heads of the grasses, fuchsias and daisies rioted, wallflowers filled the air with scent, foxgloves lit up the corners with spikes of bloom. The air was full of birdsong and the sound of bees.

Mary stood entranced, a strange feeling taking possession of her, as if the house waited for her. Like the prince in Sleeping Beauty. The children crowded close against her in the archway cut in the five-foot-thick macrocarpa hedge. She spoke as if the words were forced from her, "But why build another house when this one could be done up?"

Ninian's voice spoke behind her, quick, eager, very natural. He really was an excellent actor, never failed to pick up his cues, however unrehearsed.

"Mary, you like it, darling? You mean that?"

She swung round. His father was with him. Her eyes met his, responded. It was no good, you just got more and more involved. She couldn't let any of them down.

"Ninian, it's just beautiful. We – we could add to it. Only four rooms, the children said. It could have a modern annexe, yet designed not to detract from this. I suppose that stone can still be quarried here?"

His eyes gleamed with wicked amusement. "Yes. And of course we *would* have to add to it. After all, we plan quite a family, don't we?"

Mary managed somehow to keep her colour down. "Yes, four rooms wouldn't do us. Let's explore."

They all moved forward. The twins weren't going to be left out of anything.

It would need a lot of doing to it. The inside was shabby and festooned with cobwebs, but fundamentally it was sound. Old Joseph was delighted, like a boy. "I'll go down and get Elspeth up. She'll be over the moon. Come on down with me, children. These two will want to be by themselves to discuss it for a wee bittie."

"These two" were left regarding each other, comical dismay sitting on both.

"My family, my dear darling impetuous family!"

Mary's voice was rueful. "It's my fault, Ninian. It was so foolish. It didn't matter in front of the twins, I thought. It was just that it looked so lost and lovely as we burst through the hedge. The roses and the larkspur and the asters. I wanted to tie the hollyhocks up, trim the hedges, mow down the long grass ... the chimneys looked as if they were begging to be rebuilt, needing smoke issuing from them. The windows are so vacant and forlorn without glass, like empty eye-sockets. I love an old, old house, but it's bad enough trying to hold back your family without me positively encouraging them."

He took hold of her hands. "Mary Rose, it's all right. I got you into this, don't worry about anything that crops up. It's better this way. If Dad thinks we need a new house he'll start getting out plans right away, as it is, about this place, we can put him off, say there's no need to get cracking **on** renovations till spring. Tell him four rooms will be all right for a start." The brown eyes twinkled, remembering. "Don't worry, girl. I'd not anticipated the family getting quite so pushing about our marriage. They certainly want to get the deal clinched, don't they?"

"Yes." Mary's voice wasn't much above a whisper. It had got her by the throat. These people loved her, she loved them, but she was only playing a part. Ninian was grateful to her for that, but inwardly, remembering her foolish words about marriage, he despised her. And in any case, if he hadn't, she was only a pawn in the game.

His people wanted them irrevocably tied up because they were afraid of Nanette, afraid she would play the devil with both their sons' emotions. Ninian's and Roland's. What a horrible position for any parents.

Ninian looked sharply at her. "Don't look so terrified. You won't get pushed into marriage with me. I'll see to that. Though——"

"Yes?" asked Mary hopefully. She recognised the fact that the emotion she was experiencing *was* hope, that she wanted to know very badly what he'd thought better of saying, but didn't know what it was she hoped.

"Oh, nothing," said Ninian.

Could it be that Ninian, despite the fact that he was trying to see the funny side of things, rather wished that he could do something as final as marrying her, just to put an end to a painful situation?

His face cleared. "Listen, we'll just have to put up with their enthusiasm, try to enter into it. Go right ahead, Mary, be as free as you like, planning what you'd plan if – if this was true. They'll sense something wrong otherwise. Then, when they've spent their enthusiasm, things will die down, we don't have to get a start right away. And don't be so embarrassed, I'll not think you mean any of it."

That made it easier for her. By the time Elspeth came up the hill, with a pink bloom of excitement in her lined cheeks, Mary found she could play her part naturally.

Elspeth said, sparkling, "Oh, how Joseph's grandmother would be thrilled. She lived on in this house for years. When Joseph's father married, he built the one we live in now, copying this, but in wood. Joseph remembers his grandmother well. There are some pictures of her in the little room we use as a boxroom. I must show you. She was the sweetest thing. Isabella was named for her. I've always felt it was a crime this was allowed to go to ruin, but it's never been needed."

Every time Ninian's eyes met Mary's they were brimming with devilry. He was actually enjoying the deceit, the fun of it. She suddenly began to enjoy it too. It gave her an exhilarated feeling, something not known since childhood days when she and her brothers had so often plotted mischief and shared the slightly apprehensive delight of doing something they shouldn't.

There was a big old kitchen with a scullery off it, a sitting-room that looked west and north, which meant, seeing they were in the Southern Hemisphere, that it would get sun all day.

"Lucky, weren't we," said Ninian, "that Great-grandpapa didn't make the mistake so many of the first settlers did and build to the south?"

"Did they really?"

"Yes. You'll see a lot of the early houses in Christchurch and Dunedin built that way. Mary, what do you think about that stairway? There was never a hall here. Will it make the lounge too draughty?"

"It could, I suppose, but a stair running up from a room makes for elegance. I like it. Could we not build out a screen from the fireplace wall . . . like an inglenook?"

"Now, that's a fine idea," approved Joseph. "It's a bonnie big room and that would make it really snug. About this fireplace, would you want it made smaller, put a modern space-heater in?"

Ninian, still with the gleam of mischief in his eyes, said, "What would you prefer, Mary?"

"It would be sacrilege to have anything but an open fire there. Big bush logs burning."

Joseph's great head wagged in approval. Mary still had the feeling she must not commit Ninian too far. She added, "And I would like the fireplace left as it is. I like the rough, unpolished stone."

She thought the glance Ninian gave her was a grateful one.

"And since the windows haven't a pane of glass left in them we'll have the openings enlarged. We'll have all the charm of an old house that way, with modern light. The treads of the stairs are remarkably good, Mary. Just a little worn ... see, curved with use."

Mary looked at them and experienced a moment of inexplicable tenderness. Save old Joseph's, the little feet that had run up those stairs were now stilled, the children's and the grandchildren's. Yet there, impressed into the wood, was the evidence of their footsteps, children chasing each other, perhaps, or going up slowly in nightgowns and nightshirts, carefully carrying home-made tallow candles.

A mother, coming down to face all the rigours of pioneer farming among the mountains. Sometimes her footsteps would be slow, careful, when she was heavy with child. Sometimes she would have mounted them in apprehension, knowing her hour had come, and perhaps no one near but her man and with the fear in her heart that if anything went wrong she might leave her bairns to the desolation of a motherless home. But a few days later – for pioneer women were tough – she would be coming down with joy in her heart and a shawl-wrapped bundle in her arms.

Later, no doubt, snowy-frocked brides would have come down to weddings in the orchard ... the whole cavalcade of the years rushed in on Mary ... the busy harvest-time, with a huge table in the kitchen stocked with provender, lambing time with a tin bath full of hot water for weakly lambs, boxes of them near the big range ... Out of her dream she spoke.

"Did she have a brass rod in front of the range, Mr. Macandrew, with socks hanging to air in front of it?"

"Aye," he said, watching her face. "And my grandmother feeling she'd slipped if they were not darned and put away by the Tuesday night."

Mary said, "We had the same at home. Our house is old too. I used to dress by the range when I was small, I loved to wriggle my toes in the warm woolly softness of the old rag mat." Her colour rose as she looked up and encountered Ninian's gaze. Does he think I'm just playing up to his father? she thought.

They went upstairs. The rooms were rather dark, the

82

windows small. "That row of pines will want topping," said Ninian, "if the twins don't object. And we'll need more light, put a few extra windows in, get something designed to suit the dormers."

Mary was still in pursuit of other years. "Only two bedrooms – and they had large families. Where did they all sleep?"

"They used the sod cottage for the boys. There are two rooms there. It was still in fine repair, of course. And there was always this." He opened a door Mary had taken for a cupboard under the eaves. "That was for the current baby."

It was very tiny. Dust covered the floor and from the match-lined ceiling hung evidences of birds' nests under the eaves above it. But here and there, beneath the dust, could be seen a paper sprinkled with apple-blossom and true lovers' knots, and under the sloping ceiling a frieze of nursery cut-outs, homemade, with all the Mother Goose characters.

A sudden wild and foolish regret swept Mary. Regret that this was only make-believe, that this deserted, cold house would never be restored to its former warmth of life that there would never be a baby waking up in that room, apple-blossom outside and inside, a baby lying chuckling at its hands, talking to the tree-shadows that would pattern the ceiling, that there would never be the noisy footsteps of children on that stairway. . . . Ninian's children.

Because she was only a stand-in, an impostor. And Nanette, whom Ninian loved, was going to marry Roland, his brother. Nanette whom Ninian loved so much he would go to any lengths to give her her heart's desire.

## CHAPTER 5

MARY felt she had to get out of this darling house before her feelings got the better of her. As she led the way downstairs she heard Joseph say, "Well, work out your plans together, son, you'll hae your own ideas – they'll not be the same as ours – then when you've decided just what you want, we'll call for tenders."

As they came out into the garden a shadow passed suddenly over the sun, and the dark firs that shadowed the top storey bent before a wind that sprung up. It only lasted a moment, but Mary thought it seemed as if the little house echoed the sound of the sighing firs, a disappointed sigh. She looked back over her shoulder. Its empty window sockets were looking sightlessly at the lake.

That night Joseph, unable to help himself, said hopefully, "Do you want to start sketching out a few plans, son?"

Ninian shook his head. "Not tonight, Dad. Mary looks all in. She's tired with the travelling, I think. We'll go early to bed, there's plenty of time for plans."

Mary was glad to get to bed, on the supreme comfort of an electrically heated mattress, to read some New Zealand magazines. She felt she needed a rest from piquant situations. Yet it had been a restful evening. Ninian had merely walked with her to the stairhead to bid her goodnight.

He had said quite nicely, "Thanks for seeing me through a somewhat difficult day. You did very well – especially since you aren't a sentimental person."

He thought it was all acting, that she didn't really feel any of this. He didn't know how much she had fallen for his family, the outspokenness of them all, the simplicity of their lives, the engaging misdemeanours of the twins, the maternal solicitude of Barbara, the bond that existed between Ninian's parents; how she had fallen in love with the little forlorn house by the deserted orchard, how much she ... Mary decided it was time to clamp down on wistful, straying thoughts that could have no future. She picked up a magazine, began to read.

They managed to postpone plans for the house for the next few days. "I want to relax after all my gruelling experiences," said Ninian, looking the picture of health and winking at Mary.

Mary's manner sounded most professional. "The trip at sea wasn't really long enough. He needed weeks of it. It would do him good to be out of the house though and away out with his father, getting all the sun he can. Doctor Steedman felt his recovery was amazing considering how ill he had been, but he must take care. Have you had your tablets this morning, Ninian?"

"Yes, Sister," said Ninian meekly.

"Gosh," commented young Jonathan, "she really can manage him, can't she?"

Ninian grinned, "She got in the way of it when I was only another nuisance of a Kiwi soldier to her."

Mary smiled too. "He really was a nuisance – once he turned the corner. It would have been much better if he'd had a few broken bones. He'd have had to stay in bed then."

Ninian said to his mother, "Don't you think that's a horrible thing to say? I never knew anything so callous as nurses. My ideas of the profession underwent a change, I can tell you. No smoothing fevered brows and being sweetly sympathetic. And talk about a fierce routine! A chap just about had to ask how many times he could breathe to the hour!"

His father chuckled. "Well, you seem to have made the running just the same. Interesting and all it would be to know how you managed to fit your courting into the routine. How did you do it, son?"

"Blest if I know." Mary realised Ninian was playing for time, trying to think something up. "Every time I thought up a speech to convince her I really was falling for her, she'd shove a thermometer in my mouth or something."

"When you're nursing soldiers you take everything they say with a grain of salt. I admit you had a hard time, Ninian, and I had once sworn never to fall for a patient," said Mary.

His eyes met hers. "And, Dad, when I was convalescent enough to be allowed out – and it was her day off – what do you think she did? Went out to dinner with my Colonel!"

Joseph gave a great shout of laughter.

Mary said, "Well, a girl has to make the most of her opportunities, and I wasn't to know it would last with Ninian beyond the convalescent stage. It usually doesn't."

Ninian said to her later, "I hand it to you, Sister, you're playing up well." His mouth twisted. "But before you make any of your vitriolic speeches, I hasten to assure you that I know it's not for my sake but for my family's. You've fallen in love with them, haven't you?"

For some extraordinary reason Mary couldn't look up. "Yes," she admitted, moving away.

His voice halted her. "Dad and I are riding out to the boundary today. How about coming? Give you an idea of the extent of the place."

"Sorry," her voice held real regret, "but I promised Barbie I'd help her with that dress for the concert. She's got to be around for fittings, and so it has to be today, she's got something on later in the week."

"All right. Plenty of time to show you later."

"Yes, I suppose so.'

His fingers gripped her arm. "What do you mean? Isn't there?"

"Just that there has to be an end some time. But that we will meet when it comes.'

"Yes. Mary, tell me, what have you told your people?"

She looked out across the lake, lying bluely in the morning sun, across to the far, far mountains at its utmost rim.

"Well, naturally, I've given them no hint of a love-affair, certainly not of an engagement. They'd want to know too much. I said I travelled out on the same ship with you, to take care of you – they knew all about you, of course, your rescue made headlines even in our home town. I said the Colonel of your regiment had asked me to do so. It was quite easy then to say your family had proved very nice and most hospitable and wanted me to stay on for a bit. And there I left it."

He nodded. "Yes, I think that was fairly well thought out. Mary, that conversation I overheard – with you and Anne Meredith." He paused, and Mary's face flamed. She clenched her fingers. "Do your people – particularly your mother – know the odd slant you have on life? Your attitude to marriage, for instance. Disregarding any warmer feelings, thinking marriage can be based on nothing more than friendship?"

Her colour had subsided, leaving her pale, she looked him straight in the eye, her expression cold and hard. "I dislike people probing, Lieutenant, I'm helping you out of a sticky situation. But please keep out of my affairs, they're nothing to do with you." She turned on her heel, walked back into the house, called to Barbara that she was ready to begin dressmaking.

"Oh, good," said Elspeth. "I'll manage all the meals and the housework while you girls get on with that. Honestly, I'd rather spring-clean the house from attic to cellar than attempt that thing!"

Mary flung herself into the children's interests. With so much gone out of her life, little things helped. And it was better to be engrossed in the children's doings than to be left alone too often with Ninian. She found him an enigma. How he really regarded the situation was beyond her.

The twins were her constant shadows. She realised that despite their air of toughness they missed their mother deeply. From the moment they knew she too had been brought up on the *Anne of Green Gables* books and had actually visited Prince Edward Island, they dogged her footsteps, asking questions.

"She's just like us," they said to Ninian.

He raised his brows. "It's meant for a compliment," he said reassuringly to Mary, who was sitting on the step with them, looking dreamily at the lake and twisting the big sapphire on her finger.

Josephine and Jonathan exchanged glances. They weren't at all sure that that remark in its turn was favourable to them.

"Of course I'm like them," returned Mary serenely.

Josephine's voice held great satisfaction. "See, Ninian! We just knew she was our sort the moment she said she didn't like *Alice*."

Ninian put down his fishing flies. "Alice who? She's only just got here, she doesn't know any—"

Jonathan hooted with derision. "Alice who? *Alice in Wonderland*, of course."

Ninian looked affronted. "And that makes her a kindred spirit? Then I suppose I'm not! I read *Alice* over and over when I was a kid."

Josephine's face was earnest, not mischievous, for once. "That's what we mean, Nin. Nearly everybody likes it. We didn't. So we felt odd. But if Mary doesn't like it, too, it makes us feel good."

There was a chuckle from the bench against the wall

where Joseph was taking off his farm boots. "Nin, you're out of your depth. Dinna ye realise that shared dislikes make for more kinship than owt? Neither Elspeth nor Ros Mhairi here like dressmaking, therefore they like each other."

Elspeth came out behind them, Tiger in her arms, sat down too in the mild autumn night. "We like each other for more things than that, Father. And for likes as well as dislikes, for faults as well as virtues. Mary is just as untidy as me when she's cooking, praise be. Gets dishes strewn all over the place, but works at great speed, then with the job over and the tins full, has a grand clean-up. I could never abide over-efficiency, and if you'd brought me a daughter-in-law with a mania for tidiness it'd have driven me clean crazy. Oh, I must have my house clean, and I canna bear junk cluttering the place up, but I do no' like my house like a bandbox."

Ninian said, "Don't worry, pet, home will never be like that. And occasionally you do have fits of reform ... like a few moments ago, ordering your son newly returned from the ranks of the missing, you callous woman, to take his fishing rubbish outside."

Elspeth ignored him. "Mary'll make a good farmer's wife. You just hae to shut your eyes to a bit of dust on the mantel come harvest-time. Feeding the brutes is all that matters then. And if you get het up because you haven't polished the brass doorknobs on the right day, you'll be downright crotchety – which aye means an unhappy household."

Joseph chuckled. "Hark at her! No one'd ever think what a panic she got in, thinking that if Mary was a nursing Sister she might be all starch and efficiency, prefer kitchenettes with enamel paintwork like a hospital theatre ... ye ken what I mean, lad? – nursing Sisters often look so remote and cool."

"I ken," said Ninian, unravelling nylon line. "She gave even me that impression at first. A woman who lived by rule. But since she's been here ... well, blest if I know. It's a constant revelation. As if when the twins turned her topsy-turvy all the starch flew out of her. I used to think she had her emotions well under control, but bless my boots if I didn't go past her room this morning and Josephine's in bed with her, and they're both sitting up in bed, blowing their noses and mopping their eyes in great style. I was all concern, thought they'd developed streaming colds simultaneously, inquired about it so solicitously, only to be told to go away, they were both enjoying a howl over some daft book they were reading."

Josephine and Mary exchanged shamefaced glances, then giggled.

"It's not that we're so emotional, really," said Mary, "only that we have over-active tear-ducts!"

Ninian shouted with laughter. "Oh, Mary, Mary, you think you can explain everything away technically!"

Suddenly Mary was aware that Elspeth was looking curiously at them. She had a pondering look. She was weighing up exactly what Ninian meant. He had thought Mary starchy, her emotions under her control ... until she got here. Elspeth would be thinking how odd for a man to think a girl he was supposed to have fallen in love with at first sight cool and starchy. Mary was aware, not for the first time, that they skated on very thin ice.

It made her extremely affectionate towards Ninian for the rest of the evening. She caught him looking at her in puzzled fashion once or twice. When it came to bedtime and the others rose, she said, as any girl in love might have, "Ninian, let's go for a walk to the hill above the stables to see the mountain, it's a wonderful night."

"But put my cape on her, just the same, Ninian," said Elspeth, smiling.

Ninian turned her towards the old orchard instead. "There's an even better view up there," he explained.

The way was rutted and in the ruts gleamed tiny diamond points of frost, for the night had changed, was now clear and sparkling cold. They came up through a close-set avenue of pines with a shifting mosaic of starlight and shadow on the hard-beaten ground where the pine-needles had blown away.

They came up behind the hawthorn hedge above the little forlorn house and turned to look at Aorangi, towering above the other great peaks. A wisp of cloud like a filmy evening stole clung to it. Mary remarked on it, adding dreamily, "Pinned there with a star. I wonder if it's ever looked just like that before ... or ever will again. I wonder if your great-grandmother ever saw it like that, if your own grand-daughter will."

She turned to find him regarding her with amazement. "Mary, you *have* changed. I was a bit afraid at times that you wouldn't play up enough, that you detested me so much it might show at some unguarded moment. But since dinner-time tonight you've played your part magnificently. Mind if I ask why?"

Mary felt there was danger in this. She slipped her hand out of the crook of his arm, said coldly, "I can assure you, in case you're afraid of it, that it's not that my feelings towards you have undergone a change, Lieutenant. It was only that I thought your mother looked surprised, even suspicious, tonight, when you suddenly said you'd thought me cool and unemotional. Most men don't think those things about the women they love. You were probably off guard; you said it was only after coming here I had changed. And because I'm interested in this plot to get Roland and Nanette married, with nothing to break up the harmony of a family I admire so much, I – well – rather flung myself into disarming your mother's disquietude."

Ninian was silent. She found his silence unbearable, said hotly, "Oh, for Pete's sake don't think it was because I *am* softening towards you. It's nothing but an inborn love of doing any job I do as well as I possibly can!"

Ninian turned to her, caught her hands. He was laughing. "Oh, Mary, you spitfire! You're quite amazing. Nothing more different from Sister Rose can be imagined! I wasn't reading anything like that into it. I know you don't allow yourself any tender feelings towards men. You like all things cut and dried, all advantages weighed up. You said so. And I – of all men – am not likely to be vain about my power to attract women, am I? Nanette soon forgot to mourn me, didn't she?"

Mary caught her breath. He had said that with something of the disillusion she had felt when she knew Francis loved the Colonel's daughter. Pity stabbed at her, taking away her resentment. Ninian turned, caught the silver glint of tears.

This time his laugh had tenderness in it, not one you could resent. He caught her face between his hands. "Oh, Mary, those over-active tear-ducts!"

She looked down, blinked rapidly, tried to pull away.

"No, don't. You know even if we're not exactly kindred spirits, like you and the twins, for instance, I think we could be – pals. You're helping me out of a very sticky mess and I'm more than grateful. I must be more careful. Mother is so astute, though as she likes you so much I don't think she'll drop to a bogus situation like this engagement."

He absently turned her ring round on her finger. His ring. A ring that meant exactly nothing. That was only the visible sign of a pact that existed between them and had no future. He seemed as if he was going to say something, changed his mind, put his hand under her elbow. "Well, it's getting quite nippy now, we'll watch our step a bit closer, and if anything bothers you from time to time, Mary, bring me out like this and we'll talk it over. I know it's only a job to you, but it's more than that to me. Which reminds me, when I first proposed this I said you were to look on it as a job. Naturally, as it's keeping you from a position, from tomorrow I shall give you a weekly cheque."

As she started in protest he said, "No . . . Dad won't know. No one will know. I have my own income from part of the farm."

"I wasn't thinking of that. There is one thing you can't make me do, Lieutenant, and that is take money from you. I'm looking on this as a holiday. I had intended travelling all over New Zealand before settling down to look in real earnest for a—"

"For that accommodating husband with the bank balance. For comfort, security. I forget the rest."

"You don't have to remember it. It doesn't concern you. But I have plenty saved for what I need in the way of clothes I will not take money."

"All right, Mary, let it go for now. But if you find funds running low, will you come to me?"

"I'm not likely to run low. I'm getting my keep."

"You're earning your keep. Dad said only yesterday what a godsend it is to have you here. Mother could easily have found it too much, looking after Isabella's children all this time. And you don't irritate her the way Nanette did."

"I can find it in me to be sorry for Nanette, Ninian. She probably can't help being over-efficient. It can be exasperating, I know, but they don't seem to have made her very welcome."

"Oh, it wasn't that really. After all, Nanette lived in this district, came and went here all her life. If things had gone as they should have and her parents had let her marry Roland when she was nineteen or so, it would have been quite different. But they didn't approve our engagement because they always felt she belonged to Roland – in spirit."

There were a hundred questions Mary wanted to ask, bubbling up in her with a curious insistence she could not understand. Most of all she wanted to know how Ninian himself had felt. Had he too always known, deep down, that Nanette belonged to Roland? Had he always felt shut out, second-best? Suddenly Mary remembered that oddly hostile flicker of feeling in Nanette's eyes that day in Fairlie. Perhaps they were all wrong. Perhaps it was really Ninian Nanette loved.

Perhaps she too was desperate, caught up in a tangle made of Ninian's year-long disappearance, his ill-timed rescue, Roland's loneliness, old ties. Perhaps she was as bewildered as Mary herself.

Below them, shadowy and dark, was the forlorn house, cold and forlorn like her own heart. Empty. Mary felt panicky as the old desolation swept over her again. The happenings of the last few weeks had blotted out the memory of Francis. It must stay that way. She had come south to forget.

She heaved a sigh. "It's what the Colonel said, Ninian, a mess. We'll play for time and hope it comes out right. Maybe Roland and Nanette will get married soon. Perhaps you could talk to Roland about it. Naturally, I mean, as one brother to another. Make him feel there's no need to wait."

His voice was controlled. "It won't be Roland to fix the date, Mary. It will be Nanette. Nanette must make up her mind."

Must make up her mind. To what? To a certain date . . . or to which man was to be the bridegroom? It seemed as if Ninian knew Nanette was still unsure of herself. Or was it wishful thinking on his part?

In silence they went down the hill.

\*

But the talk had done something, had cleared the air. In spite of fresh misunderstandings that had cropped up in it, they both somehow found it easier to play their parts. Mary knew a freedom she had not known before. She was more sure that Ninian would not be embarrassed by a mock show of affection. But she still had a strange feeling, a sense of unreality, something that was to do with the fact that as she played her part all her waking hours, it seemed more real than her true feelings ... which of course, she told herself, were mainly concerned with a desire to get this job over and done with.

She and Elspeth and the twins spent a whole afternoon in the attic hunting for the photos of Joseph's grandmother. It was full of the most fascinating things, boxes of letters, photographs, greeting cards, old albums, clothes stored with mothballs ... "We're for ever re-enacting arrivals of pioneers in New Zealand," said Elspeth, "so I dare not throw them out. They were used last in South Canterbury's centennial celebrations."

Finally the twins tired of it and went out to feed the calves, and Mhairi, the black filly, their constant joy. Elspeth decided she'd have to tear herself away to start the evening meal.

Mary looked up regretfully from an old diary she had found and said, "I'll come down in a moment. This is just too fascinating. I must find out how she treated that child's diphtheria – oh, how I hope he didn't die."

Elspeth said drily, "He didn't, he lived to father Joseph." She dusted her skirt down. "Stay you there, lassie, I prepared most of the meal early on. But there's a crust to put on the apples."

Joseph and his son, coming in, were told where Mary was and went up. Elspeth said to them, "She's asked has anyone ever written up the family history. I said no, we were always saying it ought to be done. It seems she did one for their family. They *do* sound nice. I wish you two would make up your minds about that wedding date. Then we could get them over here, it's not that far across the Pacific. I'm sure she'd write it up for you, Joseph, if you asked her."

The two men changed into slippers, went up. They opened the door quietly. Mary was sitting cross-legged on the floor, with a pile of old diaries on her lap, her chin in her hand.

93

She removed the hand as they came in, leaving a smear of dust on the chin.

She heaved a sigh, eyes shining, cheeks pink. "What courage they had! Joseph, what do you think your grandmother did for your father? ... She gave him a few drops of kerosene on sugar. He was just about through – the fatal membrane was right across his throat, it was kill or cure. It cured! He gasped, turned almost black, and vomited it all up, and in an hour was sleeping peacefully!"

Joseph dropped down beside her. "Eh, lass, but you're a one. I can even be glad Ninian was missing that year, since if he hadn't been he'd never have met you. You've taken forty years off my life."

Mary blinked. There was even dust on her eyebrows and eyelashes. She rubbed at them. "How have I done that?"

Joseph glanced up at his son. "She doesn't even know. It came as natural to her as all that. Lassie, it's just that it must be all that and more since anyone as young and pretty as you called me Joseph."

Mary clapped her hands to her suddenly warm cheeks. "Oh, did I? And you don't mind? I just naturally think of you as that, not as Ninian's parents, but as Joseph and Elspeth. But I'd not have done it intentionally."

"Elspeth will love it as much as I do. When you get to our age that's one of the things that makes you feel gey auld ... that you merely become Father or Grandpa."

Ninian dropped down on the other side of her. "You've got a dirty face, darling," he said, and he took out his handkerchief.

Mary shied away from him. "I feel like the little boy ... I just *won't* be washed with spit!" she giggled.

"All right, I'll do it dry, but it won't come off properly."

Joseph leaned across and pushed Ninian away. "Give over now. Mary, will ye do it for me? Settle down to write the family history? I know many things not recorded in these. Things passed down by word of mouth from Granny to me. Things that are bound up with the history of the Mackenzie country."

"I'd like to. I do have a little know-how, Joseph. I've written quite a few articles on early settlers in Canadian magazines. I'm not a genius – far from it – but I could put real-life stuff together."

Joseph said with great satisfaction, "We've got all winter ahead of us. It'll be fine. Whenever we canna get outside we'll settle down to this."

Ninian, playing his part, pulled a face. "Looks as if I'll not get as much of her company as I'm entitled to."

"Aye. Ye may not at that, lad, but I daresay you may get wed ere winter's out and can manage a few moments alone together now and then." The old eyes twinkled mischievously. "And if you're living just up by, Mhairi and I can get on wi' the history."

Mary stood up. "I'd better have a shower and change. My skirt and jersey reek of mothballs. Ninian, if Barbie's not finished feeding the fowls, would you set the table for your mother? I think the twins are still out."

"We're not," said a voice, and a tow-head, Josephine's, looked round the door. "But if Nin's dying to set the table he can. If you're changing, Mary, be sure to put on a very full skirt, won't you? That sheath affair you had on last night'd be no good."

Ninian was mystified. "No good for what?"

Mary and Josephine grinned at each other. Josephine replied:

"For sliding down the banisters."

"Good life, you'll kill your new aunt if you aren't careful!"

The other towhead appeared beside its twin's. "Gosh, Ninian, you don't know her like we do. She got right to the top of that biggest Wellingtonia yesterday. You ought to have seen it."

"Just as well I didn't. Be bad for my blood pressure. Mary, have you no more sense? Do you know what height that is?"

"No. But a Wellingtonia is the safest tree of all to climb. If you do slip you get caught in the branches."

Ninian sighed. "But anyway, you watch that bend if you're bent on sliding down the banisters. It's tricky."

Jonathan said, "You see, she said she'd only ever come down banisters backwards, that that's the safest way, but we want her to see that it's quite easy coming down frontwards, and much more exciting, makes your tummy turn over, and if you judge your distance right, and plonk your hands on that post at the bottom and leap, you land fair in the middle of the hall."

Ninian said severely, "She could break an ankle or an arm. It's all right for kids – they're made of india-rubber. Let me tell you –"

Joseph coughed. "Now, isn't that strange. I could ha' sworn I saw you do just that yesterday morn, Ringan!"

His son gave him an exasperated look. "Well, anyway, Jo and Jonno, you're not to let her do it the first time without a great heap of cushions in the hall. And you're to tell me when you're going to do it and I'll supervise it."

Jo groaned, Jonathan muttered "Spoilsport" and dodged, and Mary said laughingly, "I must go get this shower or I'll sure be late."

The twins and Mary did the washing-up that night. As they went out of the door with the last of the dishes from the table they heard Ninian say, "Manages those holy terrors well, doesn't she?"

Mary shut the door hastily, then giggled with the twins. "Poor misguided man, he little realises that we're going to sneak off and get that one glorious swoop down the banisters without his supervision!"

They washed up at speed and departed stealthily for the big hall, happily aware that the radio was on in the big room and the folk there wouldn't notice that the clang and clatter of crockery and cutlery had stopped.

Jo said softly, "Just the same, Mary, I'm all for putting the cushions at the bottom. I wouldn't like to be us if you did hurt yourself."

Mary grinned. The twins had a wholesome respect for Ninian and also a deep affection.

Jonathan said, "This is the best banister for sliding down I've ever seen. Ours at home has a great horrible knob at the bottom so you lose the thrill of sailing off into space."

"Why, Jonno, didn't you know? Granddad sawed the knobs off this one, leaving only the things the knobs rested on ... whatdya call them? Sort of shoulders. He polished them well so it doesn't show. He did it so the kids could slide down."

96

Mary's voice was surprised. "Did he really? What a sport!"

Mary decided sport was the word. She realised the staircase would have been much more handsome with the original knobs on. They scattered the cushions clean in the centre of the hall.

"I know you land exactly there," said Jonathan, "because I always flop right in the centre of that carpet pattern."

"Shush, or we'll have Ninian out," warned Mary. "I'd really like you two to go down first to let me see exactly how you tackle that flying leap, but he might hear the thud. Come on."

"That dress is just the thing," approved Josephine.

"It's mighty old, honey," said Mary, laughing, looking down on her three-year-old white cotton splashed with cornflowers. It had a deep, heart-shaped neckline and a little jacket, and the skirt was wide and full.

They crept up the top of the stairs. Mary looked down. It seemed a lot higher from up here. But she mustn't show nervousness in front of the twins. She flung a leg over, began to slide; as she took the curve she felt a fluttering in her tummy and without knowing it gave a squeal. She kept an eye on the end of the banister rushing towards her, got her hands ready for the grip that would launch her across the hall, and was dimly aware that outside the dogs had started to bark.

Her hands touched the end, propelled her into space, and she experienced quite a thrill as she sailed through the air. She landed squarely in the nest of cushions just as Ninian flung the living-room door open, and a horde of strangers flung the front door wide.

There, in the gap, was a large circle of astonished faces as they saw someone all lacy petticoats and flying skirts fly through the air towards them and subside in a laughing heap in the middle of the floor.

# CHAPTER 6

MARY took it in ... a surprise party ... but who was the more surprised she didn't know. Ninian was beside her, crouched down on the cushions, real concern in his voice.

"Mary, you are a bad girl! I said I wanted to be there. I was afraid of that bend. It's so easy to sway."

It was no good him attempting to be cross; Mary, the twins, and the newcomers were all helpless with laughter. Ninian looked at them blankly.

Mary hastily pulled her frock over her knees. It wasn't going to be a dignified introduction to these people, but Ninian didn't seem to care.

Through the crowd her eyes met Nanette's eyes. There was a slightly triumphant expression in them, as if she was pleased Ninian's new fiancée had been caught out in a hoydenish trick. Nanette must now be out staying with her relations.

Ninian was lifting her to her feet, doing it with the utmost solicitude. He said, with assumed pride, Mary supposed, "As you can image, folks, Mary meets with the full approval of the terrible twins. With that particular feat she can now do anything they can do ... including reaching the top of the big Wellingtonia."

Mary caught a puzzled whisper, "You know, I thought she was a hospital Sister."

Ninian heard it too. The side of his mouth went up. "She was. Can't tie up a romp like that with a starched cap and an icy manner, can you? but I can vouch for it. I've seen it, even suffered it. But she soon thawed. A real Doctor Jekyll and Mr. Hyde personality."

His eyes, twinkling with fun, met Mary's. Hers twinkled back. They looked the perfectly suited couple, young, ardent, in love, brimming over with fun.

The rest of the family had crowded out into the hall. Greetings were exchanged, introductions made.

"Well," said Joseph, enjoying himself, "most surprise parties are hardly that. Nearly always one gets wind of it. But this is most certainly one."

Ninian said, "Come to think of it, Rol rang me and said he'd be ringing tonight about some stock – at nine – and would I be in? I suppose that was your way of making sure?"

"Sure was. You didn't guess at all?"

"If he did – and didn't tell me –" Mary said, laughing, "he's in for a few bad minutes later. I wouldn't be wearing this if I'd known a party was on. Even if it is suitability plus for shooting the rapids . . . I think I dusted the stairs with it."

Ninian gave a perfunctory brush at the back of her skirt. "You look sweet, my love," he said. For Nanette's and Roland's benefit, Mary reminded herself.

Old Joseph took a quick look at Mary, said, "Ros Mhairi, when you were unpacking, did I or did I not see a tartan sash?"

She smiled. "You did, Joseph."

She saw Nanette's eyes narrow and knew a quite primitive pleasure in seeing Nanette did not like their intimacy of names. Mary was rather shocked at herself, she'd thought herself above feminine cattiness.

Joseph turned to his younger son. "Ninian, go up and get it, it's all she needs for a party air. What drawer will it be in, Mhairi? And bring down my cairngorm pin from my plaid to fasten it with."

Ninian, grinning, took the stairs two at a time and was soon down, the long red sash of the Rose tartan over his arm, his pin in his hand.

The old man made quite a ceremony of it, crossing one end over the back, carrying the other across the breast, knotting both ends on the right side and pinning it on the left shoulder.

The crowd clapped when he had finished. Mary realised that they were all prepared to welcome her warmly because these were Ninian's friends, the boys and girls he had gone to school with, their parents. They too had known consternation when he had been found, and the first thought that would have flashed into their minds would have been what of Nanette, engaged to his brother. They were prepared to accept her as one of themselves, a solution, a face-saver.

They all had plates and baskets, and trooped into the kitchen with them now.

Elspeth said to Barbara, "Go and light up the big playroom, love, and push a mop over the floor to take the dust off it for the dancing."

Mary slipped off with her. The big playroom with windows on its three sides led off the lounge by double glass doors that folded back. It had been added by Joseph when his family were small, and modernised to be used for dancing later.

Mary said, "Barbie, give me that mop, and bring in the vases from the living-room and set them on the windowsills." They were chrysanthemums that Elspeth grew in her little glasshouse, sheltered from the winds that blew from the snows of the Alps. Ninian came in, put a match to the set fire of the lounge, switched on a couple of heaters in the playroom.

People drifted in, talking disjointedly, asking Ninian about his experiences, asking Mary how she liked New Zealand, what part of Canada she came from, how she liked the snows and glaciers after the heat and glamour of Malaya.

Mary hoped all her answers tallied with Ninian's. He played up well, kept by her as much as possible. Once she saw his eyes stray to Nanette, standing by Roland, her beautiful nut-brown hair with its glinting golden lights set off to advantage by the winking glass chandelier above her.

The heart-shaped face was most appealing, the eyes so starry. She had an exquisitely small waist and wore a frock of yellow taffeta patterned with tiny brown stars, perfect colouring for her, and against the creamy pallor of her skin lay an amber necklace. Bubbles of the same glowed at her ears. There was a luminous quality about her. One could imagine a painter longing to set her on canvas. And there was a Mona Lisa touch about her lips. Mary had never liked the Mona Lisa.

Ninian turned to Mary, said softly, "It's quite unbelievable that I don't know, but you do dance, don't you? I dare not admit that I don't know."

"I do. Set your mind at rest."

It was an old-time dance, more like a barn dance than a formal one. Someone played the piano extremely well, there were a couple of fiddles, and Joseph, surprisingly, brought out a concertina.

"How lovely," said Mary to Ninian. "I like nothing better than dancing to a concertina, except of course –"

"Dare I hope you're going to say 'except of course the pipes'?"

"You're right!"

"If you tell Dad that you'll be an even greater success than you are now – if that's possible. He was in the Pipe Band till about five years ago, when I took his place."

Mary had a sudden vision of how Ninian would look in a kilt.

"What tartan do the Macandrews wear, Ninian?" she asked him.

"The Anderson. But our Pipe Band wears the Mackenzie."

"Anderson . . . that's a pale blue background, isn't it?"

"Yes, and the Mackenzie is green with big blocks of blue and red check. Listen, the fiddles have got into tune. We're expected to lead off, darling."

He spoke his endearment a little loud, she thought, suddenly nervous.

She said in a whisper, "Don't stress the dears and darlings too much. It's a little overdone."

His eyes danced, he was in high spirits, she could see. "Very well, my love, I shall whisper them in your ear . . . stage whispers . . . give a good effect . . . and perhaps you could raise a blush occasionally."

To her chagrin, and Ninian's delight, she blushed vividly.

"You look like Princess Rose Red," he said, and it was not a stage whisper. She saw why. They were against Roland and Nanette. He swung her on to the floor.

It was a merry night, and she thought it a sound idea, this way she would meet most of the district at once, and it would be less strain for Ninian, trying to appear devoted for this one night instead of visiting family after family.

Taken this way there wasn't a lot of time for conversation and soon she would be part and parcel of the community. A pity, though, that Nanette had come to Lake Pukaki. Better if she had stayed in Fairlie. She would be here often in the next few days, because Roland would make Mount Hebron his headquarters. There could be awkward moments when she and Nanette would be left alone.

Roland claimed a dance with her. "I must find out how my new sister-in-law dances," he answered.

Nanette had been with him, so she automatically turned to Ninian. Mary found she was paying the pair of them more attention than to what Roland was saying. Nanette and Ninian danced beautifully together, managing even intricate steps with a sure knowledge of what the other would do.

What is the matter with you? she asked herself irritably, what can it matter to you? You're only playing a part. Trouble is, you're playing it so constantly you almost feel it's real. You actually resent Nanette being in Ninian's arms! At that moment Ninian caught her eye, solemnly winked at her, and suddenly it was all a delicious joke.

She turned her face up to Roland's. He looked down on her, said softly so no one could hear, "Mary, I wonder if you know just how much you've done for this family and particularly for me?"

She hardly knew what to say, what Ninian would wish her to say. She hesitated, then said, "Well, it was a happy solution, wasn't it?"

Roland said, "I'm so glad he met you ... loved you ... and I don't wonder he did."

Mary felt her colour deepen, and looked across the room to see Ninian watching her. Oh well, better Ninian than Nanette. She doubted if Nanette was as thankful. Yet, although she could understand any girl knowing a bit of hurt pride at being supplanted by another, in this unusual situation, if it was really Roland she loved, then shouldn't she have known relief? *If it was.*

The dance ended and Mary didn't find Ninian right away. The situation was so fraught with difficulties she felt safer with him by her side, ready to turn the too-probing question. She decided her colour was altogether too high and she'd slip up to her room to put some powder on.

As she passed a door she heard Nanette's voice in its husky, little-girl whisper, "Ninian, come outside for a few moments, don't you realise there are things I *must* ask you?"

Mary stood stock still, one hand on the stair-rail. She just had to hear Ninian's answer.

"Don't be a little idiot. It would cause talk."

She got her breath back then, but still listened.

Nanette's voice had a break in it. "But there are things to say, Nin. Things to get sorted out. It can't just finish like this!"

Ninian's voice was curt, hard. "Can't it? But it has. I thought my letter was very final, and explained everything. Listen, Nanette, you've always been inflicted with indecision and it's made a mess of Roland's life once. It's not going to this time."

"Does Roland matter more than me?"

"Yes."

Outside the door Mary clasped her hands together with sudden intensity. "Oh, Ninian, be careful, be careful. A woman scorned is unpredictable." She found she was mouthing the words.

There was a heartbroken cry from Nanette. Mary was sure it was put on. Or was that wishful thinking?

Then Ninian's voice, savage again. "Nanette, for heaven's sake! Let's get back up to the others."

Mary ran swiftly up the stairs. She must not be caught here.

She wished she knew the answer to it all. Would Nanette have ditched Roland had Ninian come back alone?

There was another question. Was it for Roland's sake that Ninian had asked her to take part in this conspiracy? Or for Nanette's? She supposed she would never know. Once Roland and Nanette were safely married, she and Ninian would stage a quarrel and she would leave the Southern Hemisphere and go back home.

It would be easier, now, to go home. Why she did not know, but Francis and the wedding that never came off seemed a long way off now. It belonged to a past that was as dead as the dodo.

She came back into the room to find Ninian looking for her. She marvelled that he could look so unruffled. "I want you to help Mother serve the supper, Mary, to take your place as the daughter of the house," he told her.

Elspeth was in the big kitchen, coffee was bubbling in two big percolators, more in saucepans, kettles were hissing on the old range.

Mary looked over the delectable array of cakes and savouries and sandwiches. "What a spread! Just as well they brought their own supper, wasn't it? Our tins were almost empty. Shall I put these in the oven to heat now? Oh, goodness, did you ever see such a confection as that? Who ever made that must be a master hand at decoration!"

She gazed at a huge Pavlova cake, set on an enormous silver wedding-cake stand. It was an immense circle, and in the centre of it, on a pool of whipped cream, were waterlilies in the shining sugared splendour of meringues.

"How could anyone get meringue into shapes like that? It's fantastic!"

Elspeth had a chuckle in her voice. "It's Nanette's. She always has to be able to display the best. Now do you know what I mean when I say I canna bear her in my kitchen, and me so slap-happy about cooking?"

Mary put her arm around Elspeth. "I bet she can't make steak-and-kidney pudding like you, you goose."

Elspeth merely said, "Oh, be off with you. Joseph canna stand hand-round suppers at parties. Could you whisk some big white cloths on to the tables?"

It was very homely and comfortable. Elspeth got Nanette to cut the big Pavlova. "I don't doubt there's an art in the cutting as well as in the making," she said, smiling quite nicely at Nanette.

"And in the eating," said Ninian in Mary's ear. "Can't stand those things. They ooze all over the place."

Mary said hastily, "But you must have a piece . . . she made it specially."

Ninian's eyebrow lifted. "Might I remind you, darling, that your days of ordering me about are over . . . when you stopped being Sister Mary Rose and became Ros Mhairi, the darling of the Macandrews. I shall have exactly the things I really like."

"Oh, dear," said Mary helplessly. "You really are in the most contrary mood."

"Time I was. Time I asserted myself. You had a long innings."

All unknowing, Nanette bent over him with a wedge of the Pavlova on a silver server.

"No, no, Nanette," he said cheerfully. "I'm off sugar. I

prefer salt these days, something with a tang to it," and helped himself to another savoury.

Mary turned hastily. "I'll have that piece, thanks, Nanette. I've never seen anything so beautiful in my life. It seems a crime to eat that water-lily."

It was one o'clock when the party that had started so early came to an end. Mary felt she knew most of the neighbours now.

Joseph said suddenly, "We must have a proper tune to end with. Son, up you go and get your pipes. It's been the one thing missing tonight."

Ninian rose, smiled down on his father. "As long as you don't insist on my donning the regalia. Take too long."

He came down again, his pipes under his arm, walked to the doorway between the rooms, took up his stand.

Mary listened entranced.

Finally Joseph said, "Now a reel for the last before Auld Lang Syne, son."

As Ninian swung into it, Mary's foot began tapping. Joseph leaned across to her. "Did ye do Highland dancing, lassie?"

She nodded. A light shot into the old blue eyes, he stood up, aged but erect, a fine figure of a man, held out his hands to Mary, who came instantly to her feet.

She shot one quick, questioning glance at Ninian. He nodded, smiling.

Up and down the room they danced, feet twinkling in and out, Mary's full skirt swirling, the end of her tartan sash swinging out. The folk in the lounge crowded to the glass doors, beat time. The music of the pipes rose, quick, merry, irresistible.

At last they came to a laughing, breathless stop, flung themselves down together on a couch. "Eh, but I havna danced like that for twenty years," said old Joseph. He had her hand.

She looked across at Ninian, said quite spontaneously, "Oh, Ninian, if I hadn't fallen in love with you I'd have fallen in love with your father!"

The moment the words were out she realised what she had said.

Ninian's eyes held hers. They widened even as hers widened. Mary's lips parted, she felt a sudden need for more air. Ninian handed his pipes to Roland, came to her, disengaged her hand from his father's, said, "Then that's enough of that. I know I could never compete against my father's charms. Next time *he* plays, *I* partner you." He looked around. "Join hands for Auld Lang Syne, folks. No music needed, I'd like everyone to join in. Away we go!"

The rafters rang. The dishes had been washed by the older women earlier. Roland was taking Nanette home. The twins were trying to postpone their bedtime still further, but were hustled upstairs by Barbara, bringing up the rear like an anxious sheepdog.

Joseph was still humming Scots tunes beneath his breath. Elspeth looked at him with love in her eyes, a look Mary noticed. As she glanced away she found Ninian had intercepted that look. He had a smile in his eyes. The two older folk went out, the smile lingered.

"It softens the heart, doesn't it, Mhairi, to watch those two."

She looked away swiftly down into the embers of the fire. "Yes, that bond is very lovely."

"You ought to be careful. It's catching. You might even change your hard-boiled notions yet."

She wouldn't look up. She said lightly, "I might at that. Oh, dear, I'm drowsy, I must go up to bed."

"Must you really?"

Was there a note of real regret in his voice? No, how could there be?

She said crisply, "Yes, I must. Roland will be back soon, and this might be the opportunity for you to have a long uninterrupted talk with him."

She began to walk away, but he reached the door with her.

"No, thanks all the same, but it's better to leave things as they are. Probing could be —" he stopped.

She finished it for him. "Probing could be painful, Ninian."

"Not necessarily. But perhaps dangerous. We have that time element in the letters to remember."

His hand came under her elbow, they began to mount the stairs. The lights were out in the children's rooms, deep breathing indicated sleep had come suddenly.

At her door, as Ninian bent towards her, Mary freed herself smartly. "No need, Ninian. They're fast asleep."

He repossessed himself of her arm, turned her round. "Mary, you're all prickles. Like a hedgehog. This might not have been pretence tonight. It might have been just my way ... a nice way, I hope ... of saying a very sincere thank-you for playing your part the way you did tonight and for giving Dad the party of his life."

He bent, brushed her lips lightly with his own, released her.

Mary felt quite unsteady as she went into her room, closed the door, leaned against it. Someone, probably Elspeth, had turned on the bedside lamp for her. So by its light her eyes met her mirrored eyes in the bureau glass opposite her. Eyes that looked away quickly from the knowledge that lay in them, eyes that wandered round the room in search of some distraction that would shake off this realisation that had been growing on her all night.

Suddenly she crossed to the bureau, leaned her elbows on it, looked searchingly at her image. And was honest. She whispered it to the reflected Mary.

"It came out of your subconscious, didn't it, you utter idiot! ... when you said that to his father ... in front of everyone. It *is* true. You *do* love him. As you never loved Francis. And he despises you for what he heard you say to Anne in a moment of utter rebellion against all that pity. Oh, Mary Rose, what have you done? Because even if he'd never heard that, you haven't got a chance. He loves Nanette. All this is for her."

She did not sleep very well.

* *

Joseph smiled at her indulgently next morning. "Too much party, it seems. Well, you must have a quiet day today. We all will."

They had had breakfast very late and Roland said he need not start out on his rounds till next day. But just as they were trying to make up their minds to clear the table, they heard a car clatter over the last lot of cattle-stops and come to a halt outside the side door.

Roland raised himself up to look out of the window. His

face lit. "It's Nanette. Fresh as a daisy, no doubt, and come to give a hand with the clearing-up."

Mary saw Barbara exchange a glance with her grandmother, then quickly assume a pleased expression as she realised Roland's glance was coming her way.

Nanette's greeting was gay. "Hul-*lo*, you old stay-in-beds. Still lingering over the breakfast table! I thought you wouldn't mind a hand this morning." She bent to give Roland a butterfly kiss, but Mary noticed her eyes went to Ninian as she did it. Mary felt swamped with a wave of indignation. That was turning the sword. For the first time Mary felt Ninian might have had a lucky escape.

Ninian said, "Well, for goodness' sake don't expect us to pitch into tidying up right now. We're relaxing. Here, have a cup of coffee and sit down for a few moments."

Nanette laughed and did as she was bid. "Might as well. It's hard to get out of the habit of obeying you, Nin."

Not tactful, and not just a slip either, Mary decided. Nanette meant to keep the former engagement in the forefront of everyone's thoughts. Why?

Nanette continued, "But we won't spend too long, will we? I mean, you've got the day off, haven't you, Rol? What about an old-time picnic this afternoon ... you and I and Mary and Ninian?"

Ninian had a drawl in his voice. "Sorry, Nanette. But Mhairi and I intend spending the whole afternoon up at the old house with some plans."

"Plans ... old house ... what do you mean? Are you pulling it down? And building on that site? Time it was down, it's just a ruin."

Mary felt her hackles rise.

There was rich satisfaction in Ninian's tone. "Not pulling it down, restoring it. Using it as the basis of our dream house."

"*Dream house*! That old relic! Why, it's crumbling to bits. The chimneys are half down."

"Chimneys are easily rebuilt. Dad and I are going to open up the old quarry and get some men in. The walls are as sturdy as ever."

Nanette looked at Mary. "Men are so impossibly impractical, aren't they? We women like modern comforts and styles. I'm sure you'd rather have a new house. Don't let Ninian stampede you into this."

Ninian would have made a first-rate actor. His voice was caressingly soft. "But it's because Mhairi wanted it that we're going to live there." His eyes came to hers, demanding she play it up.

He need not have worried. Mary had a flake of pink on each cheekbone, a spark in her eye. No one was going to decry that forlorn little house.

"As soon as I saw it I knew it was my dream house come true. It has a sense of history, of growing out of the very ground. Ninian, you will be able to attach the sod cottage in some way, won't you ? I couldn't bear to think of that completely disintegrating. It ought to be preserved for posterity. For our children's children."

Nanette said slowly, "It's a very small house, though."

Jonathan lent a hand. "Yep, but they're adding to it. They'll have to. They said yesterday they want a really big family. It's about time we had some cousins. Haven't any on Dad's side either. Gosh, I've just thought, Mary, you'd better not fix the date too early. Mum'd be as mad as a meat-axe if she missed the wedding."

Ninian said, "I'm not going to postpone my wedding for anyone, Jonno. Isabella and Gil will have to fly back instead of coming by sea if they want to get here on time."

Mary experienced a desire to laugh madly. What a family ! Roland suddenly looked more carefree. He's been worried, she thought. Is he not sure of Nanette ?

Old Joseph said, "Well, I'm not hurrying for anyone this morning. I'll have some more coffee, Elspeth, please. And Barbie, slip another slice of bread in the toaster. Anybody else like a piece ?"

Mary's eyes twinkled as they met his. "Yes, I would. Thanks, Barbie."

"I," said Jonathan, "would like some of that Napoleon cake left over from last night."

"How revolting," said Ninian. "You have the most barbarous ideas about breakfast, nevvy. And incidentally, you young ones, if you have any idea at all of saddling us with your company this afternoon, and foisting your outlandish ideas about that house on Mary and me, you can say goodbye to them right now. Mary and I are going to please ourselves. We had enough of you yesterday. We promise to do nothing to disturb your owl, but that's all."

That was quite clever, thought Mary. It meant they wouldn't have to go on making pseudo plans in front of anybody, and stymied any attempts on Nanette's part to accompany them.

Nanette seemed to have a persistence at variance with her fragile appearance. She leaned forward to Roland, put her hand on his knee, looked winning, confident.

"Rol, you needn't really work tomorrow, need you? If they are going to be so busy today, perhaps we could go on a picnic tomorrow?"

Joseph looked more rueful. "Sorry, Nanette. Ninian and Ros Mhairi won't be here. Ninian and I were putting our heads together yesterday to prepare a surprise for Mary. If they get married in winter they won't be able to go by road to Milford Sound for their honeymoon. In fact sometimes it's not open till late November. Going by air isn't the same. The road will be closed by May. So they're leaving for Fiordland tomorrow. I managed to get their bookings yesterday.

"We were going to tell Mhairi last night, but the party sent it clean out of my mind. They're going to do the lakes too, Te Anau, Wanaka, Wakatipu. No need to do Tekapo, and of course Pukaki is at our door." His eyes swept to the window and down to the lake lying bluely below the road. "They'll be better to go north in winter. Where are you thinking of, lad? Want to show Mary the thermal regions? Or Bay of Islands, Lake Taupo, or where?"

Ninian's eyes danced. "Further afield still, perhaps, Dad. Fiji, or Samoa. Or I've always had a yen for seeing the Cook Islands group, Raratonga and so on. They're all in easy flying distance from New Zealand. Or there's New Caledonia, our nearest French Colony. Bit of a novelty to hear French spoken – Oh, I was forgetting, it wouldn't be so much of a novelty to you, Mary, would it, coming from Canada. Where would you like to go?"

Her eyes were demure. "Wherever you want to, Ringan. I don't think places matter much on a honeymoon. Josephine, pass me some of that bramble jam, will you? It's delicious."

Inwardly she didn't know whether or not to be glad she would have a week or more travelling alone with Ninian. It would be so easy to reveal one's feelings. Here any betrayal would pass unnoticed, Ninian would think it part of the game.

In any case, she thought she would try to find out a little about that earlier engagement from Elspeth. If she could shake off the family – and Nanette. It looked as if she would stay all day.

\*

They were busy straightening up the house all the forenoon, Ninian insisted they go up to the old house after lunch.

Mary said to him when they were alone, "Must we?"

He grinned. "Good excuse to get away from the crowd."

She knew what he meant. To get away from the sight of Nanette and Roland together. From the sight of his ring on her finger. Diamonds. And Ninian didn't care for them.

Mary said, "Shall we take a couple of books up?"

"What for? We've got the plans to make out."

"Don't be ridiculous. That was just adding local colour to the scheme. We don't need to."

"We do. It will add a bit more."

When they got there Ninian said, "Now, let's pretend this is real. I'm all for being thorough. It will spur Roland on if he thinks our plans are cut and dried."

Mary spoke slowly. "Why should he need spurring on? Having served seven years for his Rachel, what's the point in waiting?"

Ninian's brown eyes met her blue ones. "Don't you think it would be natural if Roland had doubts! He may just wonder if – during those years he was married to Alicia – Nanette did grow genuinely fond of me. It was the very devil her people acted the way they did. Nanette and Roland should have been married years ago. It played havoc with three lives."

*Three.* Nanette's, Roland's . . . Ninian's!

He added, "Rol may think she got over him, turned to me, finding in me something of the younger Roland, then when I was missing, presumed killed, found consolation with him. He wants to be sure. I don't blame him. So we must be con-

III

vincing, Mary, and appear to plan our wedding. I hope we can make it seem so definite they'll suddenly hive off and get married themselves. They won't want a big wedding, surely. It would remind Rol too much of his first wedding. Alicia was a lovely bride . . . so frail. And so gallant."

Mary wasn't sure. She had an idea Nanette liked to be the centre of the stage. That tied up with the family's impression that she had enjoyed – somewhat – being thwarted by her parents, had enjoyed being misunderstood, most of all having Ninian come to her rescue. There were people like that. They liked having someone to blame for their own lack of decision. Those were the people who preferred being engaged to being married, someone to dance attendance but to make no demands.

But she could be wrong, of course. She didn't know Nanette well enough to pass judgment.

"Be a sport, Mary, enter into this with me. I love sketching buildings. If I hadn't been a farmer I'd have been a draughtsman."

"All right, but –"

"But what? Girl, you don't have to be afraid to speak your mind to me. I'm too much in your debt to cry you down."

"Very well. But it's just that it puts me in a false position. I love this house, I can't help loving it. Yet I'm afraid to enter into things wholeheartedly in case you think –"

He looked puzzled, then his brow cleared. "But we mentioned this before. I'm not likely to think you're falling for me. I'm not your type. You told me."

She shook her head. "No, not that. Not the emotions. Only seeing you overheard me expressing somewhat – well – what I thought were common-sense ideas about marriage, about choosing a husband – I mean if I appear too enthusiastic about the setting here you may begin to think I am – after all – considering you as extremely eligible, and it would be horribly embarrassing."

He started to laugh. "Oh, you idiot! Though you're quite a nice idiot, apart from your odd ideas about getting a husband. And in any case, what nonsense! We know far too much about each other to entertain ideas of that sort. This is merely a business arrangement. Which reminds me, I'm determined to hand you a monthly cheque. If we put it on a business footing you'll feel more comfortable."

This odd statement did nothing to make her feel that way. But before she could protest he said crisply, "Well, that's settled. Now, back to play-acting. How about this staircase, Mary? It's so filthy and scratched it ought to be stripped right down to the bare wood. How would you like it treated after that? Just oiled and polished? I know dark staining looks rich, but it gets frightfully dusty, and our nor'westers just swirl grit in. Anyway, just oiling would lighten it up."

Mary could almost hear the cogs connecting as they slipped back into their game of pretence again. They came back to the house for dinner with a most impressive array of sketches and notes. Not only that, but on the way down the hill Mary had come to a decision. She would tell Ninian, when they were away on their trip, all about Francis. About her own deep hurt, how she had hated the pity, how she had reacted, exactly why she had said what she did to Anne. It was fairer to him and – she might never have his love, but she owed it to herself to have his respect.

\*

Joseph took them into the big farm office after dinner. "Nanette's here to help Barbie wash up, and I'd like to go through these with you before you set off tomorrow. How soon will you want to leave?"

"Oh, just after lunch. We'll stay in Dunedin the first night. The rest of the bookings are fixed. Good idea going at this time of year, getting in before Easter. Good job Easter is late. Plenty of room at all hotels. Come on, Mary."

Mary backed Ninian up ably, then said, "I've things to pack, some to wash. I don't usually travel at such a short notice. Mind if I slip upstairs to do it?"

No, they didn't mind, they were deep in some constructional discussion now. What a waste of mental energy!

Mary looked into the living-room. "Elspeth, be a pet and come up and help me pack. You know this place we're going to, you can tell me what kind of stuff to take."

Elspeth rose with alacrity. In the bedroom Mary sat down on the padded patchwork quilt little Rosemary had so loved. Her Anne-of-Green-Gables quilt, she had called it.

"Sit down, Elspeth, I really want to ask you a few things," Mary invited.

Ninian's mother's eyes were shrewd. "About Nanette? Lassie, don't let her worry you. Nanette aye wanted to have her cake and eat it. She was very spoiled. I feel she clung somewhat to the luxuries of her own home. We were not so well off then, and she'd have had less if we had married Roland against her parents' wishes. They might have cut her out of their wills. If she'd been more independent and had a bit more spunk she'd have defied them. Not that I hold with that sort of thing as a rule, but there was nothing against Roland but a gap of years."

Mary said slowly, "I wanted to ask you how Ninian became engaged to her in the first place. I could ask him, but men don't like discussing affairs of the heart."

"Quite right, and we love it." She looked closely at Mary. "You won't have any doubts of Ninian's love for you, of course. I mean that no one seeing you together could have any."

Mary's hands tightened on her lap.

Elspeth continued: "You're so different. You're more like Joseph and me. Our kind. Not only that, but in the way you treat each other. Ninian and Nanette were too polite with each other. They struck no sparks. They were so careful not to fight. They knew it wouldn't stand the strain. You and Ninian aren't afraid to cross swords with each other. You tease and you disagree, you're friends *and* lovers – the ideal ingredients for a happy marriage."

Mary swallowed. Elspeth took it for emotion. She patted Mary's hand. "If you knew how happy it's made me to see you like that. I thought once that Ninian, my youngest, was to miss the best in life. Nanette had made a mess of Roland's life, and I didn't want history to repeat itself. I suffered with Roland, mothers do, though a great good came out of it. He gave Alicia some happy years and a home when she needed it most. We loved Alicia."

She looked up at Mary. "My boys are compassionate to a fault. They mistake pity for love. Ninian has made a habit of it. When he was only twenty there was a girl up here who was madly in love with someone who made a great fuss of her, then dropped her. Ninian had gone to school with her.

He just has to try to patch things up. He began to blatantly pay court to this girl. They cooked it up between them to stimulate this other chap."

Elspeth started to laugh. "But it wasn't funny at the time. It didn't deceive me for a moment. I knew he wasn't in love with her. Mothers always know. I asked him what the dickens he was up to, and he told me. I warned him it was playing with fire. This chap got mad, lay in wait for Ninian, challenged him to a fight. They both took a bit of punishment, but Ninian wanted to present this chap as a hero to the girl, and let him win. Ninian has a terrific reach – a great advantage – but did it very cleverly. It's a sort of knight-errant streak. He wouldn't let the girl breathe a word of the fact that it was a plan, and so he was regarded as the rejected and wounded suitor. It made me mad. You never think all these things will happen when you go through childbirth and hold your baby in your arms – how you'll suffer with them, all the way. And so it was the same with Nanette. Ninian came along and picked up the pieces. Just that. *Pity*. Not love."

Mary said slowly, "Thank you, Elspeth. It was awfully sweet of you to tell me. I just had to know."

Elspeth looked searchingly at her. "That satisfies you, dear?"

"It satisfies me. Now I'll get on with this packing. I wish in some ways we were not going away. I feel it's a bit much for you with the three children, and though Barbie is wonderful, she has to spend a long time on her correspondence lessons with the High School. I feel you could do with me at home."

Home. Yes, it was just that ... because home was where Ninian was.

When Elspeth had gone Mary sat on. So she wouldn't, as she had planned, tell Ninian of how she had come to Malaya. Of what she had found. Of how she had lost Francis. Of the heartbreak.

Pity was what had destroyed her most. She didn't want Ninian picking up any more pieces. She would rather have his scorn than his pity. She wanted no second-bests, so her hands were tied. Ninian would never fall in love with her because he thought that as far as marriage was concerned

she was cold, unnatural, calculating. If she told him why, he
would be stirred with compassion and it would compel him
to offer compensation ... especially as it would offer a solution.

*Pity. Not love.*

She must try to find some satisfaction in knowing she
served Ninian in this pretence. She hoped suddenly, violently,
that it would soon be over, that Nanette would marry Roland
and she and Ninian part. It would be tricky with the family so
set on it. Already Elspeth's words were tugging at her heart-
strings.

"You suffer with your children ... all the way."

They would have to do it as gently as possible. Perhaps
she would just slip away and Ninian could put up some tale
about their deciding they were not suited after all. And since
he really would not care, they would see he was not fretting,
and so it wouldn't hurt them so much.

But she wouldn't stay in New Zealand. It would be too
poignant. Perhaps she would go to Australia. You could lose
yourself there, cut yourself off altogether from these Macandrews. Forget all this.

Forget? ... The incredible blue of Lake Pukaki, ringed by
faraway mountains, Aorangi hiding its head in the clouds,
relenting, and emerging in sunset splendour; Aorangi in the
pearl and rose and gold of sunrise, its snows sparkling like a
million diamonds; Mount Hebron keeping watch and ward
over the big sheep-station, and there, beside the old orchard,
a little forlorn house with empty windows staring at the
waters of the lake. A little house that waited for small footsteps creeping up its worn stair-treads, whose garden, weedy
and overgrown, still sent out banners of hope in blooms that
sprang from seed that had first been sown more than a hundred years ago.

\*

Ninian's car had arrived, in new and shining splendour, a
week ago. They set off through the centre of the island, going
through the great earth-dam hydro works at Benmore and
down to Oamaru to join the main highway to Dunedin.

When they were well away from Mount Hebron Mary
heaved a sigh.

"What's that huge sigh for?" enquired Ninian.

"Relief. What a wonderful feeling to be away from acting a part!"

"You found it as distasteful as that? I mean the stray kisses, endearments and so on?"

Distasteful? Mary swallowed. If only he knew!

"Well, the whole thing. The deceit too. I so hate all this prevarication, trying to keep all of them from planning our wedding. One thing, this will slow things up ... our being away from home."

His eyes dropped to her lap. "You've got some letters to post. We'll wait till we get to Oamaru. It's more direct. Malaya? Who is it to?" His hand twitched the envelope round for all the world as if he had the right to know. "Oh, to Nurse Meredith. The other Canadian. Are you telling her of our engagement?"

Her tone was sharp. "I certainly am not. I wouldn't dream of telling Anne."

"Aha! What are you afraid of? Afraid of Anne thinking that after all you found you had a heart? Or of thinking you had found I possessed all the material advantages?"

"Neither of those things. You haven't got all the answers, Lieutenant! There's nothing so quick as the grapevine news of a nurses' home. It would be all over Malaya in no time. I don't want the Colonel to know."

She saw Ninian's hands tighten on the wheel, and wondered why; it was a perfectly straight road between yellowed tussocky hills.

"Oh, the Colonel!" he said.

Mary realised Ninian didn't like his Colonel.

She did not amplify her statement. After all, Ninian knew the Colonel was the only one – bar the doctor – who knew about his predicament, that his fiancée had become engaged to his brother. He would guess this was a put-up job, and the fewer who knew about it the better.

Ninian settled down in the driving seat with the tiniest of sighs. "You are the strangest mixture, Mary Rose. I don't understand you."

"You don't have to. I'm here for a purpose. When it's accomplished I'll be gone, and this will be no more than a rather madcap incident in my life. And when you are old

117

and grey you'll say to your grandchildren, 'What a pity the folk of today aren't stable and steady as they were in my young days!' And you will squash the memory of this piece of foolishness down.'"

"So you think I'm going to have grandchildren? At the present moment it doesn't look like it.'".

Mary curled her lip. "I believe, with Shakespeare, that 'Men die from time to time and worms have eaten them, but not for love.' You'll marry Ninian."

He shot her a glance. "Easy to see you've never been in love, Sister Starch! I could be a one-woman man. They do exist."

"Do they? What river is this? Let's forget the whole wretched business. Act as if we were just good friends going off on an enjoyable holiday together, and start playing our parts again as we roll over the cattle-stops at Mount Hebron on our return."

"Very well, Mary. Except that, if we should meet up with acquaintances at any of the hotels, I shall rely on you to back me up."

"Yes. But I hope it won't be necessary."

CHAPTER 7

How foolish then it was to find herself, all through their sightseeing, nostalgic for Mount Hebron. For the necessity of acting as a genuinely loving engaged couple, if she were to be honest with herself!

Ninian's caresses meant absolutely nothing, so why should she yearn for them? He was most punctilious for her welfare, paid her attentions when other people were present, for appearances' sake.

Mary reflected that if the Fiordland scenery could not induce any tender scenes, then nothing would. Mountains rose sheerly from fathomless fiords gouged out by gigantic glaciers in the Ice Age, hanging valleys spilled misty waterfalls from the laps down to cerulean waters below, the native bush was spell-binding, holding mystery and enchantment in its grotto-like green dimness. They walked among great cathedral aisles of trees reaching great heights towards sunlight, watched the moonlight fling still more beauty over hill and shore, yet still Ninian kept his distance. She might have been any newcomer to Maoriland, being shown its wonders.

Later, when she had left New Zealand, she might count every day over like pearls on a string ... the range of mountains they called the Remarkables, as jagged as cardboard cutouts over the incredible blue of snow-fed Lake Wakatipu, the dog-leg lake; Queenstown nestling in its larches and pines; the breathtaking trip on the one-way road around the Skippers Canyon where so many goldminers had lost their lives in floods and blizzards less than a century ago, the gentle dreaming peace of Lake Wanaka.

They came to Lake Hawea, booked in at the hotel overlooking the lake, put their luggage in their rooms, strolled out to look at the lake below.

Some artist had painted murals on the fence which took the same curve as the outer edge of the lake, in replica, with all the peaks named. Mary began comparing painted peaks with those across the lake, tipped with mother-of-pearl, saffron, coral, in this hour of the sunset.

The lake itself, surrounded by hills much more bare than the others, had a curious, endearing quality of its own, unornamented, shimmering. Peace descended upon Mary. Two nights here and they would go home.

They heard footsteps behind them, turned. The proprietor with a sheaf of letters in his hand. "Sorry, I should have given you these before."

Ninian took them, began sorting out which were his. It was rather endearing to find all the family had written to Mary, including the twins. Ninian paused, frowned.

"An official one for you. From our Military Headquarters, Singapore."

Mary took it, aware of quickened heartbeats. The only one who would write her would be the Colonel. And she didn't want to answer any questions about Ninian. She tore it open.

"Well, who's it from?"

She looked up, rebuke in her eyes. "The Colonel."

"Why write to you? Tell me."

She kept her tone level. "I don't have to, you know, Lieutenant."

"Don't give me any of that Lieutenant stuff. Our lives are too closely intermingled for any left-over formality."

"Perhaps, but there's still the question of good manners."

He snorted. "You said you didn't want the Colonel to know we were engaged. What would he write to you about if not that? And how would he know to write home? It sounds as if you *have* been in correspondence."

"If I had, it would have been none of your business. But I haven't. It seems he called in and got my address from Anne. He – he did ask me for it that night we had dinner together. It was nothing to do with you because he didn't even know then we would be travelling together. I didn't want to say Mount Hebron because he'd have put two and two together. So I just said I'd send him an address when I got fixed up in a billet. That was all there was to it, except that he gave me his sister's address in Wellington."

"What on earth for?"

Mary looked at him in surprise. "Merely because she happens to be something to do with the Nursing Division and he thought she'd be pleased to help me."

"Well, did you finally send our address? He's written to it."

"Are you not taking in what I say? I said he had got it from Anne."

"All right. But is there a letter from you, on your way to him, giving it?"

"No. I hope you believe that. I hope to goodness you don't think just because I'm acting a lie at the moment . . . to serve your purposes . . . that I'm in the habit of it. What are you getting at?"

"I'm just wondering if you're trying to shake the old boy off or not."

Mary was completely puzzled. "No, of course not. I think the Colonel's a pet. I'm just leaving it meanwhile. I didn't want him to know anything about our engagement at all, so I thought I wouldn't send my address till this is all over and forgotten – your brother and Nanette safely married, and myself away from South Canterbury. But he asked Anne."

Ninian seemed no more pleased than he had been before.

"Well, the situation won't resolve itself as quickly as that, do you hear? So what does he want, anyway?"

Mary's tone was quiet but firm. "I told you before it was nothing to do with you."

"It is. You've just admitted that, when you said you wanted him to know nothing of our engagement. Has he heard in some roundabout way? What does he say about it?"

"Ninian Macandrew! He does mention you at the last – but it's just a kindly inquiry any right-minded Colonel would make after one of his men. It – it – well, it happens the Colonel has a problem he – he consulted me about that night we went to dinner. It's – about his daughter, and naturally he's worried. She – she's rather disturbed over something."

"I shouldn't wonder. She's as old as you are."

Mary blinked. She couldn't sort that one out. Perhaps it didn't matter. She didn't want to prolong the argument, one thing would just lead to another, and Ninian looked angry enough to snatch the letter from her, and she had made up her mind not to mention Francis and Thea.

So she said hurriedly, clutching the letter firmly in case of onslaught, "Look, all he says about you is in the last sentence, 'Glad you went all the way with young Macandrew. I was worried about him, as you know. Evidently since you have stayed on, his people have appreciated your gesture. Let me know your next address, would you, I don't want to lose touch.' That's all, Ninian."

"All! And what does he mean by 'young Macandrew?' I'm twenty-nine. Five years older than you."

Mary giggled, she couldn't help it. "At the moment, Ninian, you sound just like a sulky four-year-old, and I can't think why."

She looked up. His face was in shadow, because he had his back to the sunset. The glorious panoply of light and cloud and lake was behind him. But his anger seemed gone. She slipped the letter into her windbreaker pocket. He took her hands.

"Mary, *you* have helped *me*. If you need help at any time with the Colonel, or the Colonel's daughter, will you come to me?"

"Thank you, Ninian, but I don't suppose I will. I'm quite capable of managing my own affairs."

She thought his face looked sad for once, all planes and angles suddenly. "I thought I could, once, too. But sometimes we have needs we don't recognize, Mhairi."

The sun went down behind the mountains.

•

Two days later they came home to Hebron at sunset-time. As they swept in at the big white gates they were momentarily blinded by a flash from somewhere.

"What on earth?" Ninian put up a hand to shield his eyes. He drew to a standstill. Mary was gazing uphill to the left of the homestead plantation.

She said slowly, "That was from the forlorn house, Ninian. The sunset catching the windows. But there weren't any windows."

They turned and gazed at each other. "I think we'll go up," he said, "before going in. They don't know what time to expect us. The old cart-track is all right this dry weather."

It wound up the hill out of sight of the homestead. They got out, took the track through the old orchard because it was easier going. They came through the gap in the hedge, stopped and marvelled. Then looked at each other in consternation.

The chimneys were rebuilt, the windows glazed. In some were new frames. The dormers had latticed panes. In fun Mary had said she would prefer them. And Elspeth had been in the garden. The tangle of shrubbery had been ruthlessly pruned, the old geraniums cut back. The asters were over and the straggly plants had been uprooted, they were lying in a heap ready for burning. Michaelmas daisies were the blue haunts of bees, the faithful daisies still bloomed.

Where the asters had been was rich, newly-formed earth, and tiny rows of pegs were set there. They moved up, bent, read:

"Crocus, narcissi, daffodils, glory-of-the-snow, ranunculus."

Elspeth's gift to them, spring in abundance, a spring that was supposed to be the first of many for them, together, a spring Mary might not ever see. By the end of winter she could be gone.

She turned quickly away from Ninian. This was ridiculous. She must gain more control of her emotions. She must *not* cry. But the tears spilled over. Ninian turned her to him, folded her against him.

"Those over-active tear-ducts again," he said, laughing, and put a handkerchief into her hand.

She shook with sobs. "You – you ought not to sympathise, Ninian. It's the wrong thing with me. I go on crying."

She could sense the smile in his voice. "All right, I'll beat you instead. Come on, snap out of it. No, don't, on second thoughts. I rather like you this way, Mary Rose. Better than hard-boiled. My family has melted the ice, hasn't it? How in the world did Dad get the workmen in as soon as this? He sure has a way with him. Let's see what else they've done inside."

Mary finished mopping up. She looked down. "Oh, I'm so glad they haven't replaced the front step. I love it curved like that with all the feet that came before our feet."

He stopped, said curiously, "You've a real feeling for old things, haven't you? That's what makes it so odd."

"Makes what so odd?"

"I'd have thought it would have had with it a sense of old values too, instead of a hard modern outlook."

She didn't answer, but stepped inside the sitting-room. They had done it exactly as the two of them had drawn the mock plans. The east wall was almost all windows now, with a seat running underneath. The pointing in the fireplace was renewed between the stones, and new flooring was down.

Ninian, investigating, gave a whistle. "I believe he's had the floor wired for heating. Mod cons with a vengeance!"

"Oh, Ninian, it's cost a fortune! Whatever shall we do?"

"Well, there's one solution. If it horrifies your Scots soul so much, you could marry me and save wasting it."

Mary turned to the window and hoped there was no shake in her voice. "That, of course, is quite ridiculous."

"Yes. People don't get married to make a house happy, do they?"

"Yes. Didn't you call it the forlorn house just now?"

"It slipped out. But this time it was the amount of money that Joseph had spent that horrifies me. I didn't dream the whole thing would snowball like this, did you?"

"No. But I don't see what we can do."

"You could get Roland to hurry up Nanette. Then we could break things off."

"I've said before it isn't Roland who needs hurrying. Look, let's stop worrying. I won't let Dad go on with the extensions. I'll make him stop here for the moment. What's he put over here?"

There was a huge old mahogany table in the window that faced west, and piled upon it were the old diaries and records Mary had found in the attic, also boxes of old photographs, and two old-fashioned oval pictures face down. Ninian turned them over.

"Dad's grandparents. The pioneers, old Ninian and Isabella."

Suddenly he turned them face downwards again, said, "Come on, let's get out of here. It's much too sentimental. I'll be catching that tear-duct complaint if we don't."

Mary took out her compact in the car, began running repairs. "It doesn't matter, Mary, I'll just say you were so overcome you burst into tears. They'll love it. We'll have to look overjoyed. Can you manage it, lass?"

"For their sakes, I can do even that."

*

The last of the autumn days rioted by in a splendid burst of colour and sunshine. Then one morning, after a night of high winds and biting cold, they woke to find it winter. The trees were bare, Mount Cook and Mount Tasman were so white you could hardly bear to look at them, even the foothills were well sprinkled.

On the station the men put on a spurt and took full advantage of the short daylight hours to get done all they could before even more bitter storms would drive them in.

Mary often went up to the old house on the hill, forlorn no longer.

"What are you thinking of calling it?" asked Joseph one evening.

Mary smiled. "How about Airdbreck House? Isn't that a name belonging to the Macandrew clan?"

"Look at Granddad," said Jonathan. "Isn't he pleased?"

"Who wadna be? Ninian getting a girl who kens all the things that really matter and has a nice sense of fitness."

"I didn't always know it, Joseph. I looked it up after studying the old diaries."

She had got thoroughly fascinated with the task now, though it was a formidable one, sifting through a mass of unimportant farm details for the living, breathing history of the family.

What a blessing Isabella Macandrew had kept a diary. They were all there, from the time she and her husband, newly-weds, had embarked on the sailing ship that had taken four months to reach the Land of the Long White Cloud. Her diaries weren't full of boring trivialities, but of emotions, even though her most poignant moments were terse.

At times the other members of the family had jotted things down. Recipes were mixed up with calving dates. It was noticeable that the recipes in the round childish hand were mostly for toffee and fudge. Later, the same hand had written in instructions for making up mutton fat and rosewater to soften the hands. "That would be my Aunt Lavinia," chuckled Joseph. "She would have to put cotton gloves on to keep the grease off the sheets. She was a gay one, that."

"And who was the one who did the sketches? They're so well done."

"My Aunt Rosemary. Our wee Rosemary inherited her talent for it." He sighed. "Let me see."

The entry for that day said, "Killed the white pig today," and there, neatly executed, was a sketch of the dear departed.

There were some very good heads of horses. Mary and Joseph looked out of the window and fancied them flying past over these very paddocks.

They chuckled together over an item that said 'a sure cure for smallpox' ... as much cream of tartar as would go on a threepence to be taken in water every night for three days!

"But listen to this ... rub beaten egg-yolk into the hair after shampooing with pure castile soap. Good heavens, and one of my birthday presents this year was called: 'Hair Duet ... an egg shampoo and creme hair rinse.' and I thought I was on to something modern!"

She turned a page, began to chuckle. "Oh, Joseph, you had a touch of sciatica last week. Listen: 'Soak flannels in vinegar and iron with a flat-iron till vaporised and apply to the unfortunate patient on the spot.' Surely they didn't iron it

125

*on* the patient. Oh, no, hardly. Um-um – and you counteract a spasm of whooping-cough by tickling the soles of the feet with a feather, and – oh, listen, Ninian, if you get struck by lightning I'm to dash cold water over you immediately.

"Now we're back to mundane things ... the mare's time was up on October 17th 1891, Yankey calved on May 16th that year ... well, I wonder why they recorded that in October. We shall never know. And a setting of duck eggs went under the speckled hen on Tuesday night. And here's a lovely recipe, 'How to pickle hams the Suffolk way.' Elspeth, it sounds lovely, let's try it."

The whole family enjoyed the diaries, but sometimes Mary went up to the old house to get on uninterrupted. She could spread the junk out there on the big old table and not have to clear it away. Ninian sawed her a huge pile of wood, had a load of coal taken up.

He came in to find her poring over Isabella's diary. He looked over her shoulder. "Why all the concentration? What's so fascinating about that? One little entry on a whole page!"

Mary looked up reproachfully. "Have you no imagination at all? Can't you see what that means? That one sentence, nothing else mattered that day. See what it says: 'Ninian went away today.' He was going down to Timaru, a terrific journey, and a terribly long time alone for her – no one to ride for the doctor if needed. It meant he would be crossing rivers that knew flash floods, that were pitted with quicksands, mountain passes where blizzards could swirl. Don't you see the emptiness in that sentence – the desolation? 'Ninian went away today.' Look at the records following it. Flat, just a record of duties done. See how she filled up the days. 'Made candles. Rubbed glycerine into my hands.' (She wanted to make herself beautiful for his return, Ninian). 'Picked rosehips for jelly. Patched Ninian's trousers. Made pickles. Polished the harness.' Then: 'Killed the goose today.' (Can't you see it, Ninian, the fatted calf?) Suddenly she writes, 'Never saw such a beautiful sunset as over Aorangi tonight. Ninian came home at noon.' Oh, I do love Isabella!"

He was laughing. "You're bringing her alive for the whole family. Mhairi. This has given Dad the thrill of his life. Is it going to take long?"

"I've most of the stuff assembled. Why? I can always take it away with me if I leave before it's done and send it back typed."

He ignored the last bit. "It's just that Dad *is* over eighty. And he doesn't spare himself. I'd like to think he saw it bound."

Mary looked distressed. "I can't think of him as that, he's so vigorous, so fascinating. And every inch a Hielan' man, even if he is third generation Colonial. I've seen it in Canada, of course. Little communities in the backwoods still retaining their Scots accent. Though now, with modern travel, that is dying out."

Ninian sat down on the opposite side of the table.

"Do you ever realise that when I brought you home, Mhairi, it was as if this place was made for you ... as far as my parents are concerned? Have you ever thought it might work out if we went the whole hog, got married?"

Mary was glad she was sitting. Her knees were shaking. She looked across at him, schooling herself to sound academic about it.

"Why should you want to marry me? To suit your parents? Most men have different reasons."

"I daresay. But not all of them for love."

"Then what is *your* reason? Is the situation just getting too complicated for you?"

He was watching her closely. "It could be that I feel Roland and Nanette are taking too long to make up their minds."

Nanette! Always Nanette.

She said drily, "I don't fancy making a sacrifice of myself merely for Nanette's sake. I don't even like her."

"But you like Roland?"

"Yes. But if he had half your go he would make Nanette marry him."

"I don't know. It looks as if *I* can't make *you* marry *me*."

"Your reasons, I would point out, are rather different. And I wouldn't consider marriage with you."

"Why? I thought you felt marriages should be entered into sensibly ... kindred tastes, bank balances and so on. My bank balance is quite healthy, my prospects good. And you wouldn't deny that you like this home of mine."

"You're quite absurd. I may have been rather scathing

127

about love, but liking at least is necessary."

"And you think you don't like me? I disagree. I think you like me very well but won't admit it." Mary's knees were like jelly now. Her tormentor's voice went on. "We like all the same things. Houses, horses, dogs, the out-of-doors, church, sheep, snow sports, even naughty children, climbing, sliding down banisters. Our religion is the same. What more could we want? And it would put an end to an intolerable situation. My people will suffer if you go. I repeat, what more could we want . . . *by your standards*?"

Mary stood up, moved the books agitatedly. "Will you stop! Will you stop making a mockery of everything I believe in! Maybe I've changed, but this I do know . . . I'd not marry without love after all. Now, get out, Ninian Macandrew. I wish I'd never consented to your hare-brained schemes. I wish I'd never set eyes on any of you. I get pushed around till I no longer have a mind of my own. I hate you, do you hear? I hate and despise and loathe and detest you!"

"If there are any epithets you can't think of," said Ninian politely, "we have a very good book of synonyms down at the house."

He came round the table. She retreated. He lunged forward, caught her, tugged her to him.

"Isn't this fun? I'm like my father. I enjoy a good slanging match. Getting all that out of your system makes room for nicer things to move in. New Zealand really is making something out of you, honestly. It's melting that Canadian ice. My block of marble is turning into a spitfire."

Mary put her hands against his chest, tried to push him away. She might just as well have been trying to move Aorangi. He kissed her very thoroughly.

When finally he let her go Mary dropped limply into her chair, put her head in her hands. Then she lifted it, said quietly, "Will you go away? Please, Ninian?"

He went as far as the door, looked out towards the lake, came back. "No, don't jump up. I'll leave you alone. But I thought I should tell you Dad is on his way up. And I don't know just how you'll react at the moment."

Mary said bitterly, "You know full well how I'll react. I love your father and you know it. You've hedged me about with obligations and I feel in a cleft stick. I warn you, Ninian, you'd better get Nanette and Roland married pretty quickly or I may suddenly run away."

Ninian sat down beside her. "Let him find us working together on the records," he said quickly.

Joseph's shadow darkened the doorway, crossed the floor, blotted out the light as he bent over the books.

"My certes, lassie, but you are getting on. But Elspeth is getting worried. She thinks I'm expecting too much of you, that you're spending time on this that you ought to be spending on getting your trousseau ready. Roland is here for tea. He's going to be in the area for a few days."

They went down to the house.

Roland said, after the meal, "Dad tells me you're getting on well with the history, Mary. I dug out some stuff myself, out of my firm's records. It's quite interesting, all about the hard times during the depression of the eighteen-eighties. I scribbled a lot down. Hope you can make out my writing, that's all."

Mary said, "As a matter of fact, I'm going up again tonight. I got right into the spirit of things today – or I did till Ninian came up and disturbed me. I'd like to get on with it. The fire would only need stirring up and restoking. I left the guard in front."

"I'll come up with you," offered Ninian. "I promise to not disturb you this time. I'll bring a book."

"You can't help yourself. Your intentions are good, but you slip."

Joseph chuckled. "Well, I don't blame the lad. I mind my own courting days. I don't know how I'd have tholed it if Elspeth had expected me to sit in a corner while she wrote. Dinna worry about it, lassie. If you just get the material together before your wedding, it'll do. You'll have all the long nights the next winter to type it."

Mary gave Joseph a saucy look. "You mean I won't find Ninian so distracting after marriage?"

"I mean nothing of the kind. You're a bad lassie, reading I don't know what into the innocent remarks of an old man."

She turned to Ninian. "But I would like to get on by myself, a night or two flat out on it at this stage would make all the difference."

He set his jaw. "I'm not having you up there by yourself.

129

It can be eerie at night. And seeing a light you might get a swagger in wanting a meal. We still do get the odd ones."

Roland said, grinning, "How about if I go up with Mary? After all, she won't find me distracting ... worse luck! I could explain these notes of mine and then just do my books at the other side of the table. I'd much rather than down here with everyone yapping flat out."

Surprisingly Ninian gave in. But out in the scullery, lifting the Inverness cloak off the hook, he said, "Watch your words. Don't let Roland guess."

"I won't. Don't worry. I'm much more tactful and cool-headed than you." Suddenly her dimple and twinkle teamed up.

"Now what?" asked Ninian apprehensively.

"I've thought of a solution." She giggled. "Roland said I wouldn't find him distracting ... worse luck! Maybe I should ... then you could marry Nanette and everyone would be happy. Roland's so easy-going."

What Ninian said was unprintable. He said imploringly, "I don't like the mood you're in. Mary, please be –"

"I will. Circumspect and demure."

＊

By now the lights were connected in the old house and they pushed the table under the centre light.

"My word, this heated floor is wonderful," said Roland. "I envy you two living here."

"This was exactly what I wanted," Mary told Roland gratefully. "I want it to be an all-round history with interest for men as well as women, and I tend to get too much diary into it."

They finished the copying and sorting, then Roland went on with his books. "Is it all right if I stay this side? The light is better."

"Yes, and we're nearer the fire."

They worked on an hour. Suddenly Mary yawned. Roland put down his pen. "Enough for me too. Mary, I've been glad of this time alone with you, but I didn't want to frustrate you in what you wanted to accomplish. I want to ask you a few things."

She hoped she would know the answers. Also the evasions.

"Yes, Roland. Go ahead."

His rather tired eyes, blue like his father's, looked into hers. "When do you think you'll get married?"

This was delicate ground. She must walk warily.

"Well, it depends on one or two things, Roland. I would like Mother and Father here, of course, and they wouldn't be able to get away in their busy time, so it will probably be late spring or early summer. And I think Ninian would like Isabella and Gil here. Why?"

"Because Nanette has some absurd feeling that she doesn't want to get married first."

It was all Mary could do not to give herself away by a tell-tale gasp. Had Nanette any suspicion that all was not as it appeared on the surface? Did it mean that after all she preferred the younger brother?

She dared not discuss Nanette's feelings with Roland, so she must keep to her own share in this situation.

"Well, I think you could safely say we'll be married before Christmas, and if I can get my people over here earlier, possibly late spring." She hesitated. "Can't you persuade Nanette to set a date before that? You've waited so long, known each other much longer than we have."

"Yes, that's true." Roland doodled on his blotter. "You know the story, I suppose, Mary? That her parents persuaded me that if I really loved her I would go away and let a younger man have a chance. That if I was out of the picture, Nanette would have the opportunity of mixing with those of her own age. So I did. Later on I married. Don't think I wasn't happy with Alicia. I was. And she never knew – about Nanette.

"Nanette stayed true to me for so long. I didn't want her to, Mary. If I had thought it could happen I'd have waited. But I honestly did think someone her own age would bring her greater happiness. Nin's age, in fact. And so – I thought – it did turn out. Then all of a sudden Ninian had this urge to do his stint of soldiering in Malaya, and went missing. Alicia died. I was horribly lonely. I'd had so much to do for her for so long I had dropped other interests. After all those months lost in the jungle we thought Ninian had been killed, we'd never thought anything else. Till he was found, not even a bit of wreckage had been traced. So Nanette and I patched up our rather broken lives.

"I wonder if you realise what it was like when we got the cable that he was found? It should have been all sheer joy. As it was, it was hell. I nearly went out of my mind."

Mary noted that he did not say Nanette had.

"It seemed as if there was no solution, Mary. Her birthday came along, and still Ninian had not been told. She got a letter from him. We thought it would just be birthday wishes. He didn't mention it. I can still see her opening that letter, opening it with dread. She wasn't exactly overjoyed at what was in it, either, for that matter. It must have been the shock of the relief.

"To me it was the heaven-sent solution. Ninian had met you, fallen for you, and not knowing Nanette and I had become engaged, had asked her to release him. He was so honest about it, so final. But now that Nanette is so reluctant to fix a day I keep thinking of her reaction when she read the letter."

"You mean," said Mary gently, "that you're just wondering if she had transferred her feeling for you to Ninian."

"Yes."

Mary smiled rather mistily. "Roland, you needn't worry. Ninian was absolutely sure it was you Nanette loved. I think it was the shock, wondering what everyone would say now and . . ." she hesitated. "Rol, you might find it hard to understand, but no girl really likes to be turned down for another. It hurts our pride. I know that. I know it so well. It happened to me, but I know now it *was* just pride, even though at the time I thought I was broken-hearted."

"You mean that when you met Ninian you found –"

"I found that what I'd thought was love had merely been a – well, a lukewarm feeling compared with what I felt for Ninian."

Mary suddenly smiled radiantly. What a relief to be able to really admit it. Because to Roland she could.

He looked at her searchingly, smiled, and for the very first time, Mary saw a resemblance to Ninian.

"I think you could be right, Mary. About Nanette finding her pride hurt. It's rather hard for a man to see it from a woman's point of view."

"She might even have felt it lowered her in your eyes,

Roland. Our minds do work that way. It's an awful shock when someone whose love you're sure of prefers someone else. I know."

"It was that way with you, Mary?"

"It was." Suddenly she found she could speak of it. "I came out to Malaya to be married, Roland. I'd delayed rather too long, nursing my grandmother. There had never been anyone else. We grew up together. Perhaps that wasn't the best, either. Perhaps I was too sure of him. I wanted to go right through my training. So far so good. But when the end was in sight Granny took ill and I knew that Mother was determined to nurse her to the end and wouldn't be able to manage with the farm work too.

"I saw it through. I still can't be sorry I did. Then I made arrangements to go out to Malaya. All of a sudden an earlier booking cropped up and I took it. To put it baldly, Roland, I tiptoed up to the door of Francis's flat, pushed it open and found him embracing the Colonel's daughter. Ninian's Colonel. Not that I knew either Ninian or his Colonel then. So I released him, there and then. That's all. I'm telling you this because it does make a girl lose confidence. That's what it will be with Nanette. If she has seemed strange and withdrawn it may be because she feels less sure of herself, even of you. You could make extra fuss of her. I don't know how articulate you are in lovemaking, Roland," she laughed mischievously, "but I think women like to be told, pretty often, how much their men care."

He nodded his head reflectively. "Then if that's been the technique, Mary, I've been all wrong. I've been letting Nanette get over it. I never dreamed she'd feel hurt, slighted. So I was giving her time. I ought to have swept her off her feet, maybe? She needed things decided for her. Perhaps I should tell her I simply can't live without her a moment longer."

"That's a procedure I should approve of entirely, Roland."

He was silent. Mary waited. He looked up, his eyes searched hers. "And you, Mary, found what you wanted with my brother?"

"Yes."

"But you had no false pride about letting him know that this Francis had preferred someone else?"

133

Mary's heart thudded against her ribs. This was something she'd not bargained for. If Roland told Ninian, then all Ninian's knight-errantry, that had got him into trouble before in his life, would come to the surface. And Mary didn't want him that way.

Her mind worked like lightning. She must think of some good reason.

She did. She said quickly, "Roland, I'm like Nanette too. I didn't relish telling Ninian someone else had tired of me. So he doesn't know. I don't want him to."

Roland said slowly, "You know, Mary, that doesn't sound much like you. It's out of character. You seem so transparently honest to me."

That stabbed. Honest! And here she was caught up in a full-scale web of deceit. But only to save a situation.

She added hurriedly, "Well, not only for my own sake but for Ninian's. He always knew Nanette's heart was yours. He told me so. I didn't want him to think he had just got me on the rebound."

Roland's face cleared. "Now, as far as you're concerned, that's more like it."

He leaned nearer her, took her face between her fingers, said very slowly, as if he were pronouncing a blessing, "Ninian has all the luck, my dear. I don't wonder he fell in love with you. You've got what this Mackenzie country needs in its women. Grit and courage and a warm heart."

As he smiled, he brushed his lips across her forehead, and at that same moment Mary heard the creak of the door as it swung wide open. She and Roland turned their heads. There, framed in the doorway against the starry night, stood Ninian and Nanette.

# CHAPTER 8

It was hard to know which pair were the more startled. They were all so frozen they looked transfixed. Then Mary giggled, giggled with real merriment in it, so that Roland dropped his hands and Ninian and Nanette stepped forward into the room, letting the door bang shut behind them.

"This," said Mary, "is like one of those corny situations on the movies. Guilty couple caught in fond embrace. I can assure you it was nothing of the kind. I've just been telling Roland, Ninian, that after all we've decided to get married in spring if Mother and Father can get here by then. So Roland was giving me a brotherly salute."

Her eyes met Ninian's.

It wasn't quite good enough for Nanette. She spoke naturally and with urgency. "But why the tribute? Why say Ninian has all the luck? That you have grit and courage and ... a warm heart?"

Mary felt sick. She'd made the situation even worse. What could she say?

Roland cut in, the once tired blue eyes dancing. "Did it make you jealous, Nan, to hear just that? Did it make you mad?"

For once colour came up in the creamy cheeks. "Of course ... what would you expect? You wouldn't imagine I'd think nothing of it, feel nothing, would you? I think the situation needs explaining."

Roland said, "It does. And we're going to explain it. Fully."

Mary dared not look alarmed, apprehensive. It would colour the suspicion of guilt if she looked any other than at ease. She realised with numb resignation that she would have to leave it to Roland.

He said, "In the first place, Nanette, I've been trying to be alone with Mary for some time. I feel we've all accepted this situation too nonchalantly. It leaves too many ends not tied up, too many knots still ravelled. Cast your mind back to the day you got Ninian's letter, Nanette."

Mary's eyes went swiftly to Ninian's face. He'd gone quite white under that brown skin. She swallowed. This might solve the Roland-Nanette situation, but it wasn't going to help Ninian much. And there wasn't one thing she could do. Roland had got the bit between his teeth for once.

Roland continued, "I realised that although the letter solved many things and that I myself was calling unnumbered blessings down upon this Mary's head, for you it wasn't all pure relief, Nan. It worried me. I tormented myself with asking myself if you had grown more fond of Ninian than of me."

135

Nanette uttered a sound of pure scorn, a sound that must have been balm to Roland and goodness knows what to Ninian. Sensitively Mary would not look at him.

"Roland," said Nanette, "you must be crazy. I – well, yes, I had mixed feelings. I don't know if a man could quite understand, I –"

"You're right there, Nan, I didn't. But Mary put me wise. She told me it would not be a withdrawal from me, that it would not be any feeling for Ninian, that it would be hurt pride. That any girl would feel just that when another supplanted her."

There was no doubt now that Nanette had lost her temper. Oddly it suited her more than that maddening placidity.

"I think, Roland, if you want to know how I feel about things you could ask me for myself, instead of asking the girl who took my place with Ninian. What can *she* know about it?"

Ninian made to speak before Nanette had finished speaking, but Roland waved him down.

"Mary knows everything about it." He turned to Mary. "I know you didn't want Ninian to know, but he's got to. I can't see anything else for it if we're going to get this straight without leaving hurt feelings and a sense of estrangement between the four of us. I don't think Ninian will feel the way you feared he might, Mary. Not now. And the time for plain speaking has come. Nanette, Mary knew because she *had* experienced just that. She came out to Malaya to marry someone she had known all her life. But she came too soon, wanting to give him a surprise, and found him with someone else.

"She told me that she realised later – when she fell in love with Ninian – that what had been hurt most was her pride. I honoured her for telling me that. It couldn't have been easy. She only did it to help the situation between you and me, Nanette. Tell me, darling: Was hurt pride the only reason for you being so maddeningly remote since you got Ninian's letter? Was it? Was it? Did you feel I might value you the less because one man had turned you down?"

The colour was flaming in Nanette's cheeks now. "Yes, it was. You seemed altogether different towards me once I got that letter. I'm sure I didn't imagine that."

He smiled, taking a step towards her. "I was giving you time to get over the great emotional strain you'd been under, you goose! It had been a ghastly mix-up. The joy of Nin's survival submerged beneath the fact that you and I had become engaged. I was trying to make allowance for natural feelings – felt that time would gradually heal all the scars. Imagine you even thinking I valued you less! It's been all I could do not to abduct you and marry you out of hand!"

Nanette's smile was like sunshine out of rain. "Roland, if only you had! Mary, did you say you would be married in spring?"

Mary gulped, caught Ninian's eye, said hastily, "Yes. It may have to be late spring, of course, to get Mother and Father here. They – they'll have to make arrangements for someone to manage the farm and –"

Nanette cut her short. "Then we'll make it *early* spring. As soon as the daffodils are out. The end of August."

"Done," said Roland with satisfaction. He stopped looking at Nanette, turned to Ninian. "I hope what I said about Mary doesn't make any difference, Nin, but I thought the time had come for plain speaking. If you're thinking of calling Mary to task for not telling you, let me tell you her reason. I think you'll like it. You'd better. And the reason *I* am telling you is that if I don't you and she might get at cross-purposes just as Nan and I did. She didn't tell you because she was afraid you might think she had been caught on the rebound, and she loved you so much she didn't want any chance of that. But you aren't likely to think that, are you?"

Mary felt nothing but admiration for Ninian, the way he made his eyes meet hers, smile, say, "I wouldn't think it. Don't you know how vain I am, Ros Mhairi?" And the laugh they all four shared broke the tension.

Roland said, sobering up, "Well, Nanette and I have things to say – and do – that won't need an audience. Come on, darling, out into the moonlight. We'll leave these two here in their own home."

There was a horrid sort of finality about the way the door shut. Mary didn't relish the coming interview with Ninian.

She walked across to the hearth. Ninian came slowly across too. She turned to face him, found him grinning.

"Phew! Of all the quick-witted girls! I didn't know how

137

you and Roland were going to handle that. I admit myself it looked pretty bad. Nanette was white-hot!"

Mary's eyes glinted. "Ninian, you don't mean *you* believe that that kiss ... on my forehead ... was anything but brotherly!"

He looked stern. "I could have. You'd said when you left me that perhaps you should make up to Roland."

At Mary's look of horror he laughed, took a step forward, caught her hands, "My love, don't be stupid, I –"

She said rather desolately, "Oh, don't, Ninian. I'm not your love."

He made an impatient gesture. "Oh, what does it matter? I've got so into the habit of it."

Mary wondered just what it would be like to have Ninian call her his love in all sincerity and truth. Truth! She didn't seem to have even a speaking acquaintance with truth since she had entered on this mad masquerade.

She looked up at him wearily, leaving her hands in his. "Ninian, it's horrible. All this lying. I just hated it tonight, but the situation began getting out of hand. Roland suddenly said he had things to ask me, said Nanette had some silly idea she didn't want to get married till we were. He asked me when. I realised they'd never get married if we didn't set a date, so I said spring, and then tried to make that a bit indefinite by saying if Mother and Father could get away. Heavens above, and the poor pets don't even know I'm supposed to be engaged to you! Then he told me how strangely Nanette had reacted when she got your letter."

Ninian's grip tightened on her fingers till it hurt. "Did he –" he began to say, but broke off. "Never mind, Mary, go on."

She moistened her lips. She must remember that all this was rubbing salt in the wound for Ninian. She must spare him all she could.

"Go on, please, Mary. You were saying . . ."

She found she couldn't go on. Ninian looked at her compassionately. "You poor little thing! You *have* got yourself embroiled in the Macandrew affairs, haven't you? I'll finish it for you."

Ninian had never called her his poor little thing before. He was sorry for her. Ninian the compassionate. He was sorry for her because she had lost Francis.

He went on. "You very wisely realised that Nanette's pride had been hurt – Rol is right, it did take a woman to see that – and to make it really convincing, you cooked up this yarn about being jilted yourself. Mary, you mixed-up, quixotic little fool, I've got you so into the habit of it, you've become an inveterate fibber. You make up stories at the drop of a hat. Never mind, some day it will come out all right. And I have a most unorthodox feeling that those same lines will just be so many more stars in your crown! Once Roland and Nanette get married you can go back to being truthful again." He smiled in quite a tender fashion. "But, Mary –"

"Yes, Ninian?"

Now what?

"Don't go back to quite the model of rectitude you were, will you? In that hospital. Stiff, starchy. I like you better this way. I dare not hint any more that New Zealand is doing you good, that you're rapidly losing those ghastly cynical ideas you once held ... in fact these days you go round match-making! I repeat I dare not. You would immediately box my ears. But stay this way, won't you?"

It was too much for Mary. She caught her lip between her teeth, rapidly blinked her eyelids, looked hastily away.

Ninian gave a great shout of laughter, entirely dispelling all strain, stooped, gathered her up, swung her round and sat down with her in the one big chintz-covered chair the room possessed.

Mary turned her head into his shoulder, sobbed quite unrestrainedly. Presently she said, between childishly hiccuping sobs, "It was dreadful, Ninian. It *did* come out all right, but I was terrified all the time that you would be furious. I felt so sorry for all of you, caught up in a tangle no one could help, Nanette, Roland ... you!"

"And Mary," added Ninian gravely. "Here, that hanky's no earthly use for such a deluge. Take mine. I must remember to carry two."

He was trying to keep things light. He must be sick of all this drama, especially as in his case it had solved nothing, except his desire to get the woman he loved safely and quickly married off to the man she wanted.

She said, "Oh dear, I wish I wouldn't. Men hate being cried on."

He chuckled. "Well, apart from getting the bosom of my shirt damp, I find I don't mind it. I seem to be good at rescuing damsels and mopping up their tears."

He was. His fatal inclination, according to his mother. There was one gleam of brightness ... he had classed her revelation to Roland about Francis as so much more make-believe. So it wasn't pity making him so nice to her.

Ninian went on, "You're the oddest thing. The things you've coped with in your nursing career! Last time the Colonel came to see me he told me that at one time – when those three chaps had been brought in after the terrorists had been at them – even he was sick and not ashamed of it. But you didn't turn a hair."

Mary said slowly, "Oh, don't think me a heroine, Ninian. I didn't – at the time. I couldn't sleep that night, though. But in uniform I can face anything. Let's go down to the house for supper."

He shook his head, his face close to hers. "No, this is very comfortable. Mother and Dad have gone to bed. Roland and Nanette are saying their sweet nothings under the moon. I daresay they'll go down to the house later, she'll make him some supper and he'll take her home to her cousin's. We'll stay up here a bit longer. I couldn't face any more sifting tonight. They won't be a bit surprised if we stay up here.

"Mary, we've done a lot of pretending for the sake of other people, why don't we do some now for the sheer fun of it? Sit on here – like this – for a while. I know you and Dad have got a tin of cookies up here, you can make us a cup of tea later.

"Meanwhile, may I say how charming you look, Sister dear? Your eyes are red, you haven't a bit of powder left on your nose, your lipstick is all smudged and is going to be more so any moment now ... for Pete's sake let me kiss you just once without a royal fight going on."

Mary thought it was like a dream. It would be something to remember later, when Roland and Nanette were married and she was gone from here.

Later that night, in the wee sma's, living that friendly hour over and over, a fragment of earlier memory tried to catch up with her but eluded her. There had been something Roland had said earlier that night that had puzzled her at the time. She had meant to question him about it later, but events had happened too quickly. It was important, she realised that. It was something she didn't understand and felt she ought to, but what it was about now she had no idea.

She woke late, rubbed sleepy eyes, became aware that a strange softer light lay in the room. She had known it too often at home not to know what it meant. Snow! She was vaguely remembering that just before she had finally fallen asleep the wind had risen.

The twins came dancing into her room. "C'mon, Mary, you old sleepyhead – breakfast's ready. Gran said just come down in your dressing-gown. We're going tobogganing. Roland and Ninian are taking us. Hurry, is this your dressing-gown?"

Mary threw a pyjamaed leg out of bed, shivered and shot back in, pulling the clothes up to her chin. The twins, thus challenged, fell on her as one man, dragged the clothes off her, pulling her out.

Jonathan leapt on to her bed, held out the pink sprigged dressing-gown, warmly padded. Mary thrust her arms into it, caught it round her, shuffled her feet into fur-lined moccasins, raced out with the twins. "The first fall of snow always exhilarates me," she said.

Jonathan leapt on the banister, Josephine followed suit, clutched him round the waist, Mary followed suit, clutching her. They were just about to sail when a hail from the spare room startled them.

"Wait for me," the voice called. "I've always wanted to do just that." Startled, they turned to see Nanette, in a pair of what were evidently Roland's pyjamas, and his dressing-gown. The pants were rolled up concertina-wise, the dressing-gown trailed on the floor.

"I spent the night. Rol said why go home. I hope he's warned his mother. I'm starving."

The twins boggled. This was a Nanette they had never seen before, ruffled, unconventional, ready to slide down with them. She flung a leg over the rail, clutched Mary's waist, gave a whoop as they started off.

The dining-room door was flung open, and framed in it

were Roland and Ninian, Elspeth and Joseph.

They sailed down at high speed, Jonathan managed to clutch the knob in approved fashion and they catapulted right into the centre of the hall in a tumbled, laughing heap, all legs and arms, before the astonished gaze of four – no, five – pairs of eyes. Barbie had come up in the rear, an egg-slice in her hand.

"Keep and save us all," said Ninian, falling back on his father's expressions as he invariably did when startled, "what a stramashing! Rol, we've got ourselves a couple of hoydens. You ought to be ashamed of yourselves! Those twins are bad enough without encouragement."

Roland laughed. "Aye. It would serve them right if they'd broken their limbs. Nanette, my love, if you aren't careful you'll lose those pyjama pants altogether."

Elspeth's face was a study. She looked from one to the other. "It looks as if the snowstorm has cleared the air," she said, and went back to her kitchen.

On the hill Ninian and Mary heard Josephine say to Jonathan, "I've never seen Nanette like this before. She's actually *fun*. What do you think has come over her? Will it last, d'you reckon?"

"Search me. Be a good thing if it did. Uncle Rol'd like it better. It's like that story. You know ... about the change-ling."

"Some changeling at that age, ninny! She must be all of twenty-five."

Mary giggled. "Quite an old lady," she said.

Ninian said quickly, "Look, brats, don't comment on it, will you? Nanette's not been very happy till now. She's had something on her mind, but she hasn't any longer. Just accept her as she is."

They agreed with an odd air of maturity that Mary found touching. She looked after them fondly as their red-tasselled heads bobbed down the snowy hill. "You can really talk to them as if they were grown-up, can't you?" she commented.

Ninian nodded. "No need to make them promise. In fact I'm not too fond of extracting promises, because occasionally one has to be frank. Situations change. Like this one here. Come on, Mary." He pulled her in front of him, set the toboggan moving.

Nanette stayed till the thaw, about three days. The family responded magnificently to this new Nanette. She laughed more spontaneously, was not so impressively efficient, even lounged about the house in relaxed fashion, had a dreamy content in her eyes, eyes that lit up whenever they met Roland's.

It was Ninian who was restless. Mary felt she alone knew what this had cost him.

The men were out a lot, moving the sheep on to sunny faces, feeding out. This hadn't been a spectacular fall; that would come later, probably in July, sometimes even in August.

"We often have our heaviest falls then," said old Joseph. "Something that's popular only with the winter sports fiends. It lengthens the season, sometimes extends it into the school holidays. But it's a right-down nuisance to us, delays the spring growth."

Mary thought, with an uplift of the heart, that it would then delay the blooming of the daffodils, and hoped for a severe and long winter. She caught herself up on the thought. She ought to be glad for Roland and Nanette's sake if spring came early.

Nanette went back to Fairlie when Roland did, and Mary had a sense of a slice of time being handed to her to make the most of. She was out a lot with Joseph and Ninian and the men, riding round the estate, watching them at their work among the sheep, among the steers, fencing, clearing watercourses, chopping back the iniquitous sweetbriers, sometimes helping them, always comparing it with similar work in Canada, answering the men's questions.

Sometimes she had duties in the house, or refused to go because she must keep working on the history of the Mount Hebron Station. Ninian had used the bitter weather as an excuse not to extend the house, had said it would be a pity to expose any of the interior to the hazards of the winter, that it was big enough to start with, anyway. They would leave it till after lambing, which was late here for New Zealand, but because of the high altitudes and low temperatures it had to be.

"But you'll get married before the lambing, won't you, son? Last year when you were away I had to get a young fellow from one of the farms to help. I could get him again. They're glad of the experience."

Ninian was careful. "Well, we've had no definite word from Mr. and Mrs. Rose yet. It may even be early summer."

Joseph was for ever digging things out of one of the barns that had been used for storing things of a bygone day. If Mary approved of them he would have them taken up to the old house. An old rocking-chair, a spinning-wheel, a warming-pan, some old horse brasses.

Ninian came up one day to find Mary not writing but sitting in the sunny window, sheltered from the icy wind off the Alps, dreamily polishing the old spinning-wheel.

She hadn't seen him come up the hill, and now he was in the doorway laughing at her. "No one to see you now would dream that you had any other thought in your mind but to restore this old house and live in it!"

He dropped down on the window-seat beside her. She coloured rosily, seemed uncertain of herself. "It's – it's just that this old house somehow got hold of my imagination. And – and I was a bit weary of the history this afternoon. I've got to a slow-moving part. Polishing is so rhythmical I thought it would help me to think."

"Yes, I suppose so." He turned to look down the lake. "You know, sometimes I think it's even more beautiful in winter."

She nodded, her eyes on the shimmering water. "Yes, and at sunset it's a miracle of colour." She added dreamily, "And what it must be like at dawn from here I can't imagine. It's a much better view than the big house. Imagine seeing the dawn light up the peaks from the bedroom window."

Ninian's hand came to hers. She could feel the callouses on his palm. "Then why go away after Roland and Nanette are married? This bogus engagement could become true. No heartbreak for anyone then. Father has become so fond of you. You're his Ros Mhairi come back. He's going to take it very badly."

Mary withdrew her hand. He might feel it tremble. "I find you absurd, Ninian. One doesn't marry a man for a view from a window, for the love of a house. In fact, not even because his old father has set his heart on the marriage. It's asking too much."

144

He was looking out over the lake again, his eyes unseeing. Mary felt a stab of pain that was almost physical, a wave of love. She thought his features would be engraved in her memory for always. The brown face, the brown eyes, the fair hair that was bleached even more at the ends . . . had he been a towhead like the twins? . . . the high cheekbones, the firm jaw, the well-cut mouth. Since he could not have Nanette, he proposed to her in this half-hearted fashion. Once before he had done the same thing. What were those unromantic words he had used? "How about going the whole hog?" Ninian, who so loved people to be happy he couldn't bear to think about his mother and father's disappointment if – when – they broke it off.

Ninian, still not looking at her, said, "Is it too much to ask, Mary?"

"It certainly is. You think too much of solutions, Ninian. Just because this would please everybody else."

"You mean it wouldn't please you?"

She made her voice sound amused. "Well, hardly. It's a very flimsy foundation to build a marriage on. It would take only one gust of feeling to spring up to destroy it."

"What exactly do you mean?"

She was glad he hadn't turned round. She might not have sounded so convincing had he been able to see her eyes.

"I mean I could suddenly fall in love with someone. Or you might." She stood up. "That's enough of a ridiculous topic."

He stood up, towering above her. "You really mean you just couldn't stand being married to me, don't you?"

"I mean exactly that, Ninian. I couldn't take vows I didn't mean. Marriage, Ninian, is –" She stopped.

His eyes were watchful. "Go on, Mary. Marriage is . . .?"

She flushed, but her eyes met his then. "Marriage is intimate. Without love it could be sheer hell."

"And with it?"

"With it you could . . . you could tread the heights. And I'd rather not know it at all than – miss the heights."

Oddly enough, she noticed, he didn't look insulted. There was even a triumphant gleam in his eye.

"So, my dear Sister Rose, at last you admit it. A bit different from the ideas you expressed to Nurse Meredith, isn't it?"

Mary had a don't-care feeling. "Oh, *that*! I might as well admit now that I never did mean that. It doesn't matter any more. So please don't say New Zealand must have mellowed me. One does – at times and because of certain circumstances and moods – make statements like that. I'm going down, Ninian. I promised Barbie I'd feed the poultry tonight."

"You really mean you don't want to stay up here now I've come."

"If you want plain speaking, yes."

As they came out of the door he asked, "Why did you say it didn't matter if you admitted it now?"

Mary looked down the sweep of the old garden and said with a wave of her hand, "That's what I mean, Ninian. There, under the trees. Thousands of them coming up. Daffodils. It hasn't been a long winter after all. They'll soon be married and I can go."

He looked, said without change of expression, "You don't know our winters. This is a false spring. We'll have more snow yet."

•

They came unnoticed into the house, paused at the kitchen door to see Elspeth busy with something Mary had never seen before. Joseph came in the back door, paused, said, "Eh, lass, it's a long time since they've come out. What are you setting up your quilting-frames for?"

"To make Mary and Ninian a quilt. I got some stuff by mail-order today. I'll get her to pick it tonight. I shouldn't be setting this one up, though. They may just prefer two singles."

Joseph chuckled. "Not they! But if they should, I'll tell Ninian something we found out long ago ... that there's many a quarrel been settled in a double bed."

Mary felt Ninian shake with laughter, his arm was against her arm. She turned and fled. Ninian could put it down to primness if he liked. But it was only that she couldn't bear it.

•

It didn't, after all, matter whether spring delayed or not. It was the next day, and Mary answered the phone to Roland's voice, a voice that sounded younger, more like Ninian's. It was full of suppressed excitement. "Is Mother there? Father too, if possible."

They were still sitting round the lunch table and Mary had answered it at the kitchen extension.

Elspeth went to the instrument, Joseph with her, his brows drawn down in puzzled fashion.

They all looked unashamedly curious. "What's he want them both for?" asked Ninian.

Then they heard Elspeth's reply to what Roland was telling her. "Married? Oh, son! No, it's all right, I quite understand. With a second wedding you might not want the fuss and flummery all over again. I think you and Nanette were very wise. But are you sure, son, that Nanette didn't want all the trimmings? O-oo-oh! It was Nanette who wanted it this way ... in case it recalled your first wedding and made you sad. Son, that was big of her. Let me speak to her ... she is there, I suppose? Oh, just a moment, your father wants to speak to you."

Joseph was very blunt. "Aye, congratulations, lad. It's what you should have done a long time syne."

They all had a turn at the phone, even the twins. Mary too managed a word or two. Nanette said to her, "It's all your doing. I was making a hash of things. Won't be long till your own now, will it? Thank you, and God bless."

Elspeth, returning to the table, didn't seem to mind being cheated out of a family wedding. "I think they'll be happier that way. It could have been an awkward function. All the district would have been there, and some are so candid. Mrs. Gemmeson, for instance. She's so old and cantankerous. She'd have said all the wrong things. Talked audibly to everyone about 'Well, who'd ha' thought she'd ha' married that brother after all. I wonder how *he's* feeling the day,' and so on."

They all laughed, Ninian too; but quite instinctively, Mary's hand felt for his, under cover of the tablecloth, and squeezed it. Then she looked at him and surprised a look of faint astonishment. Perhaps he thought her silly to be sympathetic when she had refused to let the situation go any further. Mary promptly let go his hand.

She helped wash the dishes, sorted out Barbie's lessons, told the twins, who were home from school with colds, that they'd better get cracking on their homework for the next day if they were recovered enough to fight, went out to the kitchen to mince the cold meat ready for some savoury rissoles for dinner, and all the time all she could think about was that very soon now the need for staying here would be at an end.

Ninian had the same idea. He came in from the old smithy on the property where he and Joseph had been re-shoeing Betsy, and found her upstairs in her room, staring out of the dormer.

He spoke jerkily. "You don't want to move on too quickly, Mary. It would be too pointed, undo all we set out to accomplish. Let Roland and Nanette get back from their honeymoon. He said they were having a month in Australia. Then we can discover we aren't, after all, ideally suited. No doubt some logical way of doing it will occur to us."

Mary's heart leapt at the chance not to leave too soon.

But she said cautiously, "Well, although I think you're right not to make it too soon after, there will have to be a happy medium in the timing. Your family are rather the planning sort. I would be terrified if they suddenly tried to pin us to a date. In any case, I don't want to stay over-long. I have my people to return to, my own life to live."

"And I have mine," he replied harshly.

He stood up, took a step away, turned back. "What will you do when you go, Mary? Will you want to go straight back? Even by sea it only takes about a fortnight."

"No, I won't go back right away. Though I don't think I'll tie myself down to a position. I – I thought of Wellington."

"Wellington? Why?"

Actually Wellington was the first city she had thought of and it was sufficiently remote from here, across Cook Strait, in the North Island.

Ninian's eyes had narrowed. "Oh, I remember. You were going to visit the Colonel's sister, weren't you? Well, if she likes you as well as my people have liked you, all will be well."

He went out, slammed the door.

What a thing to say. Decidedly odd. It didn't matter much whether or not the Colonel's sister liked her. It would be nothing but a courtesy call.

•

Each day now brought more signs of spring. Mary had a feeling she wanted to hold time back. She wanted the snows to cling to the foothills, the mountain slopes show nothing of the rocks beneath, but remain white-mantled, the ice on the ponds stay thick and black, the winds keen and penetrating. Because when it came in earnest, Elspeth and Joseph would be pressing about the date.

Every day Elspeth gloated over spring trying to break through, a premature crocus, the first violet, a tree of wattle breaking into fluffy golden balls.

There was to be a special Winter Show in Fairlie the first week of the August holidays. Elspeth had preserves to enter, butter made in the old-time way and patterned with oak-leaves; the crest-badge of the clan was an oak-tree and Joseph's grandmother had always done it thus. Old Joseph and Ninian were to give an exhibition of shoeing, that dying art, in the morning.

Mary elected to stay at home. "Would anyone be put out if I did? I would like to get on with the history. I was speaking on the phone to Rory Cameron – that journalist – and he said if I had it all together by a fortnight's time, he'd be able to look it over before he leaves for the States on his travelling scholarship.

"It would be good to get someone with his know-how, plus a life-long interest in the Mackenzie country, to look it over and advise me. And it will take me all my time to have it ready for him."

Ninian said, "Is it quite impossible to finish it otherwise? I think you'd enjoy the Show."

"Losh, man," Joseph rushed to Mary's aid, "the history's more important than one show. Mhairi'll be going to those shows for the rest of her life."

"You won't be nervous here, all alone all day?" Ninian persisted.

Mary looked at him in amazement. "Ninian, you're quite mad – our place at home is much more isolated."

149

"Well, this is bad enough – and anything could happen."

Mary crinkled her nose at him in derision. "Well, since I'm a nurse, if I fall and skin my knee, I shall be able to render first-aid."

Ninian gave her a sour look. His father created a diversion. He got up, went to a corner cupboard, got out a long parcel.

"Ros Mhairi, I have something to show you. It came by post today. The name-plate for your house. I had it done in beaten copper. And I've ordered a copper lantern for above the door to match it."

He undid the parcel, drew it out, laid it before her. They crowded round, looking over her shoulder.

Mary gazed at the name bewilderingly. "But, Joseph, I said Airdbreck ... the old family name of your clan. This – this is Kilravock, a name belonging to – to the Rose clan."

"Exactly." Joseph's blue eyes gleamed youthfully under the penthouse eyebrows. "I did appreciate that, lass. But I thought that when your mother and father come ower here for the wedding, it would be nice for them to think you weren't completely absorbed into our family. That there was aye a corner for the Roses."

Mary suddenly found their faces wavering at her through a mist. Oh, but they were making it hard for her to up and go.

Ninian's laugh was a nice, indulgent sort of laugh. What an actor he was! "Oh, Mhairi, Mhairi, those ducts!"

His father, always anxious no breath of criticism should fall upon his darling, said immediately, "Well, tears are womanly. Have naught to do with a woman who never sheds a tear, Ringan, she'd likely have a heart of flint."

Came Show Day and everyone on the property departed. The wives of the men were showing things too, both on their own behalf and for the Women's Institute Bays.

As they were leaving, Ninian said, "Oh, you may hear me above you this afternoon, Mary. I believe they're doing a few sight-seeing air trips from the Show. A money-making affair. If I can get a ride I will."

"Well, for goodness' sake be careful. I hate small aircraft, and you certainly ought to. I don't want to patch you up again."

He just grinned. His father said, "And you'll not forget to be within reach of the phone about one, Mary, when Parkinson will ring up about those ewes?"

She nodded. "Yes, I'm working down here today because of that."

"Better anyway," said Ninian. "I'd feel happier if you were within reach of the phone if you need anyone."

Mary had a good morning, made a snack lunch, tackled the work again. The phone call didn't come through. She discovered she had left some stuff up at Kilravock. Oh, bother, and she must have it. Well, she'd ring Parkinson's herself, and if the old man didn't have the figures she could tell him she'd be away a short time.

The phone was as dead as a dodo. Odd. It wasn't a bad day, and there had certainly been no storm or high wind to bring wires down. Oh well, maybe it happened sometimes, ordinary wear and tear. If it was reported no doubt the repair gangs would soon locate it. She went out and examined their own wires, but they seemed all right. It meant, too, that she could now go up the hill and know Parkinson wouldn't be ringing.

She put on her brogues, as the track might be muddy, and went out on to the side terrace that looked through a gap in the foothills to the back country where mile upon mile of rugged tussock-covered hills extended back into higher mountains, snow-cloaked.

Ninian had taken her a few miles into that terrain, riding the horses along narrow tracks, crossing and recrossing streams and gullies. Mary had wanted to go further, but he had said, "Not yet. When the true spring comes, yes, but it's too dangerous just now. Blizzards and storms can swoop down without warning. Horrible for flying in, too. You can get sudden white-outs. A year or two back a small Auster was forced down, further south, Central Otago way, in the Lammerlaws. Same type of country, even more remote perhaps.

"It made a forced landing because of a white-out about five one night. The plane was hardly damaged, landed in snow, but the three occupants were marooned. They had a bad time, had about eight sweets between them. They weren't sighted till two days later. Fortunate that they weren't injured. About an hour after they were sighted a Piper aircraft with Dunedin newspaper photographers aboard circled over, and believe it or not, crashed within a hundred and fifty yards of the first. Plane a wreck, but no one hurt again! Stranger than fiction! Within two minutes they were taking photos. But the rescue was really gruelling. A horse party reached the scene, but getting them to the boundary hut was a nightmare journey. Eventually they were flown out from there."

Mary thought now that Ninian knew all the risks. The trips on the joy-riding plane would be very short, they would just fly up, circle round the house, fly back. Why she should feel so nervy she didn't know.

Just as she was leaving the terrace to go up the hill she heard the drone of a plane. She shaded her eyes against the bright winter sunshine and squinted up at it. It looked like an Auster; it could be Ninian. She ran down the terrace, got on the old mounting-block, prepared to wave.

But it didn't come to circle over the station homestead. It flew on in the direction of the Hermitage, circled a bit, then went flying on into the hills. Yes, it was flying directly in line with the oddly-shaped peak they called the Four Feathers.

If it was Ninian they would probably turn ... or did you say wheel? Maybe you said bank ... anyway, come round back here. She had better stay here watching, or they would zoom round and round till she came out.

Suddenly she was aware of a change in the sound of the engine. A failing, a puttering. Alarmed, she gazed strainingly into the distance. It seemed to lose height, picked it up, soared up a little, perhaps an endeavour to gain height in case of further engine weakness and to avoid peaks. Some peaks were hidden in cloud.

Suddenly it seemed to lose height again; though it wasn't plummeting, it looked as if it was still under some sort of control. Mary had a hand to her mouth. He was going to make a crash landing, she was sure. Oh, if only one were nearer, really near enough to tell.

Then all of a sudden there was nothing in the sky any more. No dark speck. No sound. The silence seemed unbearable to ears that strained. Even the larks had stopped singing. Or was it just that there was such a buzzing in her ears that she could not hear them?

She remained where she was, trying, with all she possessed in the way of a sense of direction, to mark the exact spot. There was no tell-tale column of smoke rising, so perhaps they had been spared fire.

She came to life, unfroze. This was a time for action, not immobility. There was such a thing as the Air-Sea Rescue Organisation. She must alert them by phone. *Phone.* And the phone was dead.

Not allowing herself to panic, she rushed inside, tried it. It could have been working again. No. What a sense of isolation descended upon her. She thought of the neighbours ... if you could call them that, they were so far away. But they would all be at the Show. Besides, even to ride those miles there and back would take precious time and tire the mare.

When communication was cut like this you were just as stranded as old Ninian and Isabella had been. That wild thought gave way to a realisation. They were still on a main road. As it was a public holiday there would be no mail-van, but if she attached a placard to the mail-box the next car would see it. There was always traffic to the Hermitage at the foot of Mount Cook.

It took time. She had to think everything out clearly. She printed out a huge placard with the twins' coloured pencils. "*Help! A plane has crashed in the locality I have described in a letter inside this mailbox. Our phone is out of order. Please read and alert the rescue organisation immediately. I think it could be a plane from the Fairlie Show.*"

In the letter, although she scribbled madly, thinking all the time that a car might be passing even now, she put down as accurately as possible the location of the crash. She dared not be too technical with the points of the compass ; she of the Northern Hemisphere could easily make a mistake that could have grave consequences, not only to the safety of the men in the crash, but to members of the search parties. So she described by which peaks to take their findings and advised them to stand on the mounting-block to start with. She added that she was taking the saddle-bags with provisions, the spirit stove that was a survival unit, blankets, her first-aid kit, and a rifle which she would fire if necessary to guide rescuers to the spot.

153

When she had the placard firmly fixed to the letter-box – and she took no chances of it being blown away by the strong wind off the lake – she resisted the temptation to stop to gaze up the road in search of traffic.

She had Betsy to catch, the saddle-bags to pack, and she must forget nothing vital. She must take something along to use as splints. Her first-aid kit was a splendid one, if only, if only they were not already beyond aid. But she was sure it had been a guided landing. She prayed they had struck some not too rugged hillside, that there might have been snow, cushiony but not too deep.

She kept thinking of that earlier crash, the miraculous survival rate. Might it happen again? Could it? Ninian had survived a far worse crash, in the hidden, steamy depths of a Malayan jungle. And it might not be Ninian. But whoever it was, she had to get there.

Normally one would not venture alone in case one got lost and involved the rescuers even more, but in this case she must not lose time. Even now first-aid might be too late.

# CHAPTER 9

MARY packed the pup tent, put on eggs to hard-boil, put in a smoked ham of mutton, bread, coffee, tea, packets of soup. She filled flasks, although she had no idea if they would survive the journey or not. She found chocolate, salt, put in blankets, ground sheets, even a couple of rubber hotwater bottles. Then, as a last thought, realising she wasn't familiar with the working of the wee survival stove, she put in the thermette.

She thought she had a fairly good emergency load. Oh, if only the family had been home, if she could have had company. There were shepherds' and deerstalkers' huts among those hills, but she didn't know their situation. All she could do was try to reach the plane.

Mary, hoping desperately for the sight of some other human being before taking to the vastnesses, glanced down to the gate, and saw no welcome cloud of dust. She must go alone. She had fortified herself with coffee and a crust of bread.

Betsy was fresh and made good pace up the wide part of the beginning of the track, though Mary would not let her have her head. There were many miles to go, and at the last, among the snows, the going would be hard.

Mary's pulses gradually steadied. You couldn't remain in a state of panic too long. It sapped your energy. You planned what you must do, wasted no time longing for company, did not dissipate your needed reserves with unnecessary anxieties that tormented the spirit and took toll of the strength you needed.

She kept an eye on the sun. Darkness closed in early among the Alps.

She thought of something comforting. If the plane was from the Show they would send out scouting planes when it did not return. In fact, wherever it came from, they would alert other planes to watch for it. And if motorists passed and saw her S.O.S., even if phones were out all the way, they could go on to the Hermitage, and there of course they knew all the answers. There were Cessna aircraft at hand. Her heart lightened.

Good job she had done so much riding lately, she was in fair trim for a trip like this. But as the afternoon wore on, growing steadily colder, with the mountains becoming just a little indistinct, fear clutched at her heart. It was an awesome thing to be alone in the mountains at night, with only a pup tent between you and the elements. She had an hour or two of daylight yet. She had been on her way nearly two hours. In another half an hour she would rest and take some hot tea. Above all she prayed that she might reach the site of the crash before dark.

Suddenly, behind her, she heard a great shout. "Hoi, Mary! Hoi! Whoa there!"

Betsy stopped dead in her tracks. Mary's heart felt as if it lurched in her breast. Horse and rider turned round. Her eyes widened. It was true.

Another horse and rider, and that rider . . . Ninian.

He was coming up the gully she had just traversed, his big chestnut picking its way along the stones of the water-course, bulging saddle-bags each side.

She swung the mare's head round, turned to come towards Ninian. Betsy whinnied softly to Dickon, who whickered back. Mary dismounted, Ninian swung down smartly, came to her. As he reached her, the world about Mary, the world of mountain and tussock, boulder and stream, swung upside down for her. She gave a little sigh, buckled at the knees, toppled to the ground in a dead faint.

When she came round he was forcing her head between her knees.

She looked up at him and said crossly, as if it were his fault, "I've never fainted in my life, let me tell you."

He gave a great shout of laughter. "Oh, Mary, Mary! It's just like you to be cross. Some girls would find this romantic, you silly idiot."

She said shakenly, "I thought you were in that plane."

"Oh, Mhairi, Mhairi!" he said. There was a moment in which two pairs of eyes caught and locked, a moment in which anything might have been said. But there was work to do, urgent, not-to-be-kept-waiting work.

"Can you stand now, Mary?"

She nodded. "I was just going to stop to have a hot drink."

"Right. We'll have one. We'll have to reserve our strength if we're going to be of any assistance to those chaps."

She crossed to her saddle-bags, brought out the flasks and mugs, poured hot tea, produced biscuits. She eased her rifle off her back, flexed her muscles, stretched. The tea was glorious, scalding hot.

"I got back early, by myself," said Ninian. "I don't lay claim to any second sight, but I felt uneasy about you all day. After lunch – an early one – I decided to ring. The family thought I was mad. I couldn't get through, and found out the wires were down somewhere. I decided to come home. Dad laughed like anything, said, 'Oh, well, I know what it's like to be young and in love. Off you go.' "

His eyes met hers, smiling, over the rim of his pannikin.

"I must have got there an hour after you left. Imagine what I felt like when I saw your note. Before I finished reading it a great American car drew up. They beat it for hell down the lake road to the Hermitage. I told them from your directions the place it was most likely to be. I gave them the note to be sure. I realised you'd packed most things you

156

could need . . . what a cool, daring girl you are, Mary. Everything set out so precisely."

"I didn't feel precise."

"I know. That's where discipline and training count. Some women would have gone to pieces, at the most gone for help. And no one could have reached them before dark. A night in these altitudes, in these conditions, could be the end of them, if they're injured, and unpleasant, even if they're without a scratch.

"So I slung in a few extras – another pup tent, some more blankets, and some oats for the horses. I think you forgot that. So I set off not too long after you."

She still didn't know how he had caught her up. She looked at Dickon, flecked with foam. He had been ridden hard at first. She said so.

He smiled. "I know. I had to – I know this terrain. I was afraid if I didn't catch up on the narrow defiles, I might lose you where it spreads out. Let me put you up again."

She mounted, said, "Oh, but what a difference to have you with me!"

Ninian took the lead. Mary felt refreshed by the break out of the saddle, the tea, the joy that it was not Ninian's body she would find out there, broken, maimed, perhaps lifeless. Then she took herself to task for thinking it. It would be somebody's lover, husband, brother, son. But then she realised she wouldn't be human if she had not felt relief.

Even the sun didn't seem to be setting so fast now.

They came to snow. Now the going was hard indeed. The horses had to feel their way. In one or two gullies, still going upwards, the snow was hard-packed, frozen. "This is going to cut the horses' legs," said Ninian. They dismounted, began leading them. Their feet slipped and slid on the icy stones beneath the snow. Never had snow seemed so heavy, so clogging.

"Glad you had the sense to wind those old puttees round your legs, Mary, the snow would have got up under your jodhpurs otherwise."

He had leggings on. Mary's cheeks felt icy where the wind stung them, but inwardly she was uncomfortably hot with exertion. She could hardly lift one leg after the other.

"Round the next shoulder," said Ninian, pantingly, "we'll

157

stop for a bit. There's a plateau there that gives a good view, we might spot something. It'll be dark in less than an hour."

They rounded the shoulder, stopped dead. There, on the plateau among deep snow, was the aircraft, not so badly smashed, only crumpled, and beside it two figures awkwardly sprawled.

"That means that at least they were alive when it came down. They haven't been scattered. You can see drag-marks in the snow. They would be afraid of fire, and desperation would get them out. Perhaps they had no strength left to get back."

He cupped his hands about his mouth, shouted out, "Hoi there! Be with you soon! Help at hand!"

There was no sound, but one of the figures raised a feeble arm in acknowledgment, then was still again. They reached them, knelt down. There was a faint smile on the face of the man who had waved. "Glad you dropped in, mate. I've been trying to get Jeff back in the cockpit. Couldn't quite make it. One arm is out of commission and I was a bit scared for his ribs. I'm not sure if they're broken or not. I thought we'd have had it if we had to stay in the snow all night. He stirred a bit half an hour ago. I've been praying he'd come round before dark and we'd have another go at getting in."

Ninian was busy scraping snow away, putting a ground sheet down. Under Mary's instructions after a quick examination, they got the man on to it. The arm was broken, but near the wrist, and not too complicated. She made it immobile, attended to various minor cuts and bruises. They lifted the unconscious man across. He was only a boy. There was no bleeding from his mouth, nose, or ears. He had a nasty gash on his upper arm that the other man hadn't discovered, but it had stopped bleeding, perhaps because most of his weight was on it and it was in snow.

Mary said briskly, "I've got sutures here, Ninian. I'll have to stitch it. Can you hold it?"

"Yes, of course. Many's the dog I've had to stitch. How many?"

"Only three."

"One thing, he won't need a local. He's fairly deep, isn't he?"

"Yes. Though this may bring him out of it. If it does I'll

158

use the needle, but it's easier not to." She cleaned the wound, inserted the stitches.

He was packed round with blankets, one of the hotwater bottles was filled from the flasks.

"Now, we'll give the other chap some hot drink. Tea first, Mary, then some soup. Sop some bread in it later. I'll hold him up, you spoon it into him."

The man, George Southfield, began to get some colour back.

Ninian said, "You made a great job of landing it, old man."

They were working fast, trying to get as much accomplished as possible before dark fell. The way the aircraft was lying it gave shelter in a big angle away from the wind. They decided against trying to get them into the damaged aircraft. The floor was splintered, and Mary had grave doubts as to whether or not the young man might have internal injuries. They got the pup tents up in the lee of the plane, very close to each other.

Suddenly they heard the drone of a plane. "Gosh, they're just in time to locate us, and that's all," said Ninian. "That'll relieve everyone's mind . . . hullo, Jeff is stirring ; good man, take it easy. They'll dip down low ; I hope they take no risks. With a wee Piper like that a down draught would be disastruous. We can probably indicate that we're all right."

Jeff turned his head, looked unseeingly about him, said weakly, "George . . . are you all right?"

Tears came into the hard-bitten-looking George's eyes. "Sure I'm all right, mate. Question is, are you?"

"Yeah . . . still seeing stars, though. What –"

"We came down on Four Feathers. Help has arrived, two people from Mount Hebron. We sure are in luck, one's a nurse and a rescue plane is just coming in to plot our position.

Ninian was out away from the wrecked plane, waving his arms madly to attract attention.

They couldn't know how much the pilot got of his shouted information, or how much Ninian would get of the questions the pilot asked, but it circled round a few times, went a little way out on the plateau, dropped a bundle, flew off.

Ninian rescued it, came back, talking as he unstrapped it.

"Told him we were all right for the night, that come daybreak we'd make for Four Feathers Hut, the family would give them the location. In any case, if he didn't get all that, smoke from the hut would give it to them tomorrow. There's a flat there. They could land a small plane and take them out. We can get them there on the horses tomorrow. No more than two miles. In any case, the rescue gangs, the foot parties, will be assembled at the station right now, I imagine, and will leave for here at first light tomorrow."

Mary said in a low voice, "Ninian, I'm afraid we can only keep one blanket each for ourselves. We can huddle in it. I want them as warm as possible after the shock and the injuries. It's going to be painfully cold."

"Aye, I know, lass. We'll be right, we had the exercise. If need be, we can take some through the night. Those big torches will be a help. I've got some kindling wood in the saddle-bags, enough to boil the thermette through the night once. And we'll leave a bit of dry for tomorrow's start. We could strip a bit of stuff off the plane for that. I'll fill the thermette with snow, it may thaw a bit ready to heat then."

Jeff was recovering rapidly, though he had a lump the size of a pigeon's egg to show for his knockout. His arm throbbed and George's broken arm was hurting like hell now, he said, but when they finally got the men bedded down for the night, Mary administered some fairly potent tablets, and soon, warm and exhausted, they fell asleep, close together in the little tent.

Ninian was busy chocking the plane against wind rocking, doing it with huge boulders. Though the snow was deep, Mary helped him. It was better to keep moving, and it would make the night shorter. Ninian scraped snow away, because they had exhausted the hot water from the flasks now, set up the thermette, built rocks about it to shield it from the wind, though allowing enough for draught, made them some tea and mixed up some soup with the remaining water, and put it into the flasks for the men and themselves during the night. They ate slices of the mutton ham, hacked off and dipped in salt.

They spread the one remaining groundsheet on the floor of the other pup tent, propped up their saddle-bags and saddles to lean against, wrapped a blanket around themselves as adequately as possible. They talked in whispers, for

160

they were right against the other tent, indeed they sheltered it a little.

It was horribly uncomfortable, painfully cold. Mary thought she would never feel warm again. The ground beneath, soggy from the scraped-away snow, struck freezingly through the ground sheets, but at least kept them dry.

Finally Ninian said, "I'm going to take off your boots and puttees, Mary, and rub your feet. I've got dry woollen socks here . . . yes, all right, I've got a pair for me too. I don't want you to get frostbite. Those two are all right, they've got the hotties and three times as many blankets."

At first it was extremely painful, she almost felt like telling him he must desist, but gradually the circulation began to flow, and nothing ever felt so good as those coarse home-knitted farm socks. They talked to keep their mind off their plight. It kept the spectre of a snowfall at bay, though Ninian thought it wasn't likely. It seemed an interminable night. Draughts came under the canvas, and whistled up about them, the air was so icy it seemed tangible, they shifted position over and over again, never finding comfort. They were alert for any sound from the other tent against theirs, worried lest the men had other injuries not yet revealed. But only once did they hear them stirring; they crowded in taking the torches with them, administered hot soup, gave them more tablets, found them quite warm, swathed in their blankets, crept out again.

Ninian said, "Seems a far cry from Malaya, doesn't it, Sister?"

"Yes, Lieutenant, do you remember those stifling nights? I could use one right now."

They recalled many things to help pass the hours away, talking in whispers, Ninian asked her about her life in Canada, her family, told her something of his own childhood. Nothing was said by either of future plans. They both dozed off towards dawn, awkwardly propped against the saddlebags, and woke stiff and unrefreshed. Ninian had cramp badly in the leg that had been most injured.

Mary said anxiously, "I hope that's all it is, I couldn't bear you to have a setback now."

Ninian grinned, massaging rapidly. "For once you don't sound the imperturbable nurse. Thank goodness."

"You'll be walking too, if we manage to get the men on the horses. It'll take both of us to get them up, what with broken arms and ribs and things, though they're firmly bound. But I don't much like the idea of you walking a long distance again today."

"Now, don't get in a flap now, my love. We're as good as rescued. Once it's fully daylight and we get some breakfast into us, we'll get going. The sooner we reach the hut and decent bunks, the men can get more ease and we can pep them up a bit for the transfer to plane. I think we should get cracking now. Do us good to get moving."

They crawled out of the tent, to be met with a blast of icy air, but it was worth it for the sheer joy of standing upright. Mary reached her arms above her head, stretched, turned to the east where, far across the ranges where the foothills sloped down to the plains, somewhere above the Pacific the sun was rising.

"All thanks to the Giver of Light," said Ninian softly. "Isn't that one of the prayers of the East? And don't you think we might take a moment or two to quietly thank Him for preserving us through the night?"

Mary felt immeasurably moved.

After Ninian had given thanks they stood for a few moments, despite the intense cold, as the peaks, one after another, lit up and glittered like prisms.

"Well, we've never seen the sunrise in the Himalayas," said Ninian, "but. . . ."

"But it couldn't be more beautiful than this," finished Mary.

Ninian put an arm lightly round her shoulders. She looked up at him, to find him starting to chuckle.

"The joke?" she queried.

"I was thinking of the first time I kissed you . . . on the road to Timaru. Remember how I teased you, said your aloofness was only skin-deep? And you said with a voice like a glacier, 'As far as you're concerned, Lieutenant, *always* aloof!' Remember?"

"Yes . . . but why think of it now?"

"What a hard time you've had staying aloof, with a family like mine. And now – and now you've just spent a night with me in a pup tent!"

Mary said sarcastically, "I'm sure that was very romantic."

She tried not to laugh with him.

"Oh, Mary, Mary, quite contrary, you'll have to make an honest man of me!"

She burst out laughing. "If you were more of a gentleman you'd not even mention it."

He said, "It's going to be a good day. Look at the sunlight. This will be good flying weather."

The trip to the hut wasn't without difficulties and hazards, even a few perilous moments, though the last half mile was free of snow. They kept a tight watch on the men. Mary noticed they had to grit their teeth quite often, and the two of them looked weary and grey when they reached the hut, but within a quarter of an hour of reaching it they were beginning to regain their colour and spirits.

The fire was set with dry brushwood and in the lean-to behind was a vast stack of fuel. The cupboard was stocked with emergency rations and the tastiest and most nourishing of tinned foods. When they had breakfasted Ninian went out to clear stones and boulders away from where the plane would land. Mary went out to help him. It was ideal for the purpose. It was a lovely sight when the plane came into sight, circled round, flew off and came in again to make a perfect landing. Out got the pilot and a doctor.

He was very jovial, said, "Well, you chaps certainly knew how to pick your witness for your crash landing. What luck. A fully trained Sister, fit enough to undertake a journey like that. We'll get you properly fixed up in hospital. She's made a great job of the first-aiding, I couldn't better it. Timaru Hospital is ready for you. Just a matter of getting you into the plane. Thank goodness you're walking wounded, I've had some ticklish jobs embarking in this area before today."

He turned to Ninian. "Do you want us to send another plane in for you two, or will you go with the ground party? They shouldn't be very long, they set off earlier than us. We had to wait for local ground fog to clear. Good job conditions were good here."

Mary said, "I'd rather go back the way we came, Ninian. We can get straight home then. If they come by plane and take us it will mean going to the Hermitage and a long drive home. Besides, there's always danger landing among the peaks."

But the plane had no sooner left than another touched down – reporters and photographers. Mary didn't feel in any condition to pose for photographs.

"That's all right," one of the newspaper men assured her. "No one will expect you to look like a film star does no matter what incredible hardships she's just survived. Besides, I think you're rather something myself, even like this."

"I'll endorse that," said Ninian.

Mary shook her head at them. "You know a thing or two about psychology, I suspect. Morale boosting."

"This really is a special," said another. "Hero of the Malayan jungle and the Sister who nursed him back to life once more involved in dramatic rescue." He picked up Mary's left hand, looked at the sapphire, said, "You are engaged to each other, I suppose?"

"Too right," said Ninian solemnly, playing up to it. "From the moment I recovered consciousness in that military hospital, I knew I had met my fate."

Mary said hastily, "Take no notice of him, Mr. Munro. I wasn't there when he recovered consciousness."

"What he says is good enough for me," the reporter was scribbling madly. "Um ... let's see ... Oh yes, Mr. Macandrew and Miss Rose plan to be married ... when?"

"In spring," said Ninian firmly.

"Spring," said the reporter. Mary gave Ninian a reproachful look. She said hastily, "That's only a tentative date, it depends on whether or not my people can make it by then."

She saw Ninian's lips twitch.

The reporter said, "I'll get two lots out of this. I do a few contributions to the news letter column for the Kiwi soldiers in Malaya."

Ninian saw Mary's dismayed face. He turned away a little with her while the reporter went to confer with the photographer.

"It can't matter *now*, chump! They – the nurses over there – know you've been staying here. They'll have been scenting a romance long ago, if I know anything about nurses. What's it matter?" Then he pursed his lips. "Oh, I see. I forgot, you didn't want the Colonel to know. Well, the Colonel can jolly well make what he likes out of it."

Mary moved hastily away. That reporter wasn't far out of

earshot or above being interested. He seemed to like the human angle in news.

She was glad when the rescue party reached the hut, with fresh horses for them. The journey back was nothing like the anxiety-ridden one of yesterday. But she was weary to exhaustion, swaying in the saddle, when they reached the homestead.

She and Ninian both slept till nearly evening, then came downstairs in dressing-gowns, to old Joseph unashamedly proud of their feat, to Josephine and Jonathan starry-eyed and already wishing it wasn't the school holidays because by the time they got back the papers would have stopped featuring the rescue. It was beastly luck.

Elspeth was only thankful they were home and safe in wind and limb. "What a night we had," she said. "It didn't seem fair to sleep warm with you out there. And thank goodness it wasn't later in the year."

Ninian broke off what he was saying to his father. "What do you mean, Mother? If it had been later the weather would have been better. It wouldn't have grown dark so early, and morning light would have come sooner."

Surprisingly Elspeth appeared flustered. "I – I – well –"

Joseph, a twinkle in his eye, came to her rescue. "She means how awkward if it had come a wee bit nearer your wedding. Imagine if it had come the day afore it, and Mary with that great scratch on her cheek where she fell in the snow."

Mary thought Elspeth flashed Joseph a grateful glance.

Roland and Nanette came back from their honeymoon, spent two nights at the homestead, went down to Fairlie to set up house. Mary had a sense of time speeding up. She ought to be thinking of going back home. It must end soon, but Canada seemed so remote. There she could not even look at the stars and think the same stars looked down on Ninian.

So much had happened in her life since she set off for Malaya, a prospective bride. Would she be able to settle at home after this? She wasn't quite the same girl who had left there. Incredible now to think she hadn't even known Ninian existed ... and now he filled her whole life. Had the prodigal son ever felt completely at home again? What a stupid thing to think! She wasn't a prodigal. But perhaps it would be best to go home, to lick her wounds, to build another life.

Spring came in with a rush. The daffodils in the old orchard ran like a golden sea down to the walnut plantation. The ski slopes became soft, the ewes were heavy in lamb. Behind the house that no longer looked forlorn, old gnarled apple trees broke joyously into a froth of bridal white touched with pink and golden forsythia showered its golden rain.

The daffodils would fade, lilac and laburnum come to blooming. Mary had known Mount Hebron Station in late autumn, winter, early spring . . . she would never know high summer, garlanded and gay. The poppies and petunias Elspeth had planted so lovingly in the flowerbeds of Kilravock would bloom, but not for Mary. Would they take that name off the gate? she wondered. If they did would it be in anger or sorrow?

She thought that tomorrow she must tell Ninian that they must make their final plans for the breaking off of this bogus engagement. Tomorrow, not today. Not tonight. Tonight she wanted to savour all this . . . Ninian deep in his book beside the fire, herself in Great-Granny's old rocking-chair, darning his socks, the twins squabbling over their jig-saw on the floor, Barbie, dear, loyal mothering Barbie knitting old Joseph a tie.

Ninian looked up suddenly. "Mother darling, you're very restless tonight. You're prowling around like a marauding lion – lioness. Whatever is the matter? Are you up to something?"

Elspeth took a quick look at Joseph. "No, of course I'm not. What could I be up to?"

"You could be up to anything, my pet," said her disrespectful son. "You have the look of it. And you keep listening as if you were expecting someone. Are you? Not another surprise party, for the love of heaven. I couldn't stand it tonight."

Elspeth said quickly, "Well, I rather think Roland and Nanette might come."

"Well, what's so exciting about that? They often enough do."

Barbie said, "Is that why you were doing out the guest-room, Gran? I noticed you were even doing the top of the wardrobe."

"Well," said Elspeth defensively, "Nanette's such a good housekeeper she puts me to shame."

Ninian began to laugh. "But even Nanette wouldn't start climbing up to see if you'd dusted the top of the wardrobe."

Elspeth sounded quite cross. "Well, surely to goodness I can clean the top of my spare-room wardrobe when I like!"

Ninian laughed, patted her knee. "It's all right, honey, of course you can. Relax. I got a box of chocolates today. I'll just get them."

He was only halfway to the door when the dogs barked. "Oh, sounds like them now." He came back, went to the window, pulled the curtains back. "Yes, it's Rol's car."

They heard steps in the front hall, then the door opened. In the doorway Ninian saw a pair of perfect strangers. Yet there was a faintly familiar look about the man. A tall, handsome man of about sixty, a smiling, well-dressed woman a little younger.

Roland and Nanette were behind them, smiling. Who the —? Something made Ninian look at Mary. She stood up, scattering socks and darning wools everywhere. She had a dazed look. She took a step forward towards the couple, said in a completely disbelieving tone, "Mother! Father!" and was swept into their embrace.

Elspeth and Joseph were beaming, almost as if taking a bow as co-producers of some most successful play. Nanette had a Father Christmas look. Oh, how changed Nanette was. She was genuinely pleased to have helped in this surprise for Mary.

Fortunately, in the outcries and explanations and introductions, no one saw the completely dismayed glance which presently Ninian and Mary exchanged.

Mary had got so used to acting the part of Ninian's fiancée that although terrified at the thought of what her parents were likely to say any moment, she still managed to behave exactly as any girl might when suddenly reunited with parents dearly loved.

There would be a reckoning later, she could tell that by the occasional glint in her father's eye as it rested on her. But if he had come all this way, without demanding by cable what on earth it was all about when Elspeth Macandrew had written urging them to come as soon as possible before the wedding, he would certainly have questions to ask! She was due for a stormy session sooner or later. She was lucky that he hadn't demanded there and then what it meant, why they had not been told of this engagement. Only it had always been Father's way, when any of his children misbehaved, not to bawl them out in front of the whole family but to take them aside.

Mary was too intent on keeping things on this normal level to give much intelligent thought to it, but the fact that neither of them had demanded an instant showdown meant that the happy letter Elspeth had written them had somewhat disarmed them.

She might have known things wouldn't go as she had planned. Nothing had, the last twelve months. In her rather desolate thoughts of her future she had thought that some day, when she was back home, she might tell her mother how she and helped that Kiwi soldier out of a very sticky situation. But not till she could look at it more dispassionately when there would not be so much chance of giving herself away.

Meanwhile the main thing to do was to prevent Mother and Father giving away their lack of knowledge, especially in front of Roland and Nanette. Though at least they were married now, but what a pity to stir up doubts.

Elspeth was beaming. "Oh, dear, and I so nearly gave it away. After warning Joseph he wasn't to do so, when Mary and Ninian rescued those men, I said what a good thing it wasn't later. I meant imagine if you had turned up and your daughter was lost in the mountains! Ninian thought I'd gone mad to say such a thing. Joseph got me out of that by saying I'd meant if it had been nearer the wedding."

Angus Rose said dryly, "Do we take it then that the wedding date is fixed?"

His eye was on his daughter.

"Oh, no, Daddy, I said I didn't want to fix a date till I found just when you and Mother would be able to leave the farm. I kept putting off pinning you down to a definite date because I know how awkward it is to calculate just when you can get away. And it complicated the date too, to have to arrange a suitable time for here. Ninian didn't want to be away in the middle of lambing, even if Joseph said he could manage."

What a good thing Father had a poker face. Apart from a tightening of his cheek muscles as he heard he had apparently been consulted by his daughter, he gave nothing away.

Old Joseph started to say that he'd said before he could get help with the lambing, but Ninian cut in.

"The fact is, Mr. and Mrs. Rose, that my darling impetuous family have rather rushed Mhairi with the wedding date. They're so convinced their son will make her a good husband, they'd have liked the wedding even sooner."

Mary was sitting on the floor, looking up at her parents. Ninian dropped beside her, covered her hand with his, continued.

"But I thought that was hardly fair to her. I wanted to give her a chance to see how she liked New Zealand and New Zealanders and our way of life. If she was going to be homesick I wanted her to get it over before we were married. Didn't I, my love?"

He pinched her chin, very much the devoted fiancé. Mary felt a rush of gratitude pour over her. "Yes, darling." And she put her cheek against his for a fleeting moment in a very natural gesture. She saw her mother's eyes soften, become a little reassured. Poor darlings!

Elspeth cut in, "Well, I thought enough time had been wasted and I was dying to meet the Roses. I remembered Mary saying her father thought it wise for her to spend time here to get to know us (Mary swallowed and refused to meet her father's eye) so then I had an idea. If they came here before the wedding then they could see for themselves what nice people we are and wouldn't have another worry."

Having delivered herself of this remarkable speech, Elspeth was most amazed when everyone burst out laughing. But it cleared the atmosphere.

Ninian, sobering up, said. "Oh, Mother, Mother! At least you don't suffer from an inferiority complex."

Nancy Rose wiped her eyes. "Mrs. Macandrew, I have a feeling you're a real kindred spirit. I love people who say exactly what they think."

Ninian looked Angus Rose straight in the eye. "You'll want a talk with me, sir. I ought to have done it by letter. I realise that. But I'm an appalling letter-writer. I hate it."

Mary noted that Elspeth looked faintly surprised.

Joseph frowned. "Son, do you mean to tell me you haven't been in correspondence with Mary's father over her future?"

"I'm afraid I haven't, Father. I did mean to get around to it, but —"

Angus Rose looked across at Joseph. "I think this generation has different ideas from ours, Mr. Macandrew. And perhaps it's better discussed than written about. My word, that was a wonderful trip over. I never fancied travelling across the sea by air before. But it's certainly the way to travel. And it was grand having Roland and Nanette to meet us and to explain all the landmarks and scenery on the way from Christchurch Airport.

"As Roland's a stock-buyer I feel I already know a bit about the set-up here. I can see there will be big differences, but it will be most interesting." He turned to Mary. "Mrs. Macandrew's letter spurred us on in a decision we'd been trying to make. We've decided to retire early, and to do our travelling while we're still young enough to stand up to it. Donald is taking over the farm and we'll retire in Vancouver when we go back. Not right in the city, on the outskirts, with enough land to stop me going crazy. So we may spend a full year here."

Mary swallowed, her eyes on her father.

He continued, "Mrs. Macandrew wanted our arrival to be a complete surprise to you, so you won't know this ... they've offered us a cottage on the estate for our headquarters while we're in New Zealand. Of course we'll be away a lot, we want to see every bit of this most fascinating country. If it really has got as much variety as the tourist brochures boost, then it surely will be a great experience."

Mary felt if she said anything her voice would come out as a strangled squeak. Ninian's grip of her hand tightened as if to say ; don't panic, let it go meanwhile. Don't say anything here and now.

The conversation got disjointed, fortunately perhaps. Everyone was talking to everyone else, except the twins, who hoped by keeping quiet no one would notice how far past their bedtime it was.

Ninian said in a low voice, "We can't make a clean breast

170

of it, I'm afraid. It would be so harrowing for Roland and Nanette. Besides, your folk must be terribly tired."

Mary was too terrified to leave them all together to help with the supper in case the conversation got into deep waters again, but fortunately Nanette said, "Now, you stay right there, Mary, with your people. I'll help Barbie."

Elspeth was saying, "I think our meal customs might be a bit different from yours. We're a terrific nation of tea-drinkers, though coffee is becoming more popular than it once was. We have breakfast – Scots type of breakfast – then morning tea at ten, lunch at midday about twelve or one, according to farm needs, afternoon tea at three, and dinner about six. We have a hand-round supper just before bedtime. My daughter-in-law and my granddaughter are getting it now. Then you'll want to get off to bed and we've got a lovely long time ahead of us to plan everything."

Mary shivered. *To plan everything.*

Elspeth went on happily, "We have electric blankets on the beds. I got yours switched on early. One thing, you'll be used to cold. If we get Aucklanders down here they feel they're freezing to death. Auckland is sub-tropical. They aye say 'It *is* magnificent scenery, *but . . .*' "

Mary was trying to enter in to it all, to sound natural. She said, "Where is everyone going to sleep? With the children here too, the house is fairly full."

Ninian said, "Oh, Rol and Nanette can have my bed. It's a three-quarter. It has to be – I'm so long I have to curl up, so I like the extra width. I'll get my sleeping-bag out and put it on the floor."

"There's far too much of you for a sleeping-bag," said Mary. "You'd better let me take the sleeping-bag."

Elspeth said, "Anybody would think I'd not had everything planned for ages. I have a bed ready to put up for Ninian in Jonathan's room. I didn't want to put it up or you'd have guessed."

Barbie and Nanette came in with the supper trays. Nanette served some, then dropped down with her own cup of tea beside Mary. "No chance of getting you to myself tonight," she whispered under cover of the buzz of conversation, "but I wanted to tell you first. We're having a baby. Roland is over the moon. We didn't want to wait. Roland's not young."

Mary's hand clasped hers. "Oh, I'm so glad. Don't worry about his age. Look at Joseph, he's seen even his younger son to a fair age."

Ninian leaned forward. "What are you two getting all starry-eyed over? More surprises?"

Nanette's laugh was the most natural thing. It bubbled up from wells of happiness. "Not a mystery, Nin, a baby. It was all I could do to prevent Rol from announcing it to the whole crowd, but I didn't think our baby should steal any of the limelight from your folks, Mary. Plenty of time for that."

Ninian's congratulations sounded very sincere. Actually, poor lamb, thought Mary, he's probably feeling as numb as I am with all that has happened.

The inevitable moment came when finally the Roses went up to bed. The whole family escorted them up, still talking madly. Ninian kept close to Mary, ready, she knew, to rescue her if need be. He would be feeling terrifically responsible.

Mary had a crazy feeling that one day she would wake up to find herself married to Ninian. It seemed inescapable. Not that it wouldn't be heaven ... if it could have been the way most marriages happened ... but how absolutely horrible to live with the knowledge that your husband had been pushed into marrying you, because so many lovely people would be hurt if you hadn't married. Knowing that though you loved him, his heart had been given ago. What was it he had said once about being a one-woman man?

Wasn't it true if trite – *Oh, what a tangled web we weave when first we practise to deceive*! She wondered if Sir Walter Scott had ever found himself caught up in some tangle of his own making.

The spare room looked very cosy from the door, there was a rosy bedside lamp, the bed looked soft and inviting, the electric fire was switched on.

Everyone chorused "Goodnight," then Mary's tall father looked over their heads. "I want a word with you in a few moments, Mary," he said.

Ninian's fingers pressed her arm. She freed herself, went to her room at the end of the passage. She needed a few moments in which to pull herself together, to think her way out of it, the best way for everyone. If only – if only she could tell the truth.

She found Ninian had followed her in. She turned on him fiercely. "Ninian Macandrew! If you – if you mention a marriage of convenience again I'll – I'll choke you!"

"You'd find it very hard to do," he said mildly. "Now take that tigerish expression off your face, likewise an air of guilt. Be all sunshine and light and take a lead from me." He marched her across the passage, tapped lightly on the Roses' room door.

Her father was standing in typical male fashion in front of the electric fire. Her mother was sitting on the bed, nervously pleating the coverlet between her fingers. With a spasm of pity Mary remembered Elspeth saying how you suffered with your children. Nancy Rose would want to uphold her husband but to understand her daughter.

Mary stood in the centre of the floor, her hands behind her back, rather as if she were facing an interview with some irascible matron.

Ninian slipped one hand over her hands, disentangled them till he could hold one.

He took the initiative. "I know you asked for Mary alone, sir, but we're in this together, and I have an idea I can explain it better than she can."

Mr. Rose's blue glance was bitingly keen. "I'm sure I hope so. On the face of that very pleasant evening downstairs, I admit some of my doubts have been stilled. You seem a very fine family. But the fact that our daughter got engaged and saw fit to say nothing to her parents takes some explaining. We have never, I think, been harsh or difficult parents. We've always thought, till now, that we enjoyed the fullest confidence of our children. And from something your very charming mother said, Ninian, you were already engaged to each other when you came here, yet Mary led me to believe that she was merely escorting a convalescent soldier home. Instead of that, you've been engaged for months."

Ninian seemed perfectly at ease. "That's the whole point, sir. I'm afraid I rushed Mary off her feet. We were going to cable you from Sydney. Then Mary panicked. She thought you might think she had been carried away by mere infatuation, glamour of a man returned from the dead, surviving incredible adventures ... moonlight on the boat deck ... and so on. Any parent would have been worried. She felt that with you not being on the spot, as my parents would be, you could be very disturbed. So we agreed to wait. I think we were wrong. In fact I know we were wrong now. The idea was that when you thought we had known each other long enough to be sure, then we could tell you. But the darned scheme's gone all haywire, thanks to my darling, impetuous mother."

Mary had been looking at her feet. Now she looked up, and surprised a look on her father's face she had not expected to see ... Mirth? Yes, it was true. She stared; he was trying to repress it, trying to retain his stern look, the look of a man who has a legitimate grievance. But it was too much for him. Nancy Rose took one look at his face, and, much relieved, collapsed into laughter too.

"Oh dear," said Angus Rose, trying to sober up. "And we always thought you so sensible, Mary. It just shows what love can do to one. I'm afraid the young folk of today are quite beyond me. You tried to spare our feelings by *not* announcing it and just about gave me an apoplexy when your mother, Ninian, wrote to us talking about a wedding we didn't know was about to take place."

Ninian, out of the side of his mouth, said to Mary, "Now, watch those tear-ducts! This is *not* the moment for tears. Look overjoyed."

But as Mary came forward to her mother and father, they seemed pleased to see tears in her eyes, hear her say, "Oh, my darlings, I'm so sorry to have caused you all this anguish of heart. And it's wonderful to have you here."

Her father patted her back. "There now, there now, that's my girl."

Mary added, "And you were splendid, not giving us away in front of Ninian's family."

Ninian offered Angus a cigarette. Nancy Rose said to her daughter, "What a pity we never took up smoking, honey. I feel I need something to steady my nerves. I've been strung up all the way across the Pacific."

Angus said, "Tell me, Ninian, just as a point of interest, why didn't you tell your folks you weren't announcing the engagement to us just yet? It would have saved an awful lot of bother."

This time Mary came to the rescue. "You know, Daddy, I

174

was meeting my in-laws for the first time. I didn't want to appear to insult their son by more or less having him on approval."

Angus considered that, began to laugh again. "Trouble has been, as I see it, you've done far too much considering of other people's feelings."

Mary thought he couldn't have put it better had he known the whole truth.

Angus added, "And of course I can understand you being a bit more canny this time. Right, it's all washed up and forgotten. I've an idea I'm going to like my new son-in-law tremendously. Now, clear out, both of you, you mad, irresponsible pair."

Ninian and Mary found themselves out in the passage. They came to Mary's door.

"Phew!" said Ninian. "Well, that's cured me of lying and plotting for ever more. One thing just leads to another. I can still see the breakers ahead. I'm alarmed. I'm terrified I can't stop lying. I wish −" He stopped as if cut short.

Mary finished for him. "You wish you'd never thought the whole thing up in the first place."

He looked down at her gravely. "I don't, you know. It had to be done. For Nanette and Roland's sakes. We're at the stage now of finding all this deceit quite nauseating. It's gone against the grain, against all our upbringing, yet it's made a happy marriage, and from what we heard tonight, a happy family. So it was worth it."

Mary closed her eyes against the pain of that knowledge. It was worth it all to Ninian because it had brought Nanette happiness.

Ninian looked down on her compassionately. "You're tired ... and no wonder. Shall I get you some aspirin? No ... well, try to sleep. Don't worry too much. I saw you reading Bess Streeter Aldrich the other day. Have you ever read that one of hers where the old father always said when winding up the clock at night, 'Oh, well, everybody gets a new day tomorrow.' This won't seem so bad by morning, things never do. After all, so much has happened today that by the law of averages, tomorrow should be completely uneventful."

He was wrong.

175

# CHAPTER 10

AT first it seemed set fair. A neighbouring farmer rang Joseph up to come over to see him about something he was trying out for the first time, an experiment by the D.S.I.R. Joseph explained that they had Mary's parents from Canada, just arrived, so wouldn't be able to. The neighbour, egged on by his wife, proposed that all four should go over and stay for lunch.

"Jolly good idea," said Ninian. "It would be a pity to miss the chance of that, and after all, you've got loads of time ahead of you to show the Roses this place. Nanette's off to give her cousins a hand, but Roland's here, he'll give me a hand in the back paddock, and Greg and Maurice are already away up the hill. Mary will give us our lunch."

He smiled at Mary after they had gone. "That gets rid of them, and postpones Mother and Father showing your parents Kilravock. They might be a bit surprised to find how far we've gone with that. As it is, I'll slip in a bit about how Dad did it for a surprise when we were in Fiordland. I think Mother and Father are bound to mention to them some time or other that I was once engaged to Nanette, but I don't think they'll do it till Roland and Nanette are away again. Now I must get up the paddock, that work's urgent. Anyway, it'll do you good to have a quiet morning. When you have lunch ready give the gong an extra hard banging. Though I guess we'll be listening for it! And don't bring morning tea up, we'll take it. You're looking washed out."

A hag, no doubt, thought Mary resentfully. Well, there was plenty of tidying up to do, and the children were all away; Barbie had gone with the parents. She got the beds made, the dishes washed. She picked up a huge lambswool duster on a stick. The phone rang.

It was a call from the Hermitage. A moment's delay, then they were connected. A strong voice spoke, vaguely familiar.

"Hullo, hullo. That Macandrews'? Oh, is that you, Sister? Secumbe here."

Secumbe? The *Colonel* ... oh, help!

She swallowed. "Yes, I'm here still. No, only recovering from surprise. How do you do, Colonel? Yes, they asked me to stay on here for a while. Yes, I suppose you wouldn't be sure. His people are wonderful, so hospitable. Was ... was there something you wanted, Colonel? I'm sorry Ninian isn't in, he's up in the back paddock fencing. A bit of a fresh brought a fence down where it cuts across a gully. He's with his brother. Yes, Colonel, *that* brother. But it came out all right. The brother and the Lieutenant's former fiancée are married now. Oh, you don't want to speak to Ninian. You want to see me." She swallowed. "Why, Colonel Secumbe?"

His voice lost its military precision. Became a father's voice.

"Mary – I may call you Mary, mayn't I? It's this daughter of mine. I had to bring her back to New Zealand. The doctor thought the climate was upsetting her. Not the climate at all. I told you once she'd developed a conscience over the thing. She felt she had ruined your life, that she couldn't take her happiness at the expense of yours. Even back here she went on losing weight. So I brought her here to the mountain air, as I thought it might brace her up. It hasn't. I wanted her to come to see you. She won't. Then out of the blue Francis turned up. He's a bit under the weather too. In spirits. Are you there, Mary, can you hear me?"

"Yes, I can hear you, Colonel, go right on."

She couldn't explain that this was the last straw, that the blood was drumming in her ears. She shook her head to clear it. She must keep her mind on what the Colonel was saying.

"Well, I said we'd all come down and see you, get the thing cleared up. Francis had flown all the way from Singapore to have it out with Althea. He says he's coming to get you and is going to bring you to the Hermitage to see Althea. Says he has such confidence in you that he's sure you'll back him up and tell him he did see you in Singapore, asked for a reconciliation, but you turned him down. Althea won't believe him. He's beside himself at the change in Althea. So he's this very moment trying to see if he can borrow a car. I flew here too, you see. Will it be convenient for Francis to call about lunch-time or shortly after? I don't know just how long it will take."

Convenient? *Lunch-time?* Ninian would be in. Roland too. Or shortly after? The parents might be back.

Words almost failed Mary. How her people would react, meeting the man who had turned their daughter down and now expected her to put things right for him with the other woman, was more than she could contemplate. It was unthinkable. It just wasn't going to happen. Her brain began to function again.

She spoke quickly. "Listen, Colonel, I've a better idea. Francis is going to find it extremely hard to borrow a car. I'll come up in one of the cars here. No – it's no trouble. I'll come right away."

The Colonel thought it a good idea, and he was a very thankful man. He'd rather be in the jungle, dammit, directing operations against terrorists any day than involved in matters of the heart. Devilish ticklish, and a man without a wife was so helpless.

*

Mary wanted to get away smartly, but she wasn't going to face Francis and Althea in anything but her very best. There was the new blue suit that old Joseph had insisted on buying last time they went to Timaru to replace the one she had ruined delivering the foal. She took time over her make-up too, though despite the fact that she knew the men would not be likely to return for some time, she found herself tense.

That was what made her hurry over the note she left for them on the kitchen table. They would have to make a snack lunch for themselves. They were both capable of rustling up a meal, anyway.

She dashed it off, anchored it under a weight Elspeth used for pressing ox-tongues, hurried out to the garages, got into Ninian's car, took the lake road and drove west with the tent-ridge of Aorangi clear of cloud this morning, a glorious sight if she had been in the mood to appreciate it.

*

Roland and Ninian came down early because Roland had tipped the whole tin of staples into the creek among fine shingle that made recovery impossible.

"We'll go across to the house and get Mary to put lunch on

now, she never minds a change of plan," decided Ninian.

"I've noticed that," agreed Roland. "She'll make a wonderful farmer's wife."

They came into the empty kitchen. "What in the world's that?" asked Ninian, staring at the note. "Don't tell me *she's* run out on us too? You don't think Carmichaels have rung up and insisted on her going too?" He sounded disgruntled.

"Of course not. Mary wouldn't leave us in the lurch. No, it's something more important."

They lifted the weight off, read: "Sorry about your dinner, bacon and eggs in fridge ready to cook. The Colonel rang up. He's at the Hermitage and wanted to see me. Don't tell Mother and Father, will you? As you can imagine, I don't want him here. Hope to be back four-ish. Mary."

Ninian stared at it heavily. "You were right, Rol. It was something more important." He lifted his head. "Damned if I'll let her see the Colonel all on her own. This has gone far enough. Why the hell can't he leave her alone? Him and his wretched daughter!"

"Good on you," said Roland, adding to Ninian's mystification, "That ought to have been washed up long ago."

Ninian stared, but didn't stop to ask what he meant. He wanted to catch Mary. And travel on with her.

"Can I have your car?" he asked.

"Sure. Keys are in it. Off you go."

Ninian didn't stop to wash or to change his farm boots.

Roland shrugged. He cooked his bacon and eggs. He was just sitting down to it when the phone rang.

The Hermitage. The Colonel.

"Is Mary there?" The tone was urgent.

"No. But is that Colonel Secumbe? Yes? Well, it's Roland Macandrew here."

"Blast it! I hoped to get Mary before she started off. Do you know anything about this affair at all?"

"Well, I know that Mary used to be engaged to a chap who fell for your daughter. Someone called Francis. She told me."

"Good. Well, I rang Mary because my daughter won't come to a decision till she sees her. And Mary – bless her heart – she's a brick, offered to drive all the way up here. However, Francis has got hold of a car, and he and Althea are as good as on their way. He thinks they'll have a better chance of talking things out in a private home than in a luxury hotel. Quite right, too. Hope to goodness they don't miss each other on the way. Althea has been giving us some concern with her health. She's fretting. She simply won't say yes to Francis till she's quite convinced she hasn't ruined Mary's life."

"What?" Roland's shout nearly deafened the Colonel. "What in the world would make her think that? She's going to marry my brother. Your former lieutenant. She's simply head over heels in love with him. Her people have just arrived from Canada for the wedding ... and I hate to think what *they'll* say to Francis if he turns up here! No wonder Mary said *she'd* come to *you*!"

What the Colonel said then was unprintable, certainly not fit for any operator's ears. Roland could only hope no one was listening in.

He said, "Can you stop them, sir? Let Mary come. And my brother is probably breaking the speed limit at the moment, trying to catch up with her. He's furious!"

The Colonel stopped spluttering long enough to mutter, "Well, it's most unfortunate ... I'll do my level best to stop them," and the receiver crashed down.

Roland stood gazing at the wall. No wonder Ninian was furious. He would know all about it. But now what? That would be some meeting! Mary with Ninian in pursuit ... Althea and Francis with the Colonel hot-foot after them. By the sound of it he would simply commandeer a car. Roland decided there wasn't one thing he could do about it. But he was hanged if he'd go back to hammering staples in macrocarpa fence posts. There was no mechanical transport left. He decided he'd get Dickson out and ride over to see Nanette's cousins. He didn't think he'd say a word about this, though. It would just lead to gossip.

Meanwhile Mary was driving along the lake, fast but not too fast. She wanted time to think. Well, there was one thing — with Ninian's ring on her finger, however little it might mean, it would serve her very well this time. She would be able to convince Althea Secumbe that she was perfectly free to marry Francis. The girl must really have been remorseful to have become ill like this. Mary had no condemnation for her. Perhaps she, too, had got involved in a situation that had got out of hand too quickly. And with all the practice she had had in pretence of late, it ought to be quite easy to convince Althea she was deeply in love.

*It was true.* True, but hopeless.

She turned a bend, just before doing so noticing another car coming up steadily behind. Ahead of her was another bend. What a pretty road this was. Silly how people would speed, even in lovely scenery such as this. She was beginning to quieten down a bit herself. It was foolish on roads like this, when you never knew what might come round a corner, to keep your foot down on the accelerator.

At that moment something did shoot round the corner, but not mechanised transport ... on foot, but swift, swift with the pace lent by utter terror. A child younger than Josephine ... what in the world....? Mary instinctively slowed, felt for the brake with her foot.

The child saw the car coming, swerved to the other verge, and at that moment came into sight the cause of the terror, ugly, menacing, its head lowered to charge – a bull!

The child was almost up to the car, the bull not far behind. There was only one thing to do ... and Mary did it. Odd how in moments like this you acted instinctively, quicker than thought. Mary put a hand on the horn in an endeavour to stop the bull with fright, and drove straight between the child and the bull, wrenching the car round, hoping desperately that the combination of the blaring horn and the sight of the car would deflect the animal long enough for the child to scramble over the fence to safety.

The bull tossed its head to one side, tried, in a desperate endeavour that almost succeeded, to dodge, but its very weight and the force of its charge carried it on; it crashed sideways against the passenger side of the car, rocked it, slewed it round, almost turned it over, and then the bull made a sound between a bellow and a sob and toppled slowly to the ground, while the car stopped at a precarious angle, one wheel up on the bank.

Mary looked round dazedly. A woman had rushed out of a stone cottage close to the road, snatched at the child, hurried it inside the gate, and was now running towards the car.

Mary didn't feel anything at all. She dimly noted with satisfaction that she was well enough off the road not to constitute a danger to traffic, and she thought the driver of that car coming up would probably tell them what on earth to do with the bull. She leaned cautiously over to the passenger door to peer at the animal.

The driver's door was wrenched open. Ninian's voice, his furious voice, said, "Mhairi, Mhairi, what the hell d'you think you're doing? Charging bulls ... *charging bulls*! Here, out you come!"

He hauled her out. "Don't you realise, you idiot, that that car could topple over on its side any moment? Oh, Mhairi, Ros Mhairi, my love, the things you do! If you had any idea at all what it means to a man to see the woman he loves charging an angry bull —"

Mary's face changed. He had her by the shoulders and was shaking her.

"Ninian," she said, "oh, Ninian, what did you say? Say it again ... but you don't, do you?"

"I don't *what*?" He was shouting in sheer exasperation.

"Don't love me. You love Nanette."

The quietness of the statement, her tone, sobered him up immediately.

"*Nanette*? I *never* loved Nanette. That engagement was no more real than ours at first. It was done to save Alicia knowing. *Of course I love you*! Haven't I been trying for months and months to get you to marry me? Haven't I?" He gave her another shake. "You blind little fool, Mhairi. I fell in love with you the moment I set eyes on you. You were feeling my pulse. And as the weeks in hospital passed I knew that my farce of an engagement to Nanette must end. It has to when a real love comes into one's life. There, doesn't that ring true? But I had to ask Nanette to release me first. I couldn't say a word to you ... you'd have thought me a cad. When my rescue was in the papers it mentioned a fiancée. Then, just when I was waiting for her answer, when the time was near when I'd be free to speak to you, I heard you being scathing about marriage to Anne! And I lost my temper, thought I'd misjudged your character, and then —" He turned his head. "Oh, hell, what a moment to pick to propose! Here's Mrs. Anderson! Was ever a man so bedevilled? And anyway, we'll have to get this blasted bull off the road."

Mary's eyes were shining. "Stop swearing. It's not like you. It won't help."

"It has. It's relieved my feelings. But the Colonel – oh, hullo, Mrs. Anderson."

The woman had tears running down her cheeks. She caught Mary's hands in hers. "I've never seen anything so courageous. I saw it all from the upstairs window. I was frozen with horror. I thought you would kill yourself."

"Instead of which," said Mary, beginning to giggle with relief, "I seem to have killed the bull, poor thing." They all turned to look.

Ninian started to laugh too. The bull lifted a languid head, rolled its eyes, laid it down again, uttered a gusty sigh.

"You've only knocked him out. Lord help us, you'll be known the length and breadth of the Mackenzie as Mary the Matador! Girl who thinks nothing of knocking out a bull before lunch. I think I could get him to his feet now, Mrs. Anderson, if you open that gate. He's too groggy to do any charging. But you'd better go up and see your husband's boss and tell him this bull needs more than a barbed wire fence between him and the road."

Mary clutched him. "Ninian, you aren't going to. He might just charge again."

"Darling, he hasn't got a kick left in him. He's got the sort of head boxers have . . . only more so."

Mrs. Anderson sped across the road, opened a gate. Ninian bent over the big black bulk, grasped the ring in its nose, uttered encouraging words. Mary came close, trembling.

"It's all right, darling. He can't do anything to me while I hold him close like this. Up, Sultan . . . up, boy . . . that's it . . . come on . . . now your front legs."

Sultan got groggily to his feet, swayed a little, tried to shake his head, found it didn't pay.

Ninian said quickly, "Mary, get away from him. He may subside, and he's literally a ton weight."

He led the bull, staggering drunkenly, across the road, put him through, gave him a pat on the rump to keep him moving, shut the gate. The bull staggered on a yard or two, sank to his knees and ceased to take any further interest in the scene.

Ninian said, "Right. Off you go, Mrs. Anderson, and see to your little girl."

She said, "Will you come in for a cup of tea? It'll help you get over the shock."

Ninian said, "No, thanks. I've things to do. I'm right in the middle of prop –" a warning glance from Mary made him clamp down on the word. He finished lamely. "I was chasing her up with an urgent message."

Mrs. Anderson accepted that explanation, went off to the cottage.

"I'll wait a split second after she's shut the door, Mary, and then I'm going to kiss you. Kiss you as you've never been kissed before. Then you're going back home. You are *not* going on to the Hermitage! And the Colonel can commit suicide off the top of Aorangi for all I care! He isn't having you. The old bounder! He's twice your age and more!"

"The Colonel? Can't have me? Ninian, what in the world are you talking about?"

Ninian closed his eyes, thrust his hands through his hair. "Are you or are you not going to the Colonel? All along you've not wanted him to know about our engagement. Well, I've had it now. You're going back home and I'm going on to the Hermitage. I'm not going to tell his High-and-Mightiness that we're engaged. That our house is ready. That we're getting married in a month's time. That if he wants a wife he can go look for one his own age. And you can make up your mind to start loving me back. We're made for each other and the sooner you get that into your head the better "

Mary said softly, "I don't have to, Ninian. It's in my heart, not my head. I've loved you ever since the night of the party. Oh, before then, I suppose, but I wouldn't admit it even to myself. Why else do you suppose I'd have consented to this masquerade? I simply leapt at the chance to come to New Zealand with you. I've gone through real anguish of mind thinking that all you did was for the sake of Nanette. But what this business about the Colonel is I don't know. He –"

Ninian took a step towards her, then stopped, holding her off.

"Before we exchange this betrothal kiss, Sister Rose, yes, that's what it will be despite this sapphire of mine on your hand, we are going to get two things cleared up. The Colonel

184

and Nanette. Why are you hiving off to meet him if he isn't sweet on you? And wasn't his daughter cutting up rough because she didn't want a stepmother her own age?"

Mary was helpless with laughter. "Oh, poor man! Thank heaven you didn't meet him first. He wouldn't know what you were talking about. He's never thought of such a thing as being sweet on me. He told me that night I had dinner with him that the memory of his wife would do him for a lifetime."

"You must have been discussing most intimate things for him to tell you that," said Ninian jealously.

"We were. He said he had hoped Althea, his daughter, might some day know a love like that. But ... oh, well, nothing matters now. You see, Ninian, it was true what Roland said that night, I did understand how Nanette felt when you jilted her. I *had* been jilted too ... oh, I suppose technically I did the jilting myself. I came to Malaya to marry Francis Murchison. I'd known him since kindergarten days. I realise now, though, that what I had mistaken for love was no more than a hotted-up friendship, nothing like what I feel for you ... no, wait, Ninian. All this must be cleared up.

"I came earlier than he had expected, thought I'd give him a pleasant surprise ... remember in Sydney how much I was against your surprising your family? ... Well, I found Althea in his arms. So I took on nursing again. And Anne was from home and knew. I got so fed up with all the syrupy pity. That's why I said what I did. I was trying to be tough. But anyway, that doesn't matter, since you've found out long ago that I'm not like that. But Althea, drat her, developed a conscience. She turned Francis down. Actually, you'd better know this, he came to me in Malaya, asked me if we couldn't, after all, make a go of it. I said no. I like to think now – even if I didn't realise it at the time – that it was because I had met you. You dwarfed him, Ninian, and not only in stature of body. I'll never forget when you got that letter from your mother how your first thought was for them at home. I thought once I'd gone Francis and Althea would make it up.

"Then this morning I got a ring from the Colonel. Althea had almost had a breakdown. He'd brought her home and then down to the mountains to try to pick her up. Out of the blue Francis arrived yesterday. They wanted to come to

Mount Hebron, I think the Colonel thought I would be able to convince Althea that I wasn't still unhappy. I dared not let them come, Ninian. The situation at home is so delicate still, with Mother and Father just arrived, and not too pleased with me, anyway. How Father would have acted if he had met Francis, I didn't know. So I said I'd come up to them.'"

He had her hands now, holding them comfortingly. "But why didn't you tell me about Francis? Didn't you think I would have understood?"

"I was going to, Ninian, once. Not because I thought there was any chance of you loving me, but because I felt I must at least have your respect, that you mustn't go on thinking I had cheap ideals. But your mother told me that you'd got engaged to Nanette out of pity. That you are always one for picking up the pieces, for playing knight-errant. I wanted no more pity. If you couldn't love me for myself I'd go away."

His face was a study. "Oh, Mary, Mary, it *was* pity, but not for Nanette. For Alicia. I loved her as a dear sister. She didn't have many years of life left, and she had no one but Roland. She had never suspected he had ever cared for Nanette. He was so much older, you see. Till one day she overheard something Nanette said to me. I could have choked Nanette. She said in that wistful tone that used to enrage me – I hate people martyring themselves – 'I used to dream, as a little girl even, of being part of this family some day,' and didn't realise Alicia was sitting in the window-seat with her embroidery. She parted the curtains, looked with bewilderment at Nanette. I could see suspicion leaping into Alicia's eyes. I hand it to Nanette, she was dismayed too. I said quickly, all I could think of on the spur of the moment, 'You're the first to know, Alicia, Nanette has promised to marry me.'"

"We thought we'd better let it stand for a while." He started to grin. "History has repeated itself. But I never took advantage of that engagement the way I have with this ... I never fell in love with her. We only ever had one row, when I told her for goodness' sake to stop wearing the willow for Roland and to put it behind her, make a new life. She asked me to make it with her, that we seemed to get on very well. I should never have consented to that.

186

"But that's why I went to Malaya, Mary, to think things out. I even hoped Nanette might meet someone else. It wasn't a high-faultin' idea of serving my country." He paused, smiled. "Then I met you. I wasn't likely, Mary, having made one ghastly mistake out of pity, to make another. I nearly went mad when I heard you say those things. I'd hoped to make my wicket good with you before being sent home, hoped to get you to at least promise to visit New Zealand, to see my home. I had written to Nanette, feeling no end of a cad, even if we never had vowed eternal love, then before I got her answer, I got that letter from Mother that precipitated things. I got a scare at the time when you handed it to me. I'd written so much about you, to the home folks, that I thought my impetuous mother had anticipated things. What are you looking at me like that for?"

"I've just realised something, Ninian, something that has eluded me till now. That night Roland asked me about things. He said Nanette had got that letter on her birthday. I felt afterwards as if I had missed some important thing. That was it." Mary's face looked as if sunshine was replacing shadow. "Her birthday was some time before I got your mother's first letter, wasn't it?"

"Yes, and you nearly found that out when you offered to post my answer to Mother's, remember? You asked where Nanette's was. I had to say it was inside hers. I merely told Mother in the letter that no doubt by now Nanette had been over to tell her that I had asked her to release me. But I pretended to you I needed help. So I did, it made the situation easier arriving with you, but my main reason was not to lose touch with you when I was shipped home. Now what are you laughing at?"

"At Ninian . . . Ninian the arch-conspirator, making mistakes all round . . . and me too!"

She held out her hands. He put his arms about her, drew her close, and for a moment everything was blotted out, the lake, the mountains, the road. That kiss was everything Ninian had promised her it would be.

Finally Ninian raised his head, looked over her shoulder and said, "I rather fancy, my love, my really-and-truly love, that Althea and Francis are now walking towards us, and after witnessing that, they won't need much convincing. And

. . . so help me, here's the Colonel. In another car!"

They disengaged themselves, turned hand-in-hand.

The expressions on the three faces coming towards them were ludicrous. The Colonel was evidently trying to catch up on the other two. He made it just as they reached Ninian and Mary, but a movement caught his eye.

"God bless my soul! What in the world is wrong with that animal?"

Sultan was staggering drunkenly from side to side.

Ninian said in an offhand tone with an undercurrent of laughter, "What, the bull, sir? Sultan? Mary knocked him out half an hour ago. He has concussion. Poor Sultan!"

The Colonel boggled. Althea boggled. Francis boggled.

Ninian's voice changed. "I aged about twenty years in two seconds. Mary left a message for me about coming to see you – rather a vague one, I didn't understand – so I took my brother's car and tore after her. I got round the corner to see her driving up to the next bend, and round it tore first a little girl, then that bull charging the child. You'd have thought it fine defensive tactics, sir, but it scared merry hell out of me. Mary drove the car clean between the bull and the child as it charged. I never saw anything so foolhardy . . . or magnificent . . . even overseas. But it does something to you when you see your bride-to-be acting as if she's in a bullring."

Althea and Francis echoed it together. "Bride-to-be?"

Ninian's eyes were guileless. "Yes. We're to be married exactly a month today. Mary's parents arrived yesterday for the wedding."

The Colonel hurrumphed. "Yes. That was what I was hurrying after you for, Francis. I spoke to the homestead, Macandrew, and got your brother. Fortunately he knew who Francis was. Very quick grasp of things. Said never do to come here, told me you were engaged, parents just arrived. Upset your mother and father to meet Francis again. Very understandable. I say, we've not done any introducing. This is –"

His one-time lieutenant interrupted him without apology. "No need, Colonel. I'm sure we all know who is who." He grinned. "I'm most grateful to you, Francis, and to Althea. I fell in love with Mhairi at first sight. She was taking my

188

pulse. It would have been a real facer if I'd recovered only to find her engaged to someone else."

Mary noticed the Colonel open his mouth in surprise, close it again as if thinking better of it. Ninian smiled very nicely at Althea. "I believe felicitations are in order. I would like to wish you both every happiness."

The Colonel hurrumphed again, felt something was needed to wind things up, said, "How about coming back to the Hermitage to lunch? Very pleased to have you."

Ninian said laughing, "Sorry . . . I have often lunched there in deerstalking clothes, but I don't think I'll turn up in farm boots. I was fencing when I found Mary's note and tore after her. Besides, we can ill spare the time. The next month is just crammed, and we must go and see how that poor shaken Mrs. Anderson, the child's mother, is. She saw the whole thing from her bedroom window."

They said goodbye. Mary found that shaking hands with Francis didn't mean a thing. She said softly to Althea, "Don't wait too long before you get married. An engagement is a frightful waste of time."

They parted.

As they entered Mrs. Anderson's gate Ninian said to Mary, "I suppose I did hear aright . . . what you whispered to Althea. I hope I did, because I had an idea you were going to raise all sorts of objections to that wedding-day, Ros Mhairi."

"I have only one," she told him.

"What is it?"

"Too far off. Three weeks should be long enough to shop for a dress and veil."

Ninian stopped, said, "Mrs. Anderson must have seen plenty now . . . doesn't matter if she sees another. She'll only think it's relief from shock, from having you safe and sound."

They had lunch with Mrs. Anderson, helped her husband move the recovering bull to a paddock further from the road, drove home later in the afternoon. Ninian's car could not be driven, the mudguard was driven right into the wheel. They pushed it into a padlock.

Coming home in Roland's car, Ninian said, "Well, Ros Mhairi, I've had all this plotting and counter-plotting. Roland and Nanette must never know, of course, but I think we owe it to the parents – on both sides – to make a clean breast of it.

189

I simply can't face thinking up any more explanations. Tonight we'll take them all up to Kilravock and tell them the whole thing. Then your parents will no longer feel hurt that you didn't tell them at the first. We'll swear them to secrecy. Is it what you would like?".

"Yes, please, Ninian.".

*

They came hand-in-hand into the kitchen at Mount Hebron homestead, and something about them, the light in the eye, the spring in the step, made everyone look expectantly at them.

They were an oddly assorted pair – Mary in her soft blue tweeds, up to the minute, not a hair out of place, Ninian in farm boots caked with mud.

"She's named the day," said Ninian. "Three weeks today."

Roland was sitting by Nanette. He said, "I don't want to be too curious, of course, but was it necessary to go rushing off to Mount Cook to do it? And tell me, did the Colonel ever catch up with you?"

"The Colonel?" asked Elspeth. "You mean Ninian's Colonel? Why didn't you ask him to call?"

Mary looked frankly at them, especially at her mother and father.

"It was better not. You see, he was having trouble with his daughter. But Ninian and I have fixed it all up. She's just become engaged, with our blessing, to Francis Murchison. So all ends well.".

Old Joseph looked across at Angus Rose. "I feel there's more in this than we shall ever ken. Angus, there are times when the rising generation has me beaten, but I think that tonight we shall drink a bonnie toast to the uniting of the houses of Rose and Macandrew."

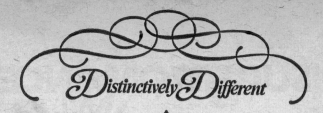